Adventures in Dating

Sara Rishforth

12 Sept. 2014

Dawn,

thank you so much for your time!
Keep up the great blog! I love
reading it & trying out the recipes.

Sara Rishforth

YamWorks Press
Adventures in Dating
Sara Rishforth
Copyright © 2014 by Sara Rishforth
All Rights Reserved

Cover Design: Thistlefish Design & Illustration
Author Photo: Timothy O. Sutherland

Address all inquiries to:
Sara Rishforth
sara@sararishforth.com
www.sararishforth.com
Library of Congress Control Number: 2013922887
CreateSpace Independent Publishing Platform
North Charleston, South Carolina
Published in the United States by YamWorks Press.

ISBN-13: 9781494339777
ISBN-10: 1494339773

To Emil, my butterbean

Acknowledgements

M y parents, JoAnn and Daryl Rishforth: I'm thankful for my mother who took me to the library every Friday to check out books. We'd climb into bed, read books, and eat cheese and Triscuits. Dad, thanks for supporting me in everything I do.

Heartfelt appreciation to Tom Rishforth, Josh Niva, Tom Bunger, Wendy Burns-Ardolino, Katie Bender, Erica Struyk, Lori Moore, Linda Orcelletto, Ron and Carrie Caramella, Patty Vogel, Pam Womack, and David Haywood Young.

1

~

"I'm so glad I moved to Alaska. I'm so glad I moved to Alaska," I chant out loud, as I stay late to work on drawings for the third night this week. My current project is the museum expansion, and I'm the typical perfectionist architect. Is there any other kind?

For a project in college, I roped in my older sister, Kimberly, to help me color in all the produce for a grocery store layout. She complained when I told her to do purple *and* green cabbage. Hello? It must be accurate. See what I mean? Perfectionist. And that's just *one* example.

But I digress. I volunteered to have these drawings revised for the 10 a.m. meeting tomorrow. My co-workers knew I would volunteer since my social life is well, not exactly hopping. Most of them have spouses and kids with evening activities, so I know staying late is harder on them.

And, it's not like I haven't tried to have a full social life. I go on dates, have several hobbies, say yes to almost any activity, and joined the Young Architects of Alaska Society. I'm the oldest person in the Society, too! Who would have thought thirty-two was old? Not I, until I went to a meeting and it was all fresh faces just out of college, still partying every weekend with kegs. Sigh.

Regardless, I still feel good about my decision to move to Alaska one year ago. Even though I haven't met some outdoorsy, build my own cabin, snowmachining type of guy with a beard (well-trimmed, of course), I'm still optimistic about living here and finding love. Plus, I'm not in a hurry to get married and have babies, but I look forward to having a guy to cuddle with on cold winter nights in front of the fireplace. It takes time to meet people … that's what I remind myself whenever I receive another wedding invitation from a college friend.

Work is super busy, and I am *far away* from my overbearing mama and dad in Charleston, South Carolina. Precisely 4,479 long miles away. Mama is the sweet Southern woman in everyone's business and constantly matchmaking me from far away. Dad just really misses me. He's a big believer in all family living close by, and I know he was heartbroken when I pulled away with a U-Haul, headed for Alaska.

Mama wonders why I haven't met The One and settled down to give them grandbabies to dote on. Most of my high school friends are married and have babies, so "what am I doing wrong," asks Mama on multiple occasions during our routine Sunday afternoon phone calls. It's funny how the "I" can either mean her or me depending on her mood. I swear she majored in manipulation at Ole Miss.

Well, excuse me for wanting to experience new places and move out of the Southern bubble. Getting hitched right out of college and having kids was never my plan. No matter how many times I tell this to Mama, it doesn't sink in. When is she going to realize I like doing my own thing and not following the crowd? Doesn't she remember how I wore Birkenstock sandals growing up while all the other girls wore pink Jellies with petite heels?

Since I'm the middle child, I'm rebellious, much to the chagrin of my parents. No drugs or binge drinking during high school, just little stuff to gain attention when I was younger. I had two other sisters to compete with for attention and praise. My parents view moving to Alaska as the ultimate rebellion and wonder when I will come to my senses. They ask when I'm moving back every single phone conversation. Boy, it's getting old.

I loved seeing Mama's face when I told her I was moving here. Her chin trembled, she sighed loudly, fixed a large vodka and tonic and retired to her room for two whole days. Southern drama at its finest.

"Can you please take another look at the window detailing in the lobby?" Jack asks, frowning, as he enters my office. He brings in the sketch and lays it on the drafting table next to my desk.

Jack is my favorite co-worker. He has a sly sense of humor, strong work ethic and *loves* chatting about food. I *love* food too, so it's fun to talk about our latest cooking adventures and favorite places to eat.

We text each other photos of our food and bring in leftovers to share. Of course, it doesn't hurt that he's absolutely adorable. He reminds me of the actor, Paul Rudd (circa *Clueless* movie days), complete with dark brown curly hair you want to run your fingers through. Plus, he has mesmerizing hazel eyes.

"Sure. I'm also worried about the lighting in there. I'm so thankful for the long Labor Day weekend. Do you have big plans?" I inquire as I look over the sketch and mark some changes with a pencil.

Then, I rub my eyes and yawn as I click on AutoCAD and bring up the file to work on. My long brown, curly hair is pulled back into a loose ponytail, and I have two pencils sticking out of my hair. Not exactly sexy and inviting, but definitely adorable. Of course, it doesn't matter since Jack and I are just friends.

"Oh, the usual. Hot yoga on Saturday morning and a trail run with my roommate on Sunday. Winter will arrive before we know it! I'm ready to break out my skate skis. So … are you excited for your blind date tomorrow night?" Jack grins, as he perches on the corner of my desk, admiring my cup full of pencils.

Okay, maybe not admiring, but amused by my pencil fetish. I love using pencils for everything … taking notes in the staff meeting, sketches, of course, and sticking them in my hair. Or, maybe it's because I can erase all the funny comments we write back and forth during the staff meeting when the boss goes off on a tangent.

"Well, it does sound promising … drinks and appetizers at The Roadhouse. I warned Lauren if this guy's a loser, she owes me an expensive lunch! I'm game for blind dates, but she's got to do a better screening job."

"I'm sure it'll go well. At least you're not committing to dinner and a movie. I assume you'll do the usual bathroom trick?" Jack smirks.

"Hey, it's not really a trick! I just time a bathroom trip when the bill is about to arrive. It's a first date, so he should pick up the tab anyway. You make it sound so bad! Seriously! In high school, they pull girls aside and tell them three things. Number one: The bathroom trick, so you don't have to pick up the tab *ever*. Number two: Girls can change their mind anytime, anywhere, about anything. Without apologies or reasons! And number three: Don't marry a mama's boy," I say, changing out the flashing detail on the window to make it more weather tight. I save the changes and close the file.

"You're so funny! Is that what all Southern schools teach?" He teases.

"I'll give you the all the details on Tuesday. Let's knock out these last revisions, so we can get out of here," I say, giving him back the sketch and adding the pencil to my hair.

I met Jack on my first day of work, and we quickly became friends. I enjoy our camaraderie, and he's my willing partner to try new restaurants in town. My general work rule is no socializing outside of work with colleagues, but I broke the rule for Jack. He's too much fun to snub for one little old rule. See? Those rules from high school apply to *so* many things in life.

I leave work at nine, pick up a veggie burrito from Tahoe South Cantina, and collapse on the sofa. My apartment has the ultimate cuteness factor since it's a corner unit and features tall windows facing east toward the mountains and wide, arched doorways. Two accent walls in the den are painted burgundy, and I chose a bright yellow for the kitchen. A sunny way to greet me every time I enter the apartment.

Clicking on TiVo to watch my favorite show, *Top Chef*, I unravel the wrapper and dive into the huge burrito filled with spicy roasted vegetables, cilantro rice, and black beans. I *love* good food, especially when I'm in my pajamas on the sofa. For dessert, I eat a bowl of black raspberry chip ice cream. After watching the chef pack up his knives on the show, I wash my face and brush my teeth before heading to bed.

My bedroom is my second favorite room in the apartment, after the well-stocked kitchen, of course. The walls are painted cornflower blue, and the bed is covered with a thick, white down comforter and white pillows. I created a little reading corner with a leather chair and ottoman. The stack of novels I'm reading is teetering precariously on the bedside table, and a vase of fresh Gerbera daisies brighten up the room.

I hope this blind date turns into a second date. Fingers crossed. I've been on four blind dates this summer. No second date with any of them. Is it me? Is it them? I like to think I'm a nice girl and not filled with drama like some of my girlfriends. Maybe guys *like* drama? As far as looks go, I'll be honest. I'm a size twelve with an ample bosom. But, I go to the gym, take good care of myself, and like the way I look.

I do have rules when it comes to dating though.

Note for tomorrow's to do list: Look at rules and analyze to see if *they* are the problem. Do this before the blind date.

2

Okay, to-do list. Write down my rules since they're just floating around in my head. I'm sitting at my desk taking a mini-break since the revised drawings received praise at the meeting and didn't spur immediate changes. I flip to a blank sheet on a legal pad and grab a pencil from the cup. As I sharpen the pencil with my handy sharpener shaped like a cupcake, I smile, feeling optimistic about tonight's date.

Kari's Rules to Dating

1. No long distance romance. I'm not driving four hours for a booty call. He must live in the same town. Driving on the icy roads in the winter for cuddling? No, thank you!

2. No ferrets. Dealbreaker. Why do people insist on having them as pets?

3. No fraternizing with colleagues outside of work. Jack is the only exception. Dating co-workers makes for really awkward situations. Trust me, I know from past experiences. Yes, *experiences*. Plural.

4. Try not to make snap judgments. I do it all the time. Doesn't everyone? If I do make a snap judgment, keep it to myself and don't broadcast it to everyone. Then I look like a total ass when

I'm wrong, and it seems to happen fairly often in my world. Hmm. Are these all of my rules? Seems like I had more than that … I mean, seriously, I'm clearly not the problem if these are the rules. I knew girls in college who wouldn't accept a second date with a guy who didn't call the next day or send flowers after a first date. Crazy! It makes my rules look absolutely acceptable and normal.

Now I can mark this off my to-do list. I open up my daytimer and flip to the notepad. My on-going to-do lists are written inside with little checkboxes next to the item. I also keep notecards, stamps, and a list of my family's birthdays in the daytimer. I'm a Type A like Mama and Kimberly. Making lists calms me. So does baking cookies. Mmmm … cookies.

"What are you marking off now, Kari?" Jack asks, as he saunters into my office and plops down in the chair in front of my desk.

"Nothing. How's your morning going?" I attempt to change the subject. *No way* do I want Jack to see this list. Easy fodder for him to tease me mercilessly. Plus, it has his name on it. I didn't tell him I broke a rule for him, and I don't want it going to his head.

"Seriously, I know your to-do list is in your little flowery pink daytimer you carry everywhere, so what did you mark off or add? Buy milk at the store or schedule your six week haircut?" Jack grins and snaps his fingers. "Oh, I know. Buy me a cookie this afternoon."

Gee, will the guy ever forget anything? I mentioned it months ago, and his steel trap mind picked up on it. I have my long, curly hair trimmed every six weeks. It keeps it healthy, and I don't want split ends. Girls worry about stuff like that. Guys have it so easy, walk into a barber shop every now and then, spend ten bucks, and call it good.

Jack picks up on the funniest little things I say or do and then teases me. *Fine*, I admit it. I love his teasing.

"Very funny, wise guy. Actually, I will buy you a cookie this afternoon if we can swing by Lauren's office on the way back.

She's lending me a shirt to wear on my thirtieth blind date," I exaggerate and roll my eyes.

"Sure! I'm dying to meet Lauren. She sounds like a hoot. Remember when she gave your business card out to the guy on the plane sitting next to her, and he emailed you a picture of him with no shirt on?" Jack guffaws. "The look on your face was priceless when you opened it."

"Don't remind me," I groan. "Anyway, I can't believe I haven't introduced you to Lauren yet. You're my closest friends. I bet she offers to set you up, so be prepared!"

"I don't need matchmaking. I'll find some girl, no big deal. The more indifferent I am to a girl, the more they want to date me."

Seriously? He just said that? What kind of a guy says something like that? Jack must be jaded from a girl stomping on his heart. Why won't he tell me about his dating adventures? I can offer feminine insight or something. Every time I ask about his past relationships, he changes the subject.

"Oh brother. Spare me. I'll ping you this afternoon for a cookie run. Now go away! I have work to do," I say, as I tuck away the list and daytimer in my purse.

⌒⍺

Later that afternoon, I send an email to Jack.

From: kcovington@bbarchitects.com
To: jharper@bbarchitects.com
Subject: Cookie Run
Ready?
From: jharper@bbarchitects.com
To: kcovington@bbarchitects.com

Sure. Meet you in 5 minutes outside.

I duck into the bathroom and dab on pink lip gloss. Pleased with the rest of my make-up, I fluff my hair and walk out of the office.

Jack's waiting for me by the atrium doors, and we head to Red Shed Coffee for a cookie.

"Work ... ergh! Thanks in advance for the cookie! I needed some fresh air," Jack says with a big sigh. He takes a deep breath in and slowly releases it. "Smells like winter."

"Sure. Listen, Lauren's expecting us, so let's hurry okay?"

"Will do, boss."

"Sorry, am I bossy? I just want to grab the shirt from her. And, I don't want you two becoming all chummy," I say defensively as we walk into Red Shed Coffee and head for the counter. All afternoon, I wondered why I hadn't introduced Lauren to Jack. I spend a lot of time with both of them, so naturally, they should meet.

"Why? Are you afraid we'll gang up on you and dissect your personal life?" Jack says with a wink, as I pay for our chocolate chip cookies and say goodbye to Lisa, the barista. She knows us by name and has our drinks memorized since we come here several times a week for coffee or cookies.

"Exactly."

We walk two blocks to City Hall, where Lauren is director of the Community Development Department. The reception-ist greets us and leads us back to Lauren's office. Lauren sits at her desk, typing furiously while she finishes up a phone call. Her straight blonde hair is cut in a chin length bob with sideswept bangs, and she's wearing a black pencil skirt with a light blue silk shirt. The blue matches her eyes perfectly.

There are brightly colored sticky notes on flip charts hung on the walls. Her office has a window with a perfect view of the

Chugach Mountains, and I notice a light dusting of snow on the highest peaks. Termination dust means summer is done, and winter is approaching fast.

"I'll take care of it by the end of the day. Look for my email," Lauren says tersely and hangs up the phone.

"Hey Lauren! Wow!" I say as I walk around her office and read numbers and acronyms written all over the sticky notes.

"Busy time for our office, Kari. New mayor. So … is this the charming Jack who I hear about constantly?" Laurens smiles and comes over to shake his hand.

"You're right, Kari, he's super cute," she pronounces, looking him slowly up and down. Jack looks amused, not even a little embarrassed by her declaration and inspection.

"Lauren!" I blush bright pink. "Jack, this is Lauren, the matchmaker of Anchorage," I smile at her. Lauren is my best friend, and I absolutely adore her.

"Very nice to meet you, Lauren. So, you're the one who convinced Kari to move up here to the last frontier. Nice job. How do you like working for the city?" Jack asks.

"Oh, you know. Depends on what the mayor wants from my department, which as you can see is plenty! Enough about my work, Kari tells me you're single. What's your type?" Lauren smiles mischievously and grabs a sticky note and pen off her desk.

Jack shakes his head. "No matchmaking for me! But, thanks for the offer." He laughs and gives her the brush off wave with his hand.

"But, I have tons of connections in town, and I know everyone! Kari can totally vouch for me," Lauren persists.

"Thanks, but I'll pass for now. Kari, don't we need to get back to the office?" Jack asks and gives me a knowing look.

"Yes, thanks for the reminder. Lauren, do you have the shirt?"

"Here it is, missy," Lauren says as she hands me a bag. "Nice to meet you, Jack! If you change your mind about a blind date, let me know!"

"Nice to meet you as well. Take care," Jack smiles and waves.

Jack and I leave her office and walk back to work. My blush just now begins to fade. I should've known Lauren would say something since she doesn't hold back anything.

"Lauren's really into matchmaking, huh? She's exactly what I pictured from your stories about her," Jack says.

"She's really fantastic and means well when it comes to matchmaking. I think she wants everyone to have a loved one, so matchmaking is a serious hobby for her. Thanks for not taking offense to it," I pick up the pace. We've been gone from the office awhile, and I'm anxious to return under the radar.

My phone chirps with a text message. I pull it out of my purse. It's from Lauren.

Lauren: He is gorgeous! Why aren't you dating him?

I sigh, and Jack looks over at me curiously. I slip the phone back into my purse. I'll wait until I'm back in my office before I reply.

Jack and I eat the cookies on the walk back to the office and chat about random topics. Seems like we never run out of stuff to talk about. We return to the office, unnoticed.

As soon as I catch up on a few emails and check voicemail, I remember to text Lauren back.

Kari: We are just friends. Period.

Lauren doesn't text me back, so I know I'll get an earful at the gym tonight. I sigh and turn my attention back to the museum expansion plans. Our team meets soon with the contractor, so I better get busy.

3

I love working out at the gym. Especially the smoothies from the juice bar after the work out. Lauren and I meet for step aerobics class three times a week. I send daily emails to remind her, and the accountability helps us both show up instead of skipping.

We stake out our usual places in the back row. The instructor is infamous for singling you out if you're talking during class or not working hard enough. We sneak chatting in before class and between songs.

"Thanks for not letting me off the hook for class tonight! I totally wanted to bail and sit on the couch with Will to watch bad reality TV," Lauren says as she bends down to stretch. She and Will have been married for five years.

"Sure, you know it helps when we push each other to go," I sit on the step bench and people watch for a few minutes before class begins.

"I laugh out loud at your emails because of the funny celebrity quote you always include in the gym reminder. Makes my day. So ... Jack is cute *and* polite. A real winner in my book if you ask me."

"Gee, it took you less than one minute to bring Jack up. Don't even think about it. I told you. We're just friends. Tons in common, but I don't think of him like that," I say, shaking my head.

"How do you know he doesn't view you as a possible Saturday night date or friends with benefits? He's single and fun. Plus, I got that flirty vibe from him. He probably flirts with you, and you don't even know it."

I roll my eyes at her and groan. "He doesn't flirt with me. We talk about food most of the time or cooking or our crazy boss and impossible deadlines."

"Well, keep it in mind, you make a striking couple, and he's not a hippie. That alone would thrill your mama."

"Ha! Speaking of Mama, did I tell you what she said to me last week?" I start laughing, thankful for the subject change. "I sent her pictures from a hike I went on with Deirdre, and she asked, 'Are you losing weight? In the pictures, your face doesn't look as round as a volleyball anymore.' Thanks, Mama. I love you too."

Mama and I have this crazy relationship. Maybe it's because we're so similar. Although, we bicker back and forth, we support each other and can talk for hours on the phone about everything. I do like to rile her up sometimes, just for fun.

Growing up, I thought my parents were pretty strict compared to my other friends. Oh, the battles we had. They won the majority of them, of course.

"Mothers … what would we do without them? I think you look great, by the way. Who cares if you're not a perfect size six? You're super active and healthy."

"You're sweet. Thank you! Oh, here comes the instructor. Don't get me in trouble again!" I warn and shake my finger at her.

"What? You're the one who stopped mid-song to laugh at me when I fell off the step!"

We make it through class without incident. Lauren wishes me luck on the blind date and reminds me to call her with all the details. She heads home right after class since it's her night to cook dinner.

I grab a pineapple banana smoothie and go home to get ready for the blind date. Last night, I tidied up the apartment and lectured myself to be on my best behavior. No snap judgments.

4

I sigh loudly as I try on the third possible outfit for my date with Brad. He'll arrive in twenty minutes, and desperation has set in. Lauren's shirt didn't fit well because I have bigger boobs than she does. I don't want the girls out there and waving to Brad on the first date.

Choose an outfit that looks casual and sexy enough to entice a second date or at least a good night kiss, I think to myself. I still need to finish my hair and make-up. Friends say my best feature is my curly hair, but I tame it for special occasions.

Tight, skinny jeans, pink silk, ruffled camisole, short black shrug sweater and black high heels. Perfect combination, flirty yet not too revealing. I relish these last days to wear cute shoes before winter hits and snow boots are the fashion statement. Oh yeah … and a whole wardrobe of coats. After my first winter up here with just a plain black coat, I noticed women wear brightly colored coats and have a different coat for each temperature range.

I stand in front of the bathroom mirror and flat iron my hair. Living in the South, my hair was curly all the time with the humidity, so I love living up here and changing my look as my mood dictates. I carefully apply make-up and blot the new lipstick I bought last week at Nordstrom.

I search my shoe closet for the Stuart Weitzman heels. Yes, I have a separate closet for my shoes. I have a fondness for expensive shoes. Don't judge. A girl has to indulge in at least one thing in life. For some women, it's purses or silk sheets. Me? Lots of beautiful shoes all lined up looking pretty.

In the living room, I gather up my cell phone and keys. I'm a little nervous and wonder about Lauren's description. How accurate will it be?

"He's tall, dark, and handsome. Will works with him and says he's nice. They skate skied almost every weekend last winter, so you know he's outdoorsy and in shape. I think he's from Colorado. Come on, you know my husband wouldn't set you up with any Joe Six Pack. Will adores you and is totally looking out for you," Lauren insists.

"Has he dated anyone lately? Is he a serial dater or just had his heart broken, and I'm the rebound girl?" I wince. Maybe knowing this information in advance will make me less nervous and apprehensive.

"I don't know. Ask him. Will has no clue. You know guys don't really talk about that stuff."

"Fine, but it's not exactly a first date kind of conversation. I just want to know what I'm in for." I'm a worrier. Can you tell?

Type A personality and a worrier can make life difficult, so I remind myself to take a deep breath and relax. I can't control everything and everyone. Even though I'd really like to.

"Relax, be yourself, and have a good time," Lauren says. Famous last words.

The doorbell rings at eight, and my stomach does a nervous little flip. Okay, think positive and smile. Remember your dating rules.

I open the apartment door. Brad is six foot two with jet black hair, slim, wearing khakis, a heather grey polo shirt, black jacket and sporting a wide smile. The shoe inspection reveals brown leather Cole Haan slip-ons. I release a deep breath and approve of his shoes. Hey! You can tell a lot about someone by their shoes. Start looking, and you'll see what I mean.

He smiles nervously and extends his hand. "Hi Kari, I'm Brad. You look terrific!"

Ten brownie points right away for the compliment. I shake his hand and no snap judgments come to mind. Good job so far.

"Very nice to meet you, Brad. Thank you so much! Let me grab my purse, and we can go."

"Perfect," Brad says, as he glances around my apartment. My den furniture consists of a tan microfiber sofa, a comfy leather chair, overstuffed bookshelves, throw pillows and fuzzy afghans. Think minimalist on a budget since most of my money is invested in the latest kitchen gadgets and top of the line pots and pans. And shoes, of course.

"You have a nice apartment."

Stop the press! Two compliments right out of the chute? This *is* promising.

I quickly text, "OMG. He's gorgeous." to Lauren as I do a final make-up check in the bathroom.

"I'm ready," I say, picking up my purse and locking the apartment door.

We walk out to Brad's silver Audi, and he opens the door for me. I sink into the plush leather seats and smile, thinking my fortune has turned.

5

~

"So, how long have you worked for *The Alaska Courier?*" I ask, as he drives to the restaurant.

"Three years, and I love it. Politics are my passion, so I love writing about the crazy stuff that goes on here. How about you? Will said you're new to Alaska. Where did you move up from?" Brad asks, conversationally.

"Charleston, South Carolina. I like it, although this is only my second winter. I've chatted with lots of people who say to wait until I've been up here for ten winters, and I may change my mind."

"This summer was pretty balmy, so maybe winter won't be too cold. Couple of years ago, we had three weeks where the temperature didn't rise above negative ten. Pretty brutal. I notice you don't have much of a Southern accent."

"Well, I say y'all occasionally and eat grits. That's pretty Southern. I guess I didn't pick up much of an accent growing up, but when I go back to visit, I come back with one," I laugh.

Brad pulls into the lot of The Roadhouse in downtown Anchorage. It's a popular restaurant among locals and a secret from most summer tourists. He opens the car door for me.

Very gracious and polite. Ten more brownie points. Keep this up, and he'll have enough points to get to second base with me tonight. Kidding, I'm just kidding.

We walk into the restaurant, and a hostess leads us to a table near the fireplace situated in the middle of the room. I gaze around the room and take in the warm interior decorated with photographs of Alaska's spectacular scenery, antique snowshoes, and Native artwork. It's one of my favorite restaurants, so I'm pleased Brad chose this for our first date.

The server comes by for drink orders, and we both order a pint of Alaskan Winter Ale, from one of the local breweries. As we look over the appetizer menu, a cacophony of sounds drifts over from the open kitchen.

"Any appetizers sound good to you?" Brad asks and sets down his menu.

"The calamari strips are really great here, and the pretzel with the ale dipping sauce sounds delicious."

"Perfect! Let's throw in some of the crab-stuffed mushrooms, too."

Brad places the appetizer order with the server and the small talk begins.

"How do you like Alaska? Can you see yourself living here for awhile?" Brad inquires.

"Everyone is so friendly here, and I like all the outdoor activities right out your back door. We don't have any mountains in Charleston. It's still early to think about long term though."

"And, I'm really glad Lauren and Will live here. They pushed me hard to apply for jobs up here when I took the plunge to move from Charleston," I say, thinking back to their numerous emails praising life in Anchorage.

I came up for a long weekend visit to check out the area, and I had my mind made up by the end of the first day. They promised to help me move and introduce me to people. It was an easy sell.

"How do you know them?"

"Lauren and I were roommates at Clemson University. She met Will there, and they moved here to Anchorage after they got married five years ago. Are you from here?"

"I grew up in Boulder, Colorado. I cross-country ski, bike, and love the outdoors, so I figured Alaska is a perfect match. The politics in Colorado aren't nearly as exciting as here." He grins, thinking of the latest local run for governor with eleven candidates. Brad had written a compass piece in *The Alaska Courier* about the election, which was picked up by the Associated Press.

"Oh, interesting," I say even though I don't like where this conversation may lead. Politics are not my strong suit, and I honestly don't know enough to hold a long, stimulating conversation.

"I have to ask. Are you a liberal or a stuffy conservative? I'm curious since you *are* from the South."

"Wow, you're direct," I pause, stalling for time since I don't know how to respond. "I don't know, I'm not really into politics much, and I haven't been up here long enough to figure out the political environment here. Is knowing which way I lean really important to you?" I ask, wondering if this is *his* dealbreaker.

"I just like to know, so I don't offend you. I have some pretty strong opinions," He runs his hand through his thick, dark hair, as he smiles smugly. Oh boy.

"Well, my parents are Republican, but like I said, I'm still trying to figure out this city and see who the honest politicians are."

Our drinks arrive, and I take a sip of beer. Is Brad going to talk about politics all night? There are other topics of conversation more suited to first dates. Okay, it's up to me to change the subject.

25

"What else do you like to do for fun?" I ask, hoping the response is something I can work with. At this point, I am *definitely* doing the bathroom trick. I have a feeling he's not going to let politics drop.

"I'm treasurer for the local Democratic Party, and I write a political blog. And I dabble in some mountaineering and rock climbing. Spent a couple of summers climbing the 14ers when I lived in Colorado. I also climbed Mt. McKinley three years ago."

"That's impressive! What was it like on top of the mountain?" I'm in awe as I haven't met anyone who has climbed Mt. McKinley.

"It was literally the best moment of my life. You actually end up climbing the mountain twice because you haul up a load of your supplies, then go back and haul up the rest of your stuff. The climbing isn't too technical, but dealing with the harsh weather conditions was the most difficult. Do you climb?"

"No climbing, but I do like hiking and camping. I'm a fair weather girl. More hiking or camping in the summer than winter."

"Yeah, winter camping is not for everyone, especially up here. What did you do last winter to keep you sane from the cold and darkness?" Brad asks. Oh yeah, I forgot about the scant six hours of daylight come mid-December. So different from the South, where you can wear Bermuda shorts and a tank top at Christmas.

"I'm learning to cross-country ski, and I picked up snowshoes at the REI sale last week. Honestly, I plan to catch up on all the stuff on my TiVo and watch the entire run of *Seinfeld* again on DVD this winter."

"*Seinfeld*? You like that show? Ugh, I can't stand it," Brad winces. "George yells his lines and totally overacts. Sorry if that offends you, but I change the channel if it comes on."

What the what? Did he just say he doesn't like *Seinfeld*? Seriously. Who doesn't like *Seinfeld*? This is not a snap judgment. It's a plain insult.

"Excuse me while I visit the ladies' room," I say, abruptly, and stand up from the table. I double-check for my phone, which I slipped into my pocket earlier.

I head to the restrooms and think about what expensive lunch Lauren will buy me next week. I pull out my phone and text her once I'm safely inside.

Me: You SO owe me!

Lauren: What? Why? You said he was cute!

Me: He hates *Seinfeld*.

Lauren: Come on, seriously? Who cares? Don't tell me it's a dealbreaker for you?

Me: Totally! Sometimes I feel like my dating life is part of that show!

Lauren: Kari. Really.

Me: And, he's super political and wants to know how I vote! He'll probably ask for my voter registration card!

Lauren: I'm so sorry! Will thought you would really hit it off.

Me: Tell Will he's cut off from my cookies and treats.

I've been gone awhile, so I slip the phone back into my pocket and walk back to the table. The server is delivering the appetizers and chatting with Brad about her thoughts on the recent mayor race. She winks at me when I sit down and quietly slips away to fetch another round of drinks for us.

"Looks delicious," I say as I slide into the chair.

"Kari, I was really rude when I spoke about *Seinfeld*. I'm not a fan, but I was wrong to put it down when you clearly like the show," Brad apologizes, looking sheepish. He reaches over to touch my hand. "I'm sorry. Not a good first impression of me."

"No worries, Brad. It's fine. These mushrooms are really yummy," I say, changing the subject and spearing another one onto my plate.

"So, back to my favorite subject, politics."

The evening wore on with Brad asking my opinions on government spending, the war overseas, the current President, and gun control. I answered the questions as best as I could, but felt scrutinized for each answer. I tried to turn the discussion back several times to learning more about him, but failed miserably. Couldn't he sense my discomfort in the topic and questions? Hello social cues!

I actually warmed up to him when he apologized for the *Seinfeld* comments, but the overzealous political questions became the dealbreaker.

After Brad paid the bill, we walk out to the car in an uncomfortable silence. I'm sure a good night kiss is not in the cards, and I'm relieved. On the way home, Brad talks about the weather and the new snow on the mountains.

When we arrive to my apartment parking lot, Brad opens the car door for me. "This was fun." Brad says awkwardly, knowing we didn't really hit it off.

"Yes, thanks for an interesting evening! I wish you the best with your political endeavors. It was definitely an educational date," I say quickly.

I shake his hand and hurry up the stairs to my apartment before he can respond. I can't wait to tell Jack about the date. Another bad one for the books.

6

"I'm telling you Lauren, he grilled me about my political views on everything. As if insulting *Seinfeld* wasn't enough," I exclaim, adamantly. "Another bad blind date for the books. One of these days, I'm going to say no to your matchmaking."

"Come on, how many questions did he really ask?" Lauren laughs and dips a chip into the spicy tomatillo salsa.

We're drinking margaritas at the Tahoe South Cantina bar Saturday night. I recant the date to Lauren and embellish a few details. Brad was a handsome snappy dresser, but too pushy on the political front for my taste. To discuss politics in a polite manner is one thing, but he was borderline obsessive and his remark about *Seinfeld* was kind of rude, despite his apology. Not everyone likes the same thing, but usually one refrains from insulting remarks, especially on a first date.

I know one of my weaknesses is making snap judgments about people after only knowing them for five minutes, but I knew at the end of the evening, there would be no second date. Brad needs to find a girl who will discuss current events and listen to NPR in the evenings with him.

"It'll be interesting to see what Brad says about the date to Will. You *have* to tell me!" I lick the salt off the glass rim and take a sip of the margarita. "I certainly didn't give him a chance to kiss me or ask me out again, though I doubt he would've done either!"

"Of course. I may have to nag Will for details, but you know I'll withhold sex until he divulges."

"I thought married people didn't have sex! Isn't that what everyone says?" I tease her. She's my only married friend here, so I like giving her a hard time.

"Very funny. It's different when you get married … you'll see. Anyway, I'm sorry it didn't work out, but I must commend you for all the blind dates I set you up on," Lauren compliments me.

"I would just love for a second date to happen, you know?" I say with a sniff and signal the bartender for another round of margaritas.

"The perfect guy is out there. I know it. Cheer up. I won't set you up on any more blind dates unless I personally screen them first," Lauren promises. "So, how's Jack doing? What's he doing this weekend?" A little smile spreads across her face.

"He's good. Don't even go there. I already told you Jack and I are just friends," I say threateningly.

"You have so much in common, and you're so comfortable with him. Why not consider it?"

I dip a chip into the salsa and chew it as I picture us as a couple. "Nope. I do adore his non-stop teasing, but it's not going anywhere between us."

"Fine. I won't bug you anymore tonight about him." Lauren gestures with a Girl Scout salute.

My phone chirps with a text message. It's from Jack. He attached a picture.

Jack: Deep fried hot dog wrapped in bacon!
Me: Seriously?
Jack: Believe it.

"Who's the text from?" Lauren asks, and I show her the picture.

"Jack. He wrapped a hot dog in bacon and deep fried it. Not sure about that," I smile and shake my head slowly.

"He sent you a picture of that awful creation?" Lauren asks, making a face.

"Yes, we send pictures of food to each other. It's kind of silly," I admit, but I love it.

"Interesting," Lauren smirks and honors her Girl Scout pledge.

We finish our margaritas, and I drive home, thinking about baking a sweet treat to share at work on Monday. I bake when I'm stressed out, and this kind of qualifies as stress. Another bad blind date resulting in no second date. I want to meet a guy and live happily ever after: do some travelling, settle down, buy a house, have children, and retire with grandchildren jumping on our laps. The usual plan for most girls, I think.

I turn on the Kitchenaid mixer after all the cookie ingredients are measured and dumped in the bowl. Chocolate chip cookies with M&M's. They are Jack's favorite cookies. Wait. Did I just say Jack, and why did I automatically mix up his favorite cookies?

OMG! This is all Lauren's fault! She keeps mentioning Jack! Nope, it's merely a coincidence. I make these cookies all the time. Wait. All the time? I consider this as I snack on raw cookie dough.

Ergh. I can't handle this right now. Jack and I are best friends and only friends. I'm reading more into this than necessary. Just bake the cookies and go to bed, I tell myself. Don't overanalyze this. It doesn't mean *anything*. To take my mind off these crazy thoughts, I turn on my favorite Fleet Foxes CD and sing along as I bake.

7

⤳

"I am *definitely* ordering the chocolate pots de crème," I say as I peruse the rest of the menu.

Jack and I sit at a corner booth at The Snowy Owl, a restaurant I've been dying to try out for weeks. Several co-workers have eaten here and raved about it. Since Jack is my dining out partner, I made us a dinner reservation after confirming his availability.

"They have an impressive selection of microbrews and Northwest wines. Do you want to share the steamed mussels appetizer?" Jack asks as he licks his lips when a server walks by with a tray of food.

"Sure," I nod and admire the restaurant décor. The walls are covered in sky blue damask, and delicate silver pendant lights hang above each table. A cluster of three votive candles sit in the middle of each table, and watercolors by local artists grace the walls. Roasted garlic and white bean puree drizzled with fruity olive oil and soft flatbread is placed in front of us almost immediately.

Jack orders us a bottle of Malbec and the mussels appetizer from the server. I like it when he orders for me. Just seems old-fashioned and sweet.

"How was work today? I barely saw you after we grabbed our morning coffee," I say and slather bean puree on a piece of flatbread.

"In addition to working on the museum expansion with the team, I got pulled into the redesign for Mountain View Elementary School. I'm working overtime until Christmas," Jack frowns and takes a sip of the wine, nodding to the server.

"Yikes. Let me know if you need anything. I'm glad we landed the school redesign. Seems like the economic downturn hasn't affected our little company, eh?"

"I know, right? Rumor has it they're going to hire two more architects early next year. So glad we have a couple of interns from the University of Alaska to help us this winter," Jack says. "I already like this restaurant. It has a good vibe."

See? This is why I like Jack so much. He's easy to talk to, appreciates good food and service, has a positive outlook, and is generally a nice guy. Why isn't he married by now or at least dating someone? He's also very handsome, but I think I mentioned that once or twice.

The server delivers a steaming bowl of mussels and sets down a basket of homemade crusty sourdough bread to sop up the broth. Jack spoons out a serving for me and then serves himself.

"Thanks! What are you going to order for dinner? I can't decide between the roasted pork tenderloin with pears and shallots or the miso grilled sockeye salmon."

"I'm going with the New York Strip with Port Mustard Sauce. Wow, these mussels are terrific," Jack says enthusiastically.

We place our dinner order, and I also pre-order dessert. Judge if you want, but imagine how disappointed *you* would be if they ran out of the dessert you were looking forward to all night. Jack laughs, but doesn't comment. He's used to me ordering dessert when I order my entrée.

I lured Jack here a little under false pretenses because I realized that I don't know much about him. I know he grew up in Seward, Alaska, down on the Peninsula, and he likes cooking, food, trail running, and skate skiing. That's it. We spend a lot of time together, but mainly chat about the same couple of topics. Tonight, I want to learn more. Especially in the romance department, of course.

"So, how did you like growing up in Seward? It's a pretty small town," I ask casually.

"Oh, you know. Small town, everyone knows everyone. It was a fun place to grow up. We all looked out for each other," Jack says as he takes another slice of bread and splits the remaining mussels between us.

Hmmm ... that's it? Not a lot of details and description.

"I realized that I've never asked you ... do you have siblings?"

"A younger sister and two older brothers. We were a handful. Maybe that's why I give Mom a really nice birthday *and* Mother's Day gift each year," Jack laughs.

"Are you close with your family? You don't mention them much."

"We're very close. In fact, my sister is coming up from Seward next weekend. I'm thinking about having a party. I'll keep you posted on the details. We'll fire up the grill and do a little prewinter grilling." Jack finishes his mussels and pushes his plate to the side. He refills our wine glasses. Perhaps a little more wine will help the flow of information from him, I hope.

Okay, enough family details. I'm going in for something good and juicy.

"What are you going to grill? Spareribs? Maybe roast a chicken? Why did you and your last girlfriend break up?" I ask nonchalantly as I mop up the rest of the broth with a piece of bread. I hope he just answers the question without even thinking about it. He has *never* mentioned past girlfriends.

"Come on, Kari. You know I don't talk about relationships. Nice try though."

"But, I want to know more about you, Jack! Our friendship can't just consist of what we're cooking, what we're eating, my crazy mama stories, and our shared love of lattes! I told you all about Brad, the blind date from hell!" I say with a huff, trying my best to look wounded.

"Kari, any chance you'll give me a hall pass, and we can talk about something else?" He lets out a big sigh.

"Nope." Stand my ground. See if he caves in. If so, I'll gladly pay for dinner. And a cookie tomorrow!

"Fine. We broke up because I wanted to get serious, and she didn't. Classic relationship scenario." Jack sounds defeated.

"Oh, I'm sorry, Jack. How long did you date?" Success! Some details.

"We dated for a year and a half. I started talking about long term, and she freaked out. Broke up with me and ran off to China to teach English. She broke my heart," Jack says tonelessly. He fiddles with the stem of his wine glass and doesn't look at me directly. Oh, crap. Now I feel kind of bad for pushing him. I'll buy him a cookie every day this week.

"I'm really sorry. You still sound really broken up about it."

"Hmm … I wonder if the food will come soon," I drop the relationship subject since I see Jack isn't up for talking about it.

"It's fine. You're absolutely right. We're friends, and we should know more about each other. You tell me all kinds of family and dating stuff. I admit to cynicism now when I think about relation-ships. It took a long time to recover from the break up, and she still tries to reach out to me. I don't want her to. She stomped on my heart, and I don't want to receive Facebook messages from her thanking me for introducing her to yoga when we dated because now she loves it. Come on!" He mutters with a frown.

Ouch. Yeah, it would piss me off too.

"I was in love with her. We spent all our time together and even adopted a dog. She took the dog, by the way. He was the coolest, laid back dog. I miss him." Jack smiles, thinking about Scout, the Labrador mix.

The server delivers our food, and we spoon some of our entrées onto each other's plate to taste. Both are outstanding, and we continue chatting.

"How about I change the subject since I've practically ruined our evening? It's your turn now. Ask me a question," I say as I cut up the asparagus. The pork tenderloin is so juicy and flavorful. I suspect they brined it and make a mental note to brine mine next time.

"Why did you choose Alaska to move to?"

"That's your burning question? Wow! I feel like you gave *me* the hall pass! Well, I know Lauren and Will really love it here."

"Seriously? Alaska is the farthest state away from South Carolina. You don't just *decide* to move up here because someone else likes it. People move up here for four reasons: to run away from the law, family, crazy exes, or some other problem. Tell the truth, Kari!"

"Fine. I really wanted to experience something different. The South is so conservative. Racial discrimination is still very much alive, and I wanted to break out and see other parts of the country."

"When Lauren and Will talked about Alaska, it sounded like this whole different world. It gives me a chance to do something on my own, far away from home, out from under the shadow of my sisters."

"So, are you happy you moved up here? 'Cause I know, I am! You're my favorite person to eat out with, and you have mad baking skills. I'll take your chocolate chip M&M cookies any day over Red Shed Coffee's cookies. Thanks for bringing them into work this week!"

"You're sweet. I *am* glad. I miss my parents, sisters and nieces, but I love it here. I feel at home," I smile. "I have one more question for you."

Jack groans and sets down his fork. "Yes?" He also sneaks in an eye roll. Typical Jack.

"Do you have plans for Thanksgiving? I'm spending it with Lauren, Will, and his folks. Do you want to come with me?" I ask, crossing my fingers under the table.

"Are you helping cook the meal?"

"As a matter of fact, yes."

"Count me in."

I smile and return my attention to dinner. We chat about random topics the rest of the time, and Jack relaxes … thanks to the wine and lack of probing questions. The server brings me the chocolate pots de crème with an extra spoon and a cup of coffee for Jack. He takes a bite and agrees it's the best part of the meal and a perfect ending to the evening.

"Maybe we can have this dessert for Thanksgiving. It's so yummy!" Jack says in between bites. Like a true gentleman, he leaves me the last bite.

"I'll look for a recipe. I'm definitely making chocolate pecan pie and pumpkin pie. I'm having lunch with Lauren tomorrow to plan out the rest of the menu," I say, licking the spoon and scraping the last bit of chocolate from the ramekin.

"Kari, you know it's only September. November is a long way off," Jack laughs. I really do love his teasing. It reminds me to not take myself so seriously and to have some fun!

"I know, I know! But we're both Type A personalities and planners, so thinking ahead is normal for us."

"You're so adorable," Jack says with a wink. I blush slightly and avoid making eye contact.

The server drops off the check, and Jack grabs his wallet from his jacket pocket and tosses down his credit card.

"My treat. I'm glad we had dinner tonight," Jack says with a big smile. He stretches, pats his nonexistent gut, and looks quite content.

"Jack! I asked you to dinner! I'll take care of the check," I insist and pull out my wallet.

"Don't sweat it, Kari. I'm happy to spend time with you. It's been a fun evening," Jack says. I put the wallet back in my purse and smile at him.

We leave the restaurant, and he drops me off at my apartment. It certainly was an enjoyable dinner out, and I'm once again thankful for my friendship with Jack.

I can't wait to surprise him with chocolate pots de crème on Thanksgiving!

8

I walk over to Lauren's office with sandwiches and chips from our favorite deli. Treading carefully, I try not to slip in the first snowfall, about two inches. My black snow boots are stylish and functional, but I'm always wary of falling on the icy sidewalks. You see people slip and fall pretty often, mostly in parking lots.

Winter is here. Time to break out the skis and hot toddies and say goodbye to sandals for nine months. Sniff. Sniff.

The receptionist ushers me in to Lauren's office and says she's running a few minutes late. She drops off some bottled water on the small conference table and returns to her desk.

On the bookshelves behind Lauren's desk, I look at pictures of her and Will from their wedding, at Clemson decked out in bright orange t-shirts and war paint for the football game, and a picture of them fishing on the Kenai River. There are also some pictures of us from the Caribbean cruise we took after we graduated college. Yikes! Me in a bikini. What was I thinking? And, how did I manage to pack on twenty pounds since college?

"Sorry, I'm late. How are you?" Lauren says, walking quickly into the office with a legal pad and an empty coffee cup.

"No problem. I just arrived. Cute outfit!" I compliment her red wraparound tie blouse she's wearing with a black pencil skirt and black Mary Jane heels I helped her pick out last week at Nordstrom. Lauren's a bit fashion-challenged and used to buy whatever outfit the store mannequin was wearing. She swears it was because she's awful at matching clothes, but I think she's just not into shopping. Lucky for her, I am!

I unpack our lunch and grab the daytimer from my purse. Lauren slides into the chair next to me after a quick scan of her emails. She has her planner in hand along with sticky notes and a highlighter. See? Type A's stick together.

"So, Thanksgiving is Thursday, November 26. What about eating at 2 p.m.? Does that work?" Lauren asks.

"Oh! Is Jack coming with you?" She unwraps the turkey and cranberry cream cheese sandwich and dumps chips onto her plate.

"Yep, he accepted! Two p.m. works fine. Who else is on the guest list?" I pause and look appreciatively at my sandwich before diving in. Thinly sliced roast beef piled high with blue cheese slices, tomato, lettuce, and spicy horseradish aioli. I take a picture with my phone and text it to Jack.

"Will's parents are driving down from Fairbanks, and my co-worker, Abby. You'll love her. Very sweet. She likes expensive shoes like you!" Lauren teases and takes a bite of her sandwich.

"All right. Will has dibs on cooking the turkey and stuffing. How about I make sweet potato casserole in addition to dessert? Jack said he would bring wine. Then, your parents and Abby can choose from the rest."

"That'll work perfectly. Are you making your Mama's famous sweet potato casserole with the pecan crumble topping?" Lauren licks her lips as she thinks about it. Sweet potatoes, vanilla, brown sugar, pecans. How can you *not* love it?

"Yes, the famous sweet potato casserole. Mama says it's the dish that got Dad to propose," I laugh and feel a sadness twang as I think about my parents. I miss them.

"That's so Southern! What did Jack say when he accepted the invitation?"

"He seemed excited, plus he's a great guest. He can chat with anyone," I say, as I admire his conversational skills. He could carry on a conversation with a wall, for goodness sake.

"Maybe you guys will end up cuddling on the couch in front of the fire."

"Lauren! You are relentless, and you also promised not to keep bringing up Jack and me as a couple! Listen, I have another unbelievable Mama story for you," I say, changing the subject.

"You and your mother. It's a love/hate relationship. Maybe you should write a book about it."

"I would, but people would think I'm making it up! Anyway, she ran into my high school boyfriend, Patrick, at the country club last week. She chatted with him, found out he was in the middle of a divorce, and gave him my email, work phone number and cell phone number. I could kill her! She has no sense of decency!" I cry out, clearly annoyed with Mama.

"Did she say how he looked? Handsome? Bald and hairy? Beer gut?" Lauren laughs.

"Did you hear what I said? In the middle of a divorce and here comes Mama playing matchmaker!"

"I heard you, but you didn't answer my question. Cute or bald with a gut?"

"If you must know, her exact words were 'charming and quite handsome'," I imitate Mama with a deep Southern twang.

"Hmmm. I bet he'll want to see you when you visit at Christmas. By the way, when do you leave? I'll mark it in my planner, too. We'll take you to the airport."

"December 20-28. I'll return for New Year's Eve. Jack's having a huge party, and I want to go. What are y'all doing?" My Southern accent shows up every now and then.

"I booked a hotel room downtown for us. We're going to eat a fancy dinner and watch fireworks." Lauren opens another bottle of water and sits back, content.

"Nice! Listen, don't go overboard on cleaning at Thanksgiving. I know your mother-in-law is a clean freak, but relax. She adores you and I'm sure the house doesn't matter. There's no need to get out the toothbrush to scrub floors."

"I know, I know. We get along well. It's just that she keeps her house super clean, and I don't want her to think Will and I live in a dirty house or I'm a bad wife because the house isn't picked up and clean all the time."

"Yes, but she's retired and has all the time in the world to clean and keep her fridge sparkling. Just promise me you won't go overboard." I savor the last bite of sandwich.

"We'll see. Thanks again for bringing over lunch! Ergh … step class tonight at the gym," Lauren makes a face.

"We have to work off all those chips we just inhaled."

We clean up our lunch mess, and I leave her tapping away at the flurry of emails that came in over the lunch hour. After I settle in back at work and change out of my snow boots to my heels, I scan my email. One of my girlfriends, Deirdre, wants to meet Wednesday after work for "Cocktails and Chasing." Chasing is her term for finding guys who will buy us drinks and engage in harmless flirting.

I reply to her and agree to meet at The Roadhouse. It's always a fun time when we go out, plus, she's my shoe shopping buddy. No judging when one of us spends half of our paycheck on cute Manolo Blahniks.

Later that afternoon, I send an email to Lauren to remind her about our gym date. No skipping out!

From: kcovington@bbarchitects.com
To: lauren.blackwell@alaska.gov
Subject: The Gym

Lauren! See you at step class tonight.

Celebrity Quote of the Day:
Dude, I go to church as much as I go to the strip club.
- T Pain

9

Lauren and I have a good workout, and we sit at the juice bar after class. The instructor pushed us hard, and my legs already ache.

We scope out the guys in the free weight area, and Lauren waves to a couple of people she knows. I'm always impressed by the number of people she knows in town.

"The new Mayor is making my life hell. Tons of work, no approved overtime, and a slew of new projects that he's branded 'Priority' from my department," Lauren says miserably and takes a long sip of her strawberry smoothie.

"Ugh, sorry to hear that, Lauren. He's not exactly popular right now with the voters since he cut back the budget on sidewalk snow clearing. Where does he expect pedestrians to walk? It was slippery today, and this was the first of many snowfalls. Brad, the infamous *Seinfeld* hater and politics lover is having a field day. Did you see his Opinion piece in *The Alaska Courier*?"

"I thought you didn't like him. Now, you're stalking him and reading his column?" Lauren gazes at me with a raised eyebrow.

"I'm not stalking him. I did take something away from the date, and that's to learn more about Anchorage and the politics. So, I've been reading his column and listening to NPR for news instead of just listening to *Wait, Wait, Don't Tell Me.* Brad will probably run for senator someday, and I can say that I once went out with him," I laugh and finish off my pineapple banana smoothie.

"You're the only moderate Republican he's ever taken out."

"Very funny. So, I'm meeting Deirdre on Wednesday for drinks."

"Just drinks? You always have some wild adventure when you meet up with her," Lauren pours us both a glass of ice water from the bar.

"She calls it 'Cocktails and Chasing,' so it makes an interesting evening for sure. We haven't really hung out since summer, other than a few Nordstrom shoe shopping runs at lunch. Did I tell you about our fishing trip in August?"

"I don't think so. What happened?"

"Her co-workers booked a halibut fishing charter, and she invited me to come along. She and a bunch of introverted guy engineers. Oh boy. She showed up with a huge cooler filled with spicy tomato juice, pepper vodka, and pickled green beans. It was a hoot! We kicked back a couple of cocktails on the way out of the inlet, and everyone eventually loosened up."

"Sounds pretty crazy. Where does she work again, and how did you two meet?"

"She's a chemical engineer for BP. We met at Red Shed Coffee, the westside location near my apartment. Just chatted in line while waiting to order lattes, and we became fast friends. Oh, and I noticed her Franco Sarto's sandals and complimented her."

"You and your shoes. I love it! Well, have fun with Deirdre! I better get going. Will and I are going out for sushi tonight," Lauren hops off the stool and picks up her gym bag.

"I'll call you tomorrow," I say and finish my water. My knees pop when I stand up to leave. I stretch my legs and limp out to the car. No pain, no gain.

⁓

Winter is definitely here in Anchorage. The two inches turned into six inches by early evening. Snow is piled up in corners of parking lots, and people have to estimate where the lanes are on the road. I really don't mind the cold so much. Wear a hat, scarf, and mittens to stay warm, and dress in layers. Many layers.

The daylight is also rapidly dwindling as we lose over five minutes a day. I find if I stay busy with work, friends, and other obligations, it's not such a big deal. Of course, there *are* times when I curl up on my sofa covered with an afghan and watch Food Network for hours.

I arrive home and change into yoga pants and a Clemson hoodie after a hot shower to sooth my aching legs. In the kitchen, I open the refrigerator and decide to make breakfast for dinner since it's my favorite meal of the day. Roasted red potatoes and a veggie egg scramble topped with sliced avocado. I snap a picture of my piled up plate and text it to Jack.

Me: B-fast for dinner!
Jack: Looks great
Me: What are you up to?
Jack: Watching football and drinking beer
Me: Have fun!

I take my plate and settle in on the sofa to watch *Top Chef.* Halfway through the show, my cell phone rings.

"Hi, Mama. How are you? Why are you up so late?" I ask, noting it's almost midnight on the East Coast. I turn the TV on mute and click the record button. Who knows how long this call will take?

"Hi, Sweetie. I'm fine. I can't sleep, so I figured I'd check in with you. Has Patrick called yet? I told him you were expecting him to make the first move," Mama says in her deep Southern accent.

"MAMA! He's in the middle of a divorce. I'm sure he has other things on his mind, and please stop giving my phone number out to every single man you meet. It makes me look desperate."

This is just one example of Mama driving me crazy. One recent example.

"You *are* desperate! You're thirty-two with no prospects. Before you know it, you'll be one of those forty-year-old women adopting a child because you want children and can't land a man. Goodness gracious, Kari. I want more grandbabies. And you live in a state where there are ten men for every one woman. I would expect you to meet a good enough man."

Ouch. Did she really research Alaska statistics to lecture me? I didn't know she knew how to do anything on the computer other than send me recipe chain emails, cat videos, or articles on how to look ten pounds thinner.

"Mama, that statistic doesn't really apply to Anchorage, maybe some of the smaller towns. Anchorage is about a one to one ratio for your information. And how do you know that anyway? And your comment about good enough ... I'm not even going there."

"Oh, don't be so dramatic. You know what I mean," Mama says with a huff.

"So, how's Kate doing in school? I never hear from her, but I read her constant Facebook posts. Is she doing any studying or just partying until May?" I quickly change the subject before I say something I'll regret.

"I know that peculiar statistic because I read up on Alaska when you announced your move there. Kate is just fine. It's her senior year at college, so she's making the most of it and enjoying herself. She mentioned meeting some boy at a party," Mama says proudly.

My baby sister, Kate, is majoring in English at the University of North Carolina at Chapel Hill. I campaigned hard for her to attend Clemson. But, her best friend was accepted to UNC, so I knew listing Clemson's assets would not help. With UNC only a few hours from Charleston, and close enough to come home for the holidays, Mama gave her blessing and helped Kate with loan applications to pay for out of state tuition.

"Good for her. I talked to Kimberly last week. The twins are a handful, but she is managing fairly well. Sounds like Mark is helping out a lot and not travelling as much," I say, happy that Kimberly picked out a wonderful man who dotes on her and treats her like a queen. They have five-year-old twin girls, and Mark is a sports writer. He travels at least one week a month to report on college games in the Southeast.

Kimberly and Mark are my role models in terms of what I want my marriage to mirror. They have equal weight in decisions about the girls, their home, careers, and more. They are respectful to each other and appreciate each others' strengths.

After college, Kimberly was the marketing director for the Stingrays Hockey Team in Charleston. She met Mark at a game he was covering for *Sports Illustrated*. After they got married and found out they were expecting twins, she decided to stay at home. She's type A like Mama and me. Rumor has it she tracked the twins poop and pee on an Excel spreadsheet. I don't need to see the spreadsheet to believe it.

"Oh Lordy! She has them on a schedule. God forbid I drop by and want to take them out for ice cream. She gets her feathers ruffled over the silliest things like that. The twins are absolutely adorable and a perfect age right now," Mama says and switches topics. "I can't wait to see you at Christmas."

"Me, too. How's Dad's golf game? Is he still playing every day?"

"You know he is; that man will be buried with his golf clubs. Is it cold there? It's cold here. Tonight it's down in the sixties. It's only September, for goodness sake."

"Yes, Mama. It's cold here, but it will only get colder. The temp is twenty-five degrees, and I'm all snuggled up on the sofa watching TV. We have six inches of fresh snow."

"All that snow! Is school and work closed?" Mama asks since any threat of snow in the South closes everything, and everyone runs to the grocery store to buy bread and milk.

"No, they don't close school or work for snow here. Only if the conditions are really bad. So, why can't you sleep?" I ask, hoping we can finish our conversation soon, so I can get back to *Top Chef*. I'm invested in this particular competition and rooting for the last woman chef.

"I don't know. Too much sweet tea at dinner, I suppose. Have you met any men lately? What about that young man, Jack, from work?"

"Jack and I are just friends. I'm going out Wednesday with my friend, Deirdre. Maybe I'll meet someone then. Who knows? You're the one in a big rush for me to get married, not me. You know, pushing me isn't helping *or* very loving, either."

"I'm just worried about you. That's all. I want you to be happy. I would prefer that you meet someone soon, move back to Charleston, and come over for dinner every Sunday with the rest of the family. You claim you're so family-oriented, yet you live so far away."

The guilt trip is in full force. I have to live my own life, and if it's far away from the family, then I'm sorry. Yes, I love my family very much and miss them, but don't make me feel guilty.

"I *am* family-oriented, but it doesn't mean I have to live in the same town as you. Y'all mean the world to me, but it's important I have some of my own adventures. Why can't you understand this?" My eyes start to tear up. It seems like we have this conversation every other month.

"As your Mama, it's my job to make sure you're happy and successful. You would be happiest near your family where we can support you. It's hard to help you from so far away. I just miss you."

"I know, Mama. I miss you, too. But, please support my decision to live here. We talk and email all the time. I'll be there for Christmas. Listen, I have to go now. Tell Dad hello for me. Can I call you this weekend?" I ask, desperate to end this conversation. I don't want to cry on the phone. Breathe in, breathe out.

"Okay, I'll talk with you on Sunday at our usual time. Love you, Honey, and I'm sorry if I upset you. I don't mean to."

I love my mama. I swear, I do. She has these iridescent blue eyes and wavy blond hair I would die for. She has this kind and willing manner, but she's a little overzealous in the marriage department. She's also an expert in the guilt department. My twin nieces, Anna and Ashley, inherited her eyes and blonde hair, not the guilt gene, thank goodness.

Mama grew up in Charleston and met my dad, Boyd, in high school. They became inseparable and were voted Homecoming Queen and King. After college, they married right away, and Kimberly, Kate and I arrived over the next six years. Non-stop diaper changes, feedings, and very little sleep. She enrolled all of us in ballet, Brownies, soccer, and piano lessons. Mama became the quintessential homemaker and even made some of our clothes.

Now, her life consists of going out to lunch with friends, attending Sunday brunch at the country club, chairing the board for the Southern Ladies Society, volunteering, and boating in the summer. It's amazing she finds time to meddle in my life and my sisters' lives. And she wonders why I moved away…

10

"What's new in your life, Kari?" Deirdre asks as she glances around the bar area. Part of the "Chasing." She rates a few guys in her head and returns her attention to me.

We're sitting at a high-top table in the bar at The Roadhouse, and it's jam-packed. I'm glad Deirdre arrived early to snag us seats before the after-work crowd arrived in force. They have the best Happy Hour in town with appetizer and drink specials.

"Working a lot! Still on the museum expansion project, and I'm *so* ready for something new. Our firm just picked up three more projects, so I'll stay busy this winter. Guess it's better now than in the summer, right?" I ask and take a sip of Merlot.

Summer is the *best* time to live in Alaska. Eighteen plus hours of daylight every day, long hikes in the midnight sun, Summer Solstice parties, fishing, biking, wildlife viewing, and camping. A co-worker told me there's no sleeping during summer. That's what winter is for.

"Absolutely! Nobody in Alaska works on Fridays in the summer, if they can help it. We're off in the wilderness soaking up the sun. Our summers are so short, we take advantage of the weather and put work on the back burner."

"How's work for you? Have they hired any extroverted chemical engineers?" I laugh, thinking of the funny engineer stories Deirdre tells. She's one of the few women engineers in a large department. Throw in politics working for an oil company, and it's an interesting work atmosphere.

"Believe me. They don't exist. Work's fine. You know, the guys really warmed up to me after our infamous drunken halibut fishing trip. However, I should've picked a different career path to find a husband. I need a gregarious, fun guy, not someone looking at their shoes as they talk to me." Deirdre sighs and picks up her martini glass and drains it. She eats the two olives and signals the bartender for another martini.

"It's not your career at all. Meeting a husband can happen anywhere, not just work. It could happen at the grocery store, church, or on a hike at Turnagain Arm. Besides, I'm a big believer in meeting people through other people."

"Perhaps. Oh, there are two guys at the end of the bar!" Deirdre exclaims. "Sneak a peek, and let me know what you think," Deirdre whispers.

Nonchalantly, I turn and look over my left shoulder. Nice. They're both wearing ties and jackets. Perhaps visiting from out of town. Anchorage-ites don't dress up to go out, or even dress up for work. It's perfectly acceptable for men to wear a long sleeve dress shirt with a fleece vest to work and call it "dressed up."

"Are they looking over here?" I ask, thinking of the *Swingers* movie, one of my all-time favorites. Vince Vaughn is a genius in the movie, and Jon Favreau is perfect in his role.

"Not yet, but the blonde guy looks familiar. Let me think a moment."

Deirdre knows everyone in town. She's on two non-profit board of directors and is heavily involved in the Petroleum Club.

An outgoing and outspoken woman engineer is kind of rare, so she likes the attention. The bartender delivers her martini, and she chews on the olives, lost in thought.

"I'm getting another glass of wine while you think about it. Do you want to order some appetizers?" I ask, since my stomach is growling. Jack and I didn't have a chance this afternoon to slip out for a cookie or an afternoon latte.

"Sure, just pick anything."

I order the pretzel with ale dipping sauce and seared ahi tuna with wasabi vinaigrette, along with my wine from the bartender. Glad Deirdre's not picky like some of my other girlfriends. No carb diets, white food diets, paleo diets, no way. Enjoy food in moderation and live life. That's my motto. Of course, ask me again after the holiday season five pound gain, and I may change my tune.

"I got it! Ron is the blonde guy, and he recently joined the board of directors for American Red Cross. I met him at a fund-raiser last month. Can I count him as a point?" Deirdre grins.

And the game begins!

We play this game called 'Who do you know?' every time we go out. One point for each person you know, but the relationship must be acknowledged, so you have to make eye contact, talk to the person, wave at each other, or do the head bob. It's a fun game to play and keeps me from being shy. Deirdre always wins since she's lived here for ten years and knows everyone, but I still like to play.

"If you want the first points on the board, then go say hi or give a little wave. No freebies from me!" I tease her.

"Back in a jif." Deirdre rises to her feet, adjusts her Albert Fermani boots, and tucks her short, blonde hair back behind her ears. With her boots, she's over six feet tall and quite stunning. Not exactly who you would picture as a nerdy chemical engineer with an impressive resume and tons of field experience.

She makes her way through the crowd and touches Ron on the shoulder. Ron is tall with blonde hair and reminds me of the quintessential California surfer. I can easily picture Deirdre and Ron with their blonde hair in an advertisement for suntan lotion, and the beach surf breaking in the background.

While they're talking, the appetizers arrive, and I contemplate digging in since I'm starving. Deirdre talks to them for a few minutes, and then she saunters back to the table. She's also sporting a huge smile and takes her purse off the chair.

"Okay, here's the deal, they're going to get us a table in the dining room. They're both lawyers. Ron's friend is Ethan, and he's really nice. I think you'll like him. He's new to town," Deirdre grins.

Uh-oh. Move over Lauren, new competition for matchmaking!

"But we just arrived, and the appetizers are here," I protest, wishing I was already on my second helping of the pretzel. My stomach is speaking for me, not my usual single self. If Mama were here, she'd scold me and push me out of my chair.

"No problem. The bartender will move our drinks and food for us," she points to the table near the fireplace where the guys are now. "Let's go!"

I sigh and grab my coat and purse. My stomach growls again.

We walk over and join them at the table. The bartender sets down our drinks and appetizers. Both Ron and Ethan stand up as we approach them.

"Hi Kari, I'm Ron Fortier. Nice to meet you," Ron shakes my hand. "This is Ethan Carrick, the newest associate at my firm."

Ethan shakes my hand while I surreptitiously look him up and down. He's wearing a navy suit with a light yellow paisley silk tie. The shoe inspection reveals shiny ECCO loafers.

"Hi Ethan, nice shoes! Oh, and nice to meet you!" I giggle nervously. OMG! Did I just compliment his shoes? He's going to think I'm crazy. Jeez. Great first impression.

"Thanks, Kari! I know I'm terribly overdressed. I recently moved here from Portland, and suits are the norm there. What do you do here in this freezing cold town?" Ethan asks with a kind smile.

He has short, brown hair, graying slightly at the temples and his face is covered in freckles. Cute in a boyish kind of manner. He also has an endearing widow's peak like Jude Law.

"I'm an architect at a small firm in midtown. I've only been here for a year. A transplant from Charleston, South Carolina."

"That's quite an adjustment in climate. How do you like Anchorage?"

"I love it. How about you? Were you here to enjoy some of the summer?" I give in trying for politeness and ladylike manners and cut off some of the pretzel and spoon some dipping sauce onto my plate. Hopefully he'll follow my lead and help himself to the appetizers.

"I managed to catch the tail end of the summer. All the daylight is really amazing. This winter, I'm looking forward to skiing and checking out some of the breweries here."

"What's your favorite thing about Alaska?" Ethan spears a couple of pieces of tuna on his plate. Saved! I'm not the only one eating here.

Deirdre and Ron are engaged in a lively debate on the best fundraiser in town since they both attend several functions a year. Suits me just fine because I'm enjoying talking to Ethan. And the pretzel is scrumptious!

"I love the fact that you can drive fifteen minutes to the mountains for a hike or drive a few hours to a quirky town like

Talkeetna and spend the day. We're accessible to everything. Do you downhill ski or cross-country ski?"

I cross my fingers for cross-country, picturing him in tight black ski pants and a fitted jacket to show off his lean physique. Toss in a hat with a cute tassel.

"Skate skiing, actually. So, what side of town is best to live on? I've been shacked up in a hotel and haven't had time to house hunt," Ethan says. "My office is here downtown, so I'd like to live nearby. I love that your rush hour lasts a half hour. My commute in Portland was forty-five minutes on a good day with no accidents or construction."

"The west side is nice, lots of housing options and one of the main highways takes you directly into downtown. I love living there. Plus it's close to my favorite Mexican restaurant, Tahoe South Cantina. They have excellent nachos," I say, trying to sound super helpful.

"Thanks for the tips! I'll keep that in mind. How about we order dinner?" He interrupts Deirdre and Ron.

Ethan signals to the server, and she hands us menus. I choose the filet mignon stuffed with king crab. After we order, Deirdre and I excuse ourselves and head to the ladies room.

"Ron is such a doll! And so successful at a young age for partner in the firm. What about Ethan? Sounds like you two are getting along," Deirdre winks at me and brushes her hair in the mirror. "Has he asked for your number yet?"

"Dee! We just met for goodness sake. I like how he asks me questions and doesn't only talk about himself like other guys. I'd definitely give my number to him," I say, putting on lipstick and fiddling with my hair.

"He's well-dressed and quite handsome. Not your usual hippie type," Deirdre laughs.

"Very funny. Why does everyone pick on me about dating hippies? Alaska is full of them! What do you expect? Let's go back or they'll wonder about us." I glance one last time in the mirror.

We rejoin them at the table just as salads are served.

"Perfect timing. So, Kari, what are some of your hobbies?" Ethan asks after he pours wine to go with the salads. They ordered wine while we were in the bathroom? Either they have an expense account, or they're trying to impress us.

"I love to cook and bake, plus I'm a voracious reader. My job keeps me pretty busy during the week, but I try to hit the gym a couple of times too. What about you?" I ask, hoping I sounded smart, worldly or at least not too nerdy.

I take a bite of my spinach salad with crispy bacon and goat cheese. Wish I could take a picture of my salad and send it to Jack. He would love the hot bacon vinaigrette dressing. Bacon makes everything better.

"I work out, too. Guess I'll have to get used to running on the treadmill this winter or buy cleats for my running shoes. I also brew my own beer, and I'm kind of a wine snob. How do you like the Merlot?"

"It's really wonderful, thank you! What prompted you to leave Portland?"

"The firm I worked for merged with a larger one, and I prefer working for smaller firms, so I floated my resume around the Pacific Northwest, and Ron's firm flew me up for an interview in May. I liked the vibe."

"Nice. I hope you stay. There are lots of transplants up here from the Portland area, so don't be surprised. It's actually hard to find someone who was raised in Anchorage. I know the oil companies attract a lot of people to move up here," I say and savor the last bite of my salad. I reach for another slice of sourdough bread and smear butter on it.

"How does your family feel about you moving so far away? Do you miss the hot weather and humidity?" Ethan asks.

Did he just ask about my family?

A. I just met the guy.
B. So sincere! Swoon!

"Every time I call home, my mama thinks it's to say I was crazy to move here and I'm moving back. Family living close by is a big thing for my dad, so it really broke his heart when I moved so far away. Mama's convinced once the temperature drops to minus ten for more than a week, I'll pack my closet full of shoes and come home."

"First of all, did you say minus ten and second of all, did you say shoes?" Ethan asks with a raised brow and an amused expression.

"Occasionally in January, the temperature will drop to minus 10 or below, but don't worry; it doesn't stay there for long. And the shoes … well, I have a lot of shoes. I love shoes. Maybe I should've listed them with my hobbies when you asked," I blush and giggle.

Ethan lets out a hearty laugh, and I can tell he's highly entertained by my shoe fetish.

"I suppose I passed your shoe test since you complimented them?" He teases kindly. "I thought you were commenting on my suit since everyone else here is in a fleece jacket."

I laugh. "You're very funny and perceptive! Yes, you have good shoes. How was your salad, by the way? This is one of the best restaurants in town, and I love everything on their menu."

"It was delicious, thanks for asking." Ethan gives me a big smile, and my heart skips a beat. Seems like we are hitting it off, and I feel comfortable talking to him.

We check in with Deirdre and Ron since we've basically ignored them since we all sat down. Ron tells us how his firm snatched up Ethan as soon as they saw his impressive resume. Deirdre regales us with tales of working with introverted engineers and the ongoing politics of working in the oil industry.

Our dinner arrives, and I'm pleased when Ethan offers me a taste of his roasted rockfish. It's perfectly cooked, and I share some of my filet with him.

The conversation shifts to skiing, the upcoming Beer & Barley Wine Festival, and the best way to avoid winter blues.

"I'm involved in a music and dinner night every Thursday," says Deirdre. "It's fun, and we encourage each other to learn new songs and become better musicians."

"What instrument do you play?" Ron asks. "I can rock out a mean bass guitar."

Deirdre laughs. "The mandolin. I know, I know, not as sexy as a guitar. I would love to start a bluegrass band someday."

"Wow, Dee, I didn't know you were so musical! That's fantastic! Can anyone come for music night? I can't play any instruments, but I love music, and you know how I like to cook," I say, thinking about my spicy pork taco recipe. Perfect for combating cold weather and dark nights.

"Sure, I'll email you the details later. Anyone else interested?" Deirdre asks and looks directly at Ron.

"Definitely. I'll bring my stack of guitar books to share with people along with my guitar," Ron says with a smile.

Ethan tells us his whole family is musical except for him. He's the athlete in the family who can't carry a tune.

Ron takes care of the bill, and we thank him profusely. "The firm expense account can handle it."

I stand up, and Ethan helps me put on my coat. He says," Kari, are you interested in driving around town and showing me some different housing areas? I would appreciate your help if you're up for it. I like to get a feel for the town from someone who lives here before I enlist a real estate agent."

"Sure, I would love to. Here's my business card," I dig in my purse for my pink leather business card holder, write my cell number on it and hand him my business card.

He glances at it and tucks it in his suit pocket. "Thanks! I'll call you."

Ron and Deirdre decide to stay behind for an after dinner drink. The flirty vibe is coming strongly from Deirdre, and I think Ron reciprocates since I see his hand resting casually on the back of her chair.

Ethan shakes Deirdre's hand. "It was a pleasure to meet you, Deirdre. Keep those fellow engineers in line! Ron, I'll see you in the morning. Kari, I'll walk you to your car."

"Thanks, Ethan. That's kind of you," I say, winking at Deirdre as I walk out with Ethan.

We make small talk on the way to the parking lot, and Ethan promises to call me. He waits until I drive away before getting into his car. Such a polite guy! Mama would approve of him.

11

Sitting at my desk, I work on additional revisions to the museum expansion and consider the new projects. The redesign of the downtown city park piques my interest because it's one of Lauren's priority projects from the mayor. I would love to work with her. We could have working lunches and gossip about our fellow employees.

I finish the revisions and click on the Internet to browse the shoes at Nordstrom. I need a new pair of dressy black heels to wear for the holidays. Yes, there are three other pairs I could wear, but I deserve a little shopping with all the hard work I've done lately. I can justify any shopping splurges.

According to my mama, I'll get off the plane at Christmas and look like a hippie since only granola types live in Alaska. Her crazy assumptions! She recently bought an issue of *Alaska Men* magazine to husband hunt for me. I received it in the mail with post it notes about the men she thought were excellent candidates. Goodness gracious.

Jack wanders into my office and plops down in the chair. He's looking so lean these days. All the yoga and skate skiing must do wonders to his metabolism. He runs his fingers through his hair and lets out a big sigh. Maybe he needs a cookie break, or he's come to tease me.

"What did you do last night?" Jack asks with a wink. What's with the wink? Does he think I had a wild night and neglected to tell him at coffee this morning?

"Deirdre and I had drinks at The Roadhouse. I should introduce you to her. You'd like her," I say, wondering if she would like him. Probably not. She would tower over him.

"Cool, is she nice? Does she ski and drink beer? Because that's all I do right now. I love winter. I love Anchorage."

"Actually, she's an alpine skier, grew up in Girdwood and competed professionally. She would totally kick your ass," I say. "So, if you love Anchorage, do you see yourself living in Anchorage for the rest of your life?" I wonder how he will respond.

Who wants to live in a state where winter is nine months a year, and construction season is the remaining three months? Not that I'm picking on Alaska, I just miss four seasons, and I'm a little homesick as the holidays approach.

"Yes, most definitely. Did you meet anyone interesting last night?"

"As a matter of a fact, I did. Thanks to a little game that Deirdre and I play. I met a cute guy named Ethan. He's a lawyer and wears good shoes."

"What game? You know I'm super competitive. Tell me." Super competitive? That's an understatement. Jack scoots up to the edge of the chair, and he looks ready to pounce.

"It's called 'Who do you know?' and you receive one point for each person you know. It involves a wave, conversation, or head nod with the person to prove you know them to get the point."

Jack points at me. "I bet she kicks your ass since you've only been here for a short time. Heck, I would beat you on the way to coffee every morning!" He snickers and sits back.

"Gee thanks, Jack. Give me *some* credit. I know a few people around here, and I occasionally beat her. We play every time we go out, whether it's shoe shopping, drinks after work, or whatever."

"Sounds fun. Count me in. How many points for kids? Most of my friends have kids," Jack rubs his hands together already scheming how to beat me in the game.

"No points for kids. Sorry."

He pouts. "Come on! They should totally count."

"Nope, Deirdre and I made the rules, so if you want to play, deal with it," I say.

I've unleashed a monster. He'll beat me every time at this game, and I bet we'll play every single time we go anywhere. Sigh.

Trying to change the subject, I ask, "What did you do last night?"

"Hung out at Kahiltna Brewery and played pub trivia. You should come sometime. It's fun, and Pabst Blue Ribbon pitchers are two dollars. Our team name was 'I love Justin Bieber.' We came in second place."

"That was your team name?" I laugh. "I'll keep it in mind. Thanks for the invite!"

"When are you and the fancy lawyer going out on a hot date? You won't need to do the bathroom trick with him," Jack guffaws.

Ha. Ha. I'm so glad my personal life induces so much amusement from him.

"I gave him my business card, so we'll see how many days it takes for him to call. He asked me to show him around Anchorage and the different neighborhoods. He's not *exactly* my type, although he *is* cute."

"Kari! You're already writing him off because you think he's not your type. That's a snap judgment right there! Jeez, give the brother a chance, will you? And, hippie guys, your so-called type," Jack curls his fingers for air quotes, "don't generally hang out at The Roadhouse."

"I know, I know. I'll give him a chance. I admit he was kind of intriguing because of the questions he asked me. I guess I could Google stalk him in the meantime," I say.

Jack bursts into laughter. "Google stalk him? I thought only guys did that. You know, Google stalk and Facebook stalk."

"We do it, too. So, is pub trivia every Wednesday? Maybe I'll meet you there next week."

"Yep, it starts at 7 p.m. Well, I better get back to it. Catch you later."

Jack leaves my office with a quick wave, and I turn my attention back to the Jimmy Choo's I just added to my Nordstrom shopping basket. After purchasing them, I add Pub Trivia next Wednesday to my Outlook Calendar and daytimer.

Following a packed afternoon of meetings, I drive home on the slick, snow-covered roads. Lauren and I were supposed to meet for step class tonight, but she had to cancel due to an Assembly meeting, and I decide to skip.

I change out of my work clothes into running pants and a bright orange Clemson hoodie. After pushing play on my iPod, Ray LaMontagne belts out a ballad, and I open up my cookbook. I flip to the chicken pot pie recipe. Perfect comfort food on a cold wintry night.

After I prep the ingredients and pop it in the oven, I sit on the sofa with a glass of Chardonnay and open the latest book from Anita Shreve. My cell phone rings, and caller ID says unknown number.

"Hello?" I say, with a little trepidation.

"Hi Kari? This is Ethan. I met you last night at The Roadhouse. You know, the only guy in a tie and jacket in the restaurant," Ethan laughs.

"Hey Ethan. How are you doing?" I'm shocked he called within three days, thinking of the famous scene from *Swingers*, the movie.

"Wonderful, how was your day today? Guess the cold weather is here to stay, eh?" Ten points for asking how my day was, and I barely know the guy.

"Yes, I'm glad I didn't have errands to do after work. Or had to pump gas in the cold weather," I giggle. OMG! Did I giggle like a five year old? Kari! Get it together!

"I agree. So, I'm wondering if you're available for dinner tomorrow night. I know it's kind of late notice..." Ethan trails off.

"Sure, I'd love to," I answer quickly. "What did you have in mind?" Ten more points for boldness and asking for *this* weekend.

"Do you like sushi? My co-workers told me about a great place called *Sushi Maki* in South Anchorage."

"Sushi sounds good. I've never been there, but the review in *The Alaska Courier* gave it four stars."

"Fantastic! I'll pick you up at seven if you want to give me your address. Maybe we can drive around town on Saturday morning, too? I'll buy you a latte to start the day."

I give him my address, and we chat for a few more minutes before hanging up. I learn he's staying at the Residence Inn and most of his belongings are in storage until he finds a permanent place to live. I'll find out more details when we go out on Friday. Jack would be so proud of me for keeping an open mind and giving Ethan a chance.

The oven timer rings, and I take out the chicken pot pie from the oven. After it cools a few minutes, I dish out a serving, plus grab the bowl of salad I made earlier.

While I sit at the table and eat, I mentally go through my closet and pick out an outfit for the date. Ethan is a sharp dresser, so I want to look extra nice.

My cell phone chirps with a text message from Jack.

Jack: Saw Channel 2 weather girl at the gym. 100 points.

Me: 1 point per person, AND I have to be with you.

Jack: Celebrities are worth more points. And, she was in running shorts. Woop!

Me: 1 person, 1 point.

Oh, Jack. Playing the game with him will be interesting! Maybe I will hook him up with Deirdre, so she can give him a run for his money.

I call Lauren and fill her in on my night out with Deirdre and embellish a few details when I describe Ethan. She tells me about the Assembly meeting and the long line of people waiting to testify on a couple of hot issues.

"By the way, Brad was at the Assembly meeting. He asked about you," Lauren reports.

"Really? We had zero connection on our date. Maybe he was being polite," I say, casually, although my heart skips a beat. "What did you tell him?"

"I told him you were doing very well. Kept it short, sweet, and a little mysterious."

"Maybe he's had a change of heart and wants to see how a Republican is in bed!"

Lauren laughs, and we hang up after making a lunch date for tomorrow. I love having a friend who is amused at my attempt at jokes. That's what best friends are for!

12

On the way to Red Shed Coffee the next morning, Jack is surprised when I tell him Ethan called me last night.

"Probably a good sign he didn't wait a week to call you." Jack shivers, despite his North Face down coat and wool beanie. We walk quickly to keep warm.

"Yes, I think so too! It's been awhile since I've had sushi, so I'm excited. What are you doing this weekend?" I ask.

We enter Red Shed Coffee and wait in line with the other caffeine addicts. Jack waves to a few people in the café, and he has three points. Game on.

"A group of us rented a cabin at Hatcher Pass, so we'll ski all weekend, maybe sled and definitely drink beer. Where are you going for sushi?" Jack asks, looking around for other points.

"Sushi Maki in South Anchorage. Have you been there?" We edge up in line.

"Yes, it's the best sushi place in town. You'll dig it. Give me some deets on Ethan. One point for Lisa, by the way." We give our coffee cups to Lisa, and Jack pays for our drinks. We take turns paying for coffee.

"You can't count baristas or servers. Quit trying to change the game rules. So, Ethan's from Portland and new to

Anchorage. That's about it." I smile and look around for someone I know, so I can count them. Skunked! I don't know anyone in here.

"Right on. Well, I hope it goes well. Text me and let me know, will ya?"

"I will. Your cabin weekend sounds like a blast," I say. We wave goodbye to Lisa and trudge back to work on the snowy sidewalks, sipping our coffee.

"In the vault, Kari, another architecture firm is courting me to work for them," Jack says, quietly.

"WHAT?" I shriek. We stand outside the office building, warming our hands on the coffee mugs.

"Shhh. I know, crazy, huh? I'm not looking for a new job, but the other architecture firm working with me on Mountainside Elementary School approached me."

"JACK! Are you going to quit and work for them? What will I do without you?" I'm about to cry. Seriously. I can feel the tears about to squirt.

"Kari, I'm not sure yet. Still thinking about what to do. The offer is super attractive, but I like working for B&B Architects," Jack shakes his head slowly and wrinkles his brow.

"When do they want an answer?" I turn my head to watch the cars navigate the icy roads. Tears are now officially welling up in my eyes, and I don't want him to see it.

"Monday. So, I'll ski this weekend and think about it. Please don't tell anyone."

"Of course, I won't. It's in the vault. Let's go in, I'm freezing," I say and open the door to the atrium.

We walk inside and head in separate directions to our offices. As I sit down in my office, my phone chirps with a text from Jack.

Jack: Are you okay?
Me: Yes
Jack: Are you sure?
Me: I'll really miss you if you quit.

I click on "New" and write a quick email to Lauren.

From: kcovington@bbarchitects.com
To: lauren.blackwell@alaska.gov
Subject: Jack

OMG! Jack might quit and go work for another firm!

Side note: Yes, I know it's in the vault, but telling your best friend doesn't count. She'll make me feel better.

From: lauren.blackwell@alaska.gov
To: kcovington@bbarchitects.com
Subject: RE: Jack

WHAT??? Oh no! Is it here in town? Is he moving?

From: kcovington@bbarchitects.com
To: lauren.blackwell@alaska.gov
Subject: RE: Jack

Thankfully, it's here in Anchorage. He's going to think about it this weekend. What will I do without him? He's my work buddy, and one of my best friends. We go for coffee practically every day and eat lunch together all the time. ARGGGHHHHH…

From: lauren.blackwell@alaska.gov
To: kcovington@bbarchitects.com
Subject: RE: Jack

Maybe he won't take it. I know he adores you too, so don't spend all weekend worrying. You have a hot date tonight, plus we're going snowshoeing on Saturday; plenty to keep your mind off of him. Cheer up and quit worrying! There's nothing you can do about it.

From: kcovington@bbarchitects.com
To: lauren.blackwell@alaska.gov
Subject: RE: Jack

You're right, I know. Okay, I'll try not to think about it. You are such a good friend! We'll talk more at lunch. See you at noon at Miller's Deli.

⌒◦

Of course, I spend the rest of the day alternately thinking about Jack and my date with Ethan. Lauren reassures me at lunch, and I feel slightly better. At 3 p.m., my email dings, and it's from Ethan. Hmmm, I hope he's not cancelling on me tonight.

From: Ethan.winston@sktlaw.com
To: kcovington@bbarchitects.com

Hi Kari,
Looking forward to seeing you tonight-
Ethan

Well, this is a first. A pre-date email. I kind of like it. Confidence. That's my favorite characteristic in a guy. Plus good-looking and tall.

From: kcovington@bbarchitects.com
To: Ethan.winston@ktslaw.com

Ethan,
Me too! See you tonight!
Kari

I keep the email response short even though I want to compliment him on sending it. Now, I'm really excited for tonight. I skip the gym *again*, so I can wash my hair and flat iron it before my date. That totally trumps working out.

13

Ethan rings my doorbell ten minutes early, and I'm running around without shoes or lipstick. An inauspicious beginning for sure. I open the door, and he's smiling and holding a bouquet of stargazer lilies.

"Hi Kari. You look beautiful," Ethan says and steps inside.

"Thanks, Ethan. You're very kind. I'm almost ready," I say and approve of his black, dress slacks and blue button down shirt with black loafers.

He hands me the flowers. "These are for you. I hope you like lilies."

I take them into the kitchen. "I love these lilies. They are my favorite! Thank you!" I quickly arrange them in a vase with water and set them on the kitchen table.

"Make yourself comfortable. I'm almost ready," I say and dash into the bathroom.

I'm so glad I decided to flat iron my hair. It looks more sophisticated and goes well with my dressy outfit. I put on my lucky M*A*C Russian Red lipstick and open my closet door to choose shoes. My outfit consists of a blue beaded drape neck blouse and a black satin pencil skirt. Hmmmm … which shoes? I grab the Vera

Wang Black Patent Heels and cross my fingers that we won't have to walk too far in the snow or ice.

"Ready to go?" I ask and walk into the den. Ethan is looking at the pictures of my family and friends on the bookcases.

He picks up his coat from the couch. "Sure. I made us reservations for eight o'clock, so we have plenty of time to navigate the snowy roads. Guess I better get used to it!"

I grab my black wool dress coat from the hall closet, and he helps me put it on. We walk out to his green Range Rover, and he opens the door for me.

On the drive to the restaurant, we talk about different areas of town as we drive toward South Anchorage. I point out Tahoe South Cantina and other places of interest.

"You sure do know a lot about this town for only living here a year," Ethan compliments me. "Have you made a lot of friends here?"

"I have a few close friends. That's how you survive the long winters. Hanging out with friends, game nights, weekend trips, planning a tropical vacation, and skiing. Then you don't go crazy from the darkness or cold."

"My friend, Jack, and I eat out pretty often, so we try new places," I say. Why did I bring up Jack in the first five minutes of my date? Hopefully, Ethan doesn't ask who Jack is, not that it matters, but I should concentrate on Ethan.

"I love gourmet food and cooking. On a cold day, I like whipping up a big pot of soup and uncorking a bottle of Shiraz." OMG! He likes to cook too? I've totally hit the jackpot. Goodbye granola-type of guys. I have a crush!

"Me, too! Cooking is a stress releaser for me. I enjoy spending all day in the kitchen with a complicated recipe." Does it sound like I'm bragging?

"I noticed your kitchen. Looks like you have it stocked with fancy pots and pans and the biggest knife collection I've ever seen," Ethan says, appreciatively. "Maybe we can invite some folks over and cook together sometime."

He's inviting himself over to cook? Already? This is the first date! Doesn't he know there can only be one cook in the kitchen? Okay, Kari. Simmer down, and roll with it. He just mentioned it nonchalantly. It's not like he's already invited friends over and planned the menu.

"Ummm ... sure. That sounds fun," I say slowly, wondering if his confidence is still attractive or a dealbreaker. I know what I said earlier about confidence, but it's coming on a little strong.

We arrive to Sushi Maki, and he offers to drop me off at the front door, since the parking lot is crowded, and it's cold outside. I'm thankful and take him up on the considerate offer.

He tells the hostess his last name for the reservation, and she leads us to a table by the window and hands us menus. Sushi Maki is brightly lit with a contemporary setting of silver accents, bright green bamboo trees, and black banquettes lining the outer wall.

"Would you like to start off with saki?" Ethan asks and opens the menu to look at the options.

"Sure. They have quite a large menu. How did you hear about this place, again?" I ask. My mouth waters as I read through the roll descriptions.

Ethan places the saki order with the server. "Ron took me here when I came up for the interview. And, it's a favorite among my co-workers. How about we start with some edamame and yakisoba?"

"Perfect. What kind of rolls do you like?" I ask. I've decided his confidence and taking the lead *is* attractive. I hate those conversations that are "I don't know. What do you want to order? I don't know. Whatever you want." Spare me.

"I like tuna or salmon sashimi and the spider roll. Oh, the dragon and spicy scallop rolls are my favorites, too. Save room for dessert. I want to take you to this new dessert café for the best cheesecake ever. Since you're a baker, I think you'll appreciate it," Ethan says with a smile.

Wow. Is he trying too hard, or is this how dates are supposed to go and I've been on really bad ones this past year? I feel like I'm in some alternate universe and should proceed with caution, or I'll wake up.

"All of those sound wonderful. I also like the crunch rolls and the ocean roll."

Ethan places the appetizer and roll order with the server, and he picks up his saki for a toast. "To a fun night!" We clink glasses and sip the warm saki.

"Kari, thanks for giving me a tour tonight on the way here. Are you still up for driving around tomorrow morning?" Ethan asks.

"Sure. I just need to be home by 1 p.m. since I have a snow-shoeing date with my friend, Lauren."

"No problem. I'll make sure we finish by noon."

"So, do you have family in Portland?" I ask, wanting to know more about Ethan. Is he truly as perfect as he seems?

"Yes, my parents and two younger brothers still live there. I'm glad it's a fairly short flight back, so I can visit often. How often do you get back to Charleston?" Ethan asks.

"I try for twice a year, but it's such a long flight. Takes all day and two layovers. Jet lag coming back is worse than going there though," I say.

"Must be tough living so far away from your family. Are you close with them?" Ethan asks.

"Yes, I talk to my mama every week, and my sisters and I email a lot. I really miss my twin nieces. They are five years old and quite precocious."

"Sounds like you have a tight knit family. I love kids. Both of my brothers have three kids each, so I love being Uncle Ethan. My mom is ready for more grandkids though," Ethan laughs. "She loves the grandma role and babysits whenever possible."

I laugh. "My parents are the same! They love spoiling the girls."

The server delivers the edamame and yakisoba. Ethan puts a portion of each dish on a plate for me before he serves himself.

"Sounds like our families are pretty similar," I say, as I navigate the yakisoba with my chopsticks, trying not to get sauce on my blouse.

Oops! Too late! I splash a bit of sauce on my blouse. Hopefully my cleavage will distract Ethan away from the spot. Ha!

We chat more about our families and some of our favorite foods to cook. I'm having a wonderful time, and I wonder if Ethan is The One.

14

Lauren and I snowshoe at Russian Jack Park, huffing and puffing. When we arrive to the other side, we take a break, and I take out a thermos with hot chocolate and peppermint schnapps from my backpack.

"So, what did you do after dinner?" Lauren asks and takes the steaming cup from me.

"He took me to Sugar, this little dessert café that just opened, and we had the most amazing cheesecake," I take a sip from my cup. "He had the date all planned out, and I was really impressed. He is a perfect gentleman."

"Hmmm. Sounds like a winner. Any red flags? Did he try to kiss you at the end of the date?" Lauren asks with a wink.

"Lauren! No! It was our first date, totally a 'get to know you kind' of date. No red flags or dealbreakers so far. Oh, I forgot to tell you. This morning, he showed up at my apartment with a latte, and we drove all over town. He's looking for a place to live, so we drove through the different neighborhoods."

"Wait? Isn't that what a real estate agent does?"

"Yes, but he said he wanted insight from a local," I smile. "He's really smart, considerate *and* cute. I was downright impressed with him taking me to Sugar. He remembered that I like to bake!" I say and take a sip of my drink.

"When are you going out again?"

"I don't know. He said he would call me tomorrow. I guess the one possible red flag is that he mentioned inviting friends over to my place and cooking up a big meal together. I mean, we just met, and he's already looking into the future as a couple. Is that what normal guys do, and I've just been dating losers?" I ask.

"No, that's not *exactly* typical, but he must like you or feel comfortable around you to bring up dinner with friends. Interesting. I'll ask Will and get his thoughts."

"Are you ready to snowshoe back to the car? It's getting colder out here, and there are ice crystals in our hair," Lauren asks and hands me back the cup.

"Sure, but let's take a picture of us, so I can send it to my family," I say and repack the thermos in my backpack.

Lauren snaps a photo of us close up to capture the ice crystals, and she takes one of me with the snowy mountains and bright blue sky in the background.

15

O n Sunday, I clean the apartment and do errands since the temperature is a balmy forty-two degrees. Thank you, Chinook Winds for bringing the warm blast of weather. According to the locals, the Chinook Winds blow through a few times each winter and warm up the air temperature. People appreciate the sight of ice and snow melting until the temperature drops and ice skating rinks form everywhere.

After going to the grocery store, I relax on the sofa in the afternoon and check email. I send the picture of Lauren and I snowshoeing to my family, and I include a quick note about what I've been up to and ask about their Thanksgiving plans.

The coq au vin simmers in the oven, and I hum a little song. Life is good right now. I met a guy, went out on more than one date with him (kind of), and am relatively content. The only wrinkle in my thoughts is Jack. I wonder how his weekend at the cabin went, and if he's made a decision about leaving B&B Architects.

I guess our relationship wouldn't change too much. We would still go out to lunch and dinner several times a week, but I would miss our coffee runs in the morning and talking about random stuff.

I want the best for him so if he leaves, I will wish him well and *try* not to take it personally. But, I like having a work husband, and it certainly keeps me sane at work to have a confidante.

However, I can't wait until Monday to see if he's made a decision. I decide to text him.

Me: Quitting or staying?

I hold onto my phone for a few minutes for a response, but he doesn't respond back. Maybe the cell phone coverage is spotty at the cabin, he's driving, or too hungover.

My cell phone rings, and I answer it quickly without looking at the caller ID, hoping it is Jack with good news.

"Hello?"

"Hi Kari, it's Ethan. How are you?" Ethan says.

"Hey, Ethan. I'm fine. What are you up to?"

"Just got back from the gym, and I thought I'd check in with you. Are you up for hanging out tonight?"

Whoa. I saw him on Friday night and Saturday morning. Is he into me? Or, is he bored and going stir crazy living in a hotel? I'm optimistic, so I'm going with the former.

"Well, I have coq au vin cooking in the oven. Do you want to come over for dinner?" I ask. I would enjoy having someone special to share this fancy meal with tonight.

"I'd love to. What can I bring, and what time?" Ethan says eagerly.

"How about a salad and wine? I bet you know the perfect wine pairing for dinner. Come over around six," I say, with a smile.

"Perfect! See you then!" Ethan hangs up.

This is an interesting turn of events. I go from random blind dates to a guy who wants to spend a lot of time with me. *And,* I didn't have to call him. Mama would be so proud.

⌒⊙

Before Ethan arrives, I slice up a crusty baguette and measure ingredients for polenta to serve with the coq au vin. I also change out of my cozy fleece pants and put on jeans and a red turtleneck. A skinny black headband holds back my curly hair, and I throw on some bronzer, so I don't look so pale. Welcome to winter in Alaska!

Ethan rings the doorbell promptly at six, and he's holding a paper bag of groceries.

"Welcome, come on in. You look nice," I say, noting his tan corduroys and long sleeve blue polo shirt. He's such a dapper dresser. I love it!

"Thanks, Kari. It smells heavenly in here," Ethan says, setting the bag of groceries on the hall table and slipping off his Timberland boots. "I hope you don't mind if I prep the salad here. The kitchen in my hotel room is pretty limited, and I'm dying to try out your knives."

"Sure, no problem," I say. I open the cabinet to retrieve a cutting board and bowl and grab a peeler from the utensil drawer. The knives are displayed on a magnetic strip next to the stove.

He pushes back his sleeves and starts peeling and cutting vegetables.

"Is there something I can help you with?" I ask, watching in amazement as he juliennes a carrot and then expertly dices a cucumber.

"No, I've got it. Sit back and relax. I'll open the wine and let it breathe, if you show me where your wine opener is. The flavor will really open up once you expose it to air. Mellow, full-bodied. Sorry, if I get carried away about wine," he blushes.

I grab the wine opener from the silverware drawer, and he opens the wine. I go over to my iPod and choose the latest Adele album. It's kind of romantic music, but I don't care. I'm throwing caution to the wind.

After checking on the coq au vin and starting the polenta on the stove, I sit on a stool and watch Ethan finish the salad. He also makes a honey mustard vinaigrette. While he washes the cutting board and knife, I take a quick photo with my phone and send it to Jack.

Me: Salad AND dressing made by Ethan!
Jack: Nice
Me: So, are you going to take the job?

No response. Why is he like this? Is it because he doesn't want to text bad news? I try not to worry. Focus, Kari! A guy is in your kitchen, washing dishes, and you're gripping your phone tightly and frowning.

Ethan pours us a glass of Pinot Noir, and I set the table. This is totally like a 'couple' thing. I'm loving it!. I even pull out the blue paisley cloth napkins and set the table with candlesticks. The lilies are holding up well, and all of the buds have opened, releasing their heady fragrance.

"What did you do today?" Ethan asks and sits on the sofa. I click on the gas fireplace and then sit down next to him.

"Errands. Grocery store, Bed Bath and Beyond, and met a friend for coffee."

"What about you?" I ask, pleased that he asks about my day each time we see each other. Okay, it's only been like twice, but still.

"Worked this morning on a deposition. I like my job here, but I see working many weekends in my future," Ethan says, wrinkling his brow.

"Are you working on some interesting cases? I know you can't really tell me much about them."

"A couple of them have some fascinating facts. Can I be honest with you?" Ethan changes the subject and looks me in the eyes. "I really like spending time with you. I know we just met, but I feel really comfortable with you."

"Me, too. You're incredibly considerate, sweet, and kind," I smile. Wait, is he leaning in?

Yep, he's leaning in.

Ethan leans over and gently kisses my cheek, and then my lips. I kiss him back, and he pulls me into him. His tongue probes my mouth softly, and I melt into his arms. He groans and gently caresses my cheeks with his soft hands, as the kissing becomes more passionate.

Now, I'm sitting in his lap, and my arms are wrapped around his neck. His skin is warm from sitting next to the fireplace, and he begins kissing my neck. My breathing is shallow, and I am *so* enjoying the moment.

Ding! And then the oven timer rings.

We stop kissing, and I giggle softly and extract myself from his lap. As I stand up, he smiles at me, and I come back for one more kiss before I go to the kitchen.

"I better go check on the chicken and turn the timer off," I whisper. "We don't want to eat a burned dinner."

"Go turn off the timer and then come back. We can always order pizza," Ethan grins mischievously.

I walk quickly to the kitchen and turn off the timer, oven and stove. Then, I take the heavy enameled pot out of the oven and set it on the stovetop. The polenta is ready, as I give it a final stir and walk back to the sofa.

Ethan smiles, pulls me back onto his lap, so I'm straddling him. He plays with my curly hair as he leans in to kiss me.

"You are so beautiful, Kari. I'm so lucky to have met you." Ethan looks me in the eyes and then kisses the palms of my hands.

"Oh, Ethan," I say, breathlessly. He gently massages my lower back with his hands, and I can feel his groin pressing against me as we kiss.

16

At work the next morning, I walk directly to Jack's office without stopping at my office to drop off my purse or change out of snow boots.

He's sitting at his desk, flipping a mechanical pencil in between his fingers and whistling. He stops whistling when I storm in, drop my purse, and close his office door.

"JACK! You ignored my text messages all weekend!" I cry.

Jack grins at me. "Not true. I texted back when you sent me a picture of the goopy salad the lawyer made for you."

"First of all, it wasn't goopy at all. It was delicious even if it was a little soggy since he dressed it and then we didn't eat right away as it turned out. Whatever. Did you make a decision?"

"About what? Why didn't you eat right away?" Jack smirks and gives me a sideways look.

I practically scream this time. "JACK!" Then I lower my voice and ask, "Are you quitting?"

I cross my arms and stand there tapping my foot impatiently. I don't have time for games. Why is he torturing me?

"Kari, calm down. No, I declined the offer right before you came in here freaking out. I like working here, so why change it up?" Jack says calmly.

I could kill him. I could hug him. Which should I do first? He drives me crazy!

"Phew. I'm glad for you. I mean I would've wished you good luck if you took the other job, but I'm happy you're not leaving." I let out a deep breath and collect my purse from the floor.

"Let's go grab a coffee," Jack says. "I'll treat since you're so traumatized."

"Very funny. Give me a few minutes in my office to check email first," I say and walk out of his office. I hear the whistling start back up as I walk down the hallway. Why no one has complained about his whistling baffles me. This is a workplace!

Over coffee, I chastise him again for making me wait all weekend for his answer. He says he was too busy drinking beer, skiing, and eating. Flimsy excuse, but I'm too happy to call him on it.

My day flies by with sketch revisions and meetings in the afternoon. I do admit that I don't go to lunch with Jack on the off chance Ethan calls to invite me. No such luck, but I'm still on a high from last night.

That evening, Lauren and I browse the clothes racks at Classic Consignment. She's attending the Mayor's Charity Ball next week and needs a new snazzy dress.

"So, I made out with Ethan last night," I say nonchalantly, looking closer at the price tag of a black dress.

Lauren whips around and cries, "WHAT?" She pulls on my elbow to bring me standing directly next to her and hisses. "Spill it, Kari."

"Well, he came over for dinner last night. I made a new recipe, coq au vin. It was really easy to put together. I'll email you the recipe," I grin mischievously.

"I don't care about the damn recipe! Is he a good kisser? Did you make out after dinner in front of the fireplace? Tell me you didn't give it up to him."

"Lauren!" I shush her and look around to see if anyone heard her last question. "We kissed before we even ate dinner. Then the oven timer went off. We ended up eating reheated coq au vin in front of the fireplace, snuggled under an afghan."

"Did he spend the night? I *knew* something was up with you when I saw you. You're glowing! No one here glows in the winter," Lauren laughs.

"No, we kept it strictly PG, no overnight. I just met him for goodness sake. Give me a little credit."

"Yet, you sucked face with him after meeting him on Friday. Good for you! It's time you got some action. What's the plan for seeing him again?" Lauren moves onto the skirt rack now that the juicy news is over for the most part.

"He said he would call me this week. I really like him," I admit. "He also sent me a sweet email this morning saying how much fun he had."

"Kari, I'm so happy for you! He sounds like a winner. When do we get to meet him?" Lauren asks.

"I don't know. I can ask if he wants to grab dinner this week with you and Will," I say this, but secretly wish for another repeat of last night instead. I browse the shirts and select a chiffon blouse to try on. It's flirty and romantic looking. Why not? Romance is in the air, and I'm feeling good about Ethan and the future.

"Good. I'm going to try these dresses on. Let me know what you think, okay?" Lauren asks and walks into a dressing room.

I go in to the other dressing room and try on the blouse. It's too tight in the chest. Ergh. Sometimes I curse my ample chest while other times I love it. Having to buy a larger size in shirts frustrates me. I change back into my work clothes and wait for Lauren on the bench outside the dressing rooms.

My phone chirps with a text, and my pulse quickens thinking it might be from Ethan. But, the message is from Jack.

Jack: I saw the mayor skiing on the downtown trail. 500 points.
Me: Negative points. Did you trip him?
Jack: No, but I totally wiped out in front of some cute girls. On purpose, of course.
Me: 100 points
Jack: Funny

"Who are you texting, Kari? I can hear your fingers tap a mile a minute out there," Lauren calls out.

"Just Jack," I say and slip the phone back in my purse.

"Speaking of Jack, what's the latest on his job? Is he leaving B&B Architects?" Lauren asks.

"No, thank goodness. He declined the other firm's offer. I'm so thankful, but also want to wring his neck for making me wait all weekend, not knowing," I say.

"I'm glad he's not leaving. Otherwise, who would you go on coffee runs with?"

"I know, right?" I giggle and think about Jack. Our morning conversations are the highlight of my day.

Lauren comes out in the first dress. It's black and sleeveless with a gathered waist. "What do you think?"

"I love it! Turn around. It looks really good, and the length works well," I say, admiring the dress on her.

Lauren agrees and goes back into the dressing room. "Are you going to tell Jack about kissing Ethan?"

I wrinkle my brow. "No, he doesn't kiss and tell, so neither will I."

Two can play at this game, plus I don't know what Jack's reaction will be. Would he even care? Would he tease me?

"Fair enough," Lauren says and goes to the counter to pay for the dress. She also selects a deep purple shawl to go with the dress.

"I can't wait to tell Will about Ethan! He loves spending time with you, so we can double date to dinner, movies, and everything!" Lauren bubbles over with excitement.

"You bet. I feel giddy, but I don't want to jinx anything."

"Don't worry. He sounds perfect, so relax and enjoy the moment," Lauren says and gives me a hug.

After we leave the store, Lauren drops me off at my apartment. I'm humming a song and smiling. The romance department is looking up! Just in time for winter and snuggling season.

17

No call from Ethan that evening, but I'm not worried. He mentioned he's in court all day on Monday, so I'm sure he's really busy.

The next morning at work, I scan emails and then check my calendar. Oh yeah! Trivia night at Kahiltna Brewery. I decide to invite Deirdre to pub trivia tomorrow night, so she can meet Jack and play the 'Who do you know?' game. Jack is going with his roommate and some friends, and they promised to save us a couple of seats.

From: kcovington@bbarchitects.com
To: Deirdre.weston@bpoil.com
Subject: Trivia

Hey Dee!

Are you up for pub trivia tomorrow night at Kahiltna Brewery? It starts at 7. Jack and his friends are going. Should be fun. You can handle all the science and engineering questions.

Kari

From: Deirdre.weston@bpoil.com
To: kcovington@bbarchitects.com
Subject: RE: Trivia

Kari,
Sure! Are any of his friends single and cute?

Dee

From: kcovington@bbarchitects.com
To: Deirdre.weston@bpoil.com
Subject: RE: Trivia

You know, I actually haven't met any of his friends, but I'll find out! I'll see you there.

Kari

I send a short email to Jack to confirm our attendance. I haven't gone to pub trivia since Clemson, so I'm looking forward to it.

My office phone rings at lunch. I'm struggling to change a segmented arch using AutoCAD, and it's proving quite cumbersome.

I answer, "Kari Covington."

"Hey you. It's Ethan." Hey you? Did he say Hey you? My heart flutters.

"Hi, how are you?" I ask, minimizing AutoCAD so I can concentrate on my phone conversation.

"Good. I'm calling to say hi and see if you want to have dinner this week."

"Sure, I would love to. How did it go in court?" I ask, pleased with myself for asking about his day since he's so considerate to ask about mine.

"The judge threw out the case, so I'm very happy. How about dinner on Thursday?" Ethan asks.

I click on my Outlook Calendar. Wide open for Thursday.

"Sure, I'm going to the gym with Lauren after work, so I can do dinner after 7 p.m."

"Perfect. Is this the Lauren you went snowshoeing with on Saturday afternoon?" Ethan asks. Wow. He remembers every little detail.

"Yes, we also go to the same step class. She's one of my best friends up here. Her husband, Will, is teaching me to ski, too!" I say.

"Well, if they're free, we can all go out. Sound good?" Ethan asks.

"Ummm. Sure. I can ask her," I say slowly. Dang! I was hoping for just the two of us with more kissing. Guess that can wait until after dinner.

"Okay, I better let you get back to work. We can figure out the details later. Have a good afternoon, Kari," Ethan says.

"You too. Bye!" I say and hang up the phone. I add dinner to my calendar and wonder if Jack will ask me about it when he stalks my calendar. We stalk each other's calendar daily. Lunch dates with famous actresses are often on his calendar. What a funny guy.

I click on "New" and send an email to Lauren. She won't believe what I'm about to tell her. Wish I was there to see her face when she reads my email.

From: kcovington@bbarchitects.com
To: lauren.blackwell@alaska.gov
Subject: Dinner with Ethan and Me

Hi Lauren,

Ethan called me. HE suggested dinner with you and Will. Are you available on Thursday?

Just so you know, I didn't prompt him to ask you. He did it all on his own! I'm finally dating a grown up! Life is good.

Kari

From: lauren.blackwell@alaska.gov
To: kcovington@bbarchitects.com
Subject: RE: Dinner with Ethan and Me

Seriously??? He invited us all on his own?
Of course, we're available. I HAVE to meet him.
WOO HOO!

So, we're on for Thursday. I send Ethan a quick email to confirm dinner, and he emails right back and asks me to pick a restaurant. I'll have to think of a place with a superior wine list. A sweet surprise for Ethan.

On Wednesday's coffee run, I ask Jack about his friends, so I can give Deirdre a preview.

"My roommate, Darren, and a couple of guys from the ski club are going. What's the deal with your friend, Deirdre?" Jack asks as we enter Red Shed Coffee and stand in line.

"She's gorgeous. Tall, short blonde hair, smarter than you. The only extroverted engineer to exist," I say, as we give our coffee cups to Lisa.

"Hey Lisa! Morning!" Jack says and hands over his credit card.

"Hey, you two! Busy morning, guess everyone needs extra caffeine today," Lisa laughs. We chat for a few minutes after she hands us the steaming lattes.

On the walk back to work, I update Jack on the museum expansion, since he was pulled off the team to work on another assignment in addition to the school project. The project end is in sight, and I'm ready for a new challenge.

"Hey, are any of your friends single? I want to give Deirdre a heads up," I say.

Jack smirks and rolls his eyes. "You, girls! Yes, as a matter of fact, they're all single. But, please don't play matchmaker. I just want to win at trivia, relax, and drink beer."

"Don't worry. I won't," I promise.

We brainstorm on some team names, and come up with two winners: Bailin' Palin or Suck it, Trebek.

Back in the office, I send a quick email to Deirdre.

From: kcovington@bbarchitects.com
To: Deirdre.weston@bpoil.com
Subject: Trivia

Dee,
Bring your A game tomorrow night! All of Jack's friends are single.

Kari

From: Deirdre.weston@bpoil.com
To: kcovington@bbarchitects.com
Subject: RE: Trivia

You know I will.

Dee

18

W hen I arrive at trivia, Jack, his friends, and Deirdre are sitting at a large table near the big screen TV. They're laughing and drinking pints of Pabst Blue Ribbon. A nearly empty pitcher and menus are on the table.

"Hey Kari!" Deirdre calls out to me. I take off my green down coat and black scarf and join them at the table.

"Kari, this is Darren, Hugh, Chris, and Jeremiah. Everyone ... my favorite co-worker and fellow caffeine addict, Kari," Jack says and gives me a big smile.

"Hi, guys. Nice to meet you," I say and quickly scan faces and memorize names. "Deirdre, you and Jack have never met. How did you pick each other out from all these people?"

Deirdre pours me the last of the beer. "Jack called out my name when I was scoping out the tables looking for you. Guess you gave him a good description of me." She laughs. "By the way, Jack was first to know someone here, so now it's my mission to kick his ass."

"Are you bitter, Deirdre? I hope not because we need you for the science questions," Jack teases.

"You wish, Jack," Deirdre laughs and looks around the room for people she knows.

"How does pub trivia work here?" I ask, taking a sip of beer and scanning the menu.

"There are seven rounds of questions. We write the answers down, turn them in, and they tally the results at the end of each round. Up on the stage is a board with team names and the running tally. Each round usually has a theme," Darren says.

"Thanks, Darren. What's our team name?" I ask, noting he's cute in a nerdy kind of way with black-rimmed glasses.

On our afternoon cookie run, Jack gave me the lowdown on everyone. Darren is an accountant for one of the Native Corporations.

"We already picked it out. Suck it, Trebek," Hugh says and high fives Chris. "Jack said you guys came up with the name earlier today, and we liked it."

"It was all Kari's idea. Let's order some food!" Jack says and flags down the passing server.

We order two baskets of hot wings, beer battered halibut chunks, smoked salmon dip, and another pitcher of beer.

The first round is all about U.S. Presidents and their hometowns, policies, and years in office. Since I slept through U.S. History in high school, I don't contribute much and concentrate on the hot wings and blue cheese dressing. Chris teaches history at University of Alaska, and he knows every answer. Off to a good start.

In between rounds, Deirdre and I chat with everyone. Our food is delivered, and we all dive in.

"So, Hugh, what do you do for a living?" Deirdre asks after polishing off her second beer.

"I'm a real estate agent. How about you, Deirdre?" Hugh asks and takes another chicken wing from the basket. He is the most dressed up out of all the guys, with a pressed button down shirt and tie loosened around his neck. His blond hair is slightly receding, and he has striking blue eyes.

"Chemical engineer at BP. How's the housing market? Moving in a more positive direction yet?" She asks.

"Well, it's on an upswing for sure, just slow. How do you like working for a big oil company? I couldn't deal with all the politics."

"Nah, the politics aren't too bad in my department. I just have to deal with introverted engineers who look at my high heels when we talk," Deirdre laughs and crosses her legs. I notice she's wearing new UGG Skylair boots.

"Kari, Chris is also a ski coach at the University. He can give you some good tips, I'm sure," Jack says, as he spreads salmon spread onto bread.

"Come on, Jack! You're an excellent skier," Chris blushes. "What kind of skiing are you learning, Kari?"

I wipe the wing sauce off my lips with a napkin. I know, graceful. "Cross-country, just classic style. I'm still really scared of going down big hills."

"Yeah, kind of intimidating, huh? Just keep your knees bent, loose and floppy, equal weight on your skis," Chris says. He stands up and demonstrates.

Wow, what a nice guy. See? This is what I love about Alaska. Everyone is friendly and willing to show you, help you, or give you advice on anything.

"Thanks, Chris. I'll keep that in mind," I say, smiling. "I appreciate the demo." What a nice guy and cute! He reminds me of the Ken Barbie. Tall, short, brown hair, fair complexion, clean-shaven, and trim.

Why are all these guys single? I don't see any red flags emerging from our conversations so far. Hmmm.

The second round of trivia is Classic TV Shows, and we all contribute to the answers. The pub quiz girl can hardly spit out the questions fast enough. Seems like everyone knows the answers, and we're ready for something harder. Perfect score again.

We order another pitcher of beer. Jack and Deirdre are tied with six points each on the 'Who do you know?' game, and the competition is heating up between them.

Darren is shy, but I try to engage him in the conversations between rounds. Jeremiah is super talkative, and he's hoping for a sports-themed round to show off his expansive knowledge. Guess I'm not surprised since he's built like a football player, husky, broad-shouldered, and loud.

After the sixth round, we are tied for second place with another team. We're pumped up and excited for the last round. Jack and Chris walk around and check out the other teams.

Deirdre and I excuse ourselves from the table and head to the ladies room. I overhear Jack ordering another basket of wings with extra blue cheese. We need some high caloric energy to get us through the last round.

"Jeremiah is a cutie! He's really outgoing and smart. I like that in a guy!" Deirdre says and touches up her make-up in the mirror. "He works up on the North Slope as a Safety and Health Director. We know a lot of the same people."

"Yes, I hope the last round is sports for his sake. He's dying to answer some baseball and football questions. What do you think of Jack?" I ask, hoping she appreciates his quick sense of humor like I do. They seem to get along, probably due to their shared competitiveness.

Deirdre stops and looks at me. "Jack adores you. It's so obvious. He's witty, sarcastic, and nice all rolled into one. Although, I really want to kick his ass in the game."

"He *is* great. Chris is kind, too! I can't believe he gave me his email and phone number and offered to take me skiing. What a sweet gesture! Of course, Will might be jealous since he's the one teaching me to ski. I should ask Hugh for his business card and pass it on to Ethan since he's looking for a house."

"Oh yeah! How is dreamy Ethan? Has he called you yet?" Deirdre asks while she's digging in her purse for lipstick.

"We've gone out three times already! It's crazy! I really like him. I'm so glad we went to The Roadhouse that night. What about you and Ron? Did you stay out late after we left?"

"Nah, we just had one more drink. He's a serial dater. My friend knows him, and she gave me the dish on him. Good looking and rolling in the dough, but I'm not interested. I'm glad you and Ethan hit it off. He helped you put your coat on and walked you out to your car! Who does that these days?"

We chat for a few more minutes and then return to the table. Round seven is Sports, and Jeremiah pounces on each question, sure of every answer.

After we turn in our answer sheet, there's a long wait for the tally, so we polish off the remaining chicken wings. The server drops off the bill, and we all pitch in cash to cover it.

The pub quiz girl announces the winners. Third Place is Lawyers, Guns & Money. Second Place is Snowboarding off the Fiscal Cliff. She pauses before announcing the first place winner, and Jack looks like he's about to have an aneurysm, sitting on the edge of his seat. First place is Suck it, Trebek!

We won! We won! We're jumping up and down and whooping it up. Jack pulls me in for a big hug, and he runs up to the stage to collect our prizes. It's a fifty dollar gift card to Kahiltna Brewery and a reserved table for next week's pub trivia.

And, Deirdre won the 'Who do you know?' game on the way out to the parking lot. She saw a friend coming into the pub. And, she knew the bouncer (which doesn't count, but I secretly count it for her). Score!

19

Ethan and I are meeting Lauren and Will at Turnagain Heights Steakhouse for dinner. I selected this restaurant after I researched their wine list and read some on-line reviews. None of us have been there before, so I wanted to make sure it had several positive reviews.

I open my closet and choose grey wool pants and an emerald green ruffled wrap cardigan. My black lacey camisole pairs well under the cardigan. Lace always invokes romance, right? I also select the lucky pearl necklace from my jewelry box.

I flat iron my curly hair and tuck one side behind my ear. After putting on my make-up, I choose the Stuart Weitzman black high heels, so I'm almost the same height as Ethan.

Ethan rings the doorbell at seven, and I grab my purse and black dress coat from the closet.

"Hi Ethan!" I say, and he steps inside the entryway.

"As usual, you look gorgeous, Kari!" Ethan compliments me. He's wearing navy slacks and a white button down shirt with a blue tie, loosened around the collar. "Hope you don't mind the tie. I had to work late and didn't make it home to change."

"You look very handsome," I say. Ethan pulls me in close and kisses me on the lips. "Mmm ... you taste good."

I blush and pull away. "We should probably go, or we'll be late."

Ethan sighs. "Okay, promise me after dinner, we can pick up where we left off." He helps me with my coat, and we walk out into the chilly evening.

We arrive at the restaurant, and Lauren and Will are already seated at the table. I can tell Lauren is excited to meet Ethan.

"Hi y'all!! I'd like you to meet Ethan," I say and sit down in the chair that Ethan pulled out for me.

Will stands up and shakes Ethan's hand. "Nice to meet you, Ethan. I'm Will, and this is my wife, Lauren."

"Hi Ethan. Nice tie," Lauren says and winks at me. I kick her shin under the table.

Ethan sits down and points to the tie. "I know. I'm overdressed for Anchorage. Kari clued me in the night we met. I didn't have time to change clothes before picking up Kari, so my apologies."

"No apology necessary, I like it!" Lauren says, smiling.

Will clears his throat. "Ethan, she's used to seeing me go to work in jeans, t-shirt, and a fleece vest."

Lauren rolls her eyes at me, and I giggle. They are such a cute couple, and I adore their teasing and lightheartedness toward each other.

The server comes by for drink orders and tells us the dinner specials.

"Shall we order a bottle of wine? I'm a bit of a wine snob, so I promise to pick out something good," Ethan says.

We agree to have Ethan pick out the wine. After he places the order with the server, we look over the dinner menu.

"Will, you mentioned going to work in jeans. Where do you work that affords the nice luxury of casual attire?" Ethan asks.

"I'm the Business Editor at *The Alaska Courier* newspaper. Kari mentioned you recently moved here. What do you think of Alaska so far?" Will asks conversationally.

"I'm really enjoying it despite the snow and cold weather. I was also lucky enough to meet Kari. She's wonderful," Ethan says and rubs my shoulder with his hand.

"Yes, I agree. She keeps me on my toes and sane," Lauren says, grinning. I can tell she approves of Ethan already.

The server brings over the wine, and Ethan tastes it and nods to the server. After the wine is poured, he raises his glass. "Here's to new friends, new experiences, and the last frontier. Hope we all survive winter."

We laugh and clink glasses.

"How did you two meet?" Ethan asks, and Will starts to respond, but Lauren interrupts Will.

"I tell the story better than you, so I'll do it. Will, Kari and I all went to Clemson University. Kari and I were roommates. Just imagine ... she's from Charleston, the deep South, and I'm from Colorado and a ski bum. We became inseparable right away. She's also responsible for introducing me to sweet tea, which I still make all the time."

"Get to the good part of us meeting!" Will cries. "Ethan doesn't want to hear about you and Kari goofing off and your addiction to sweet tea." We all laugh.

"Hold your horses, Will Blackwell! Anyway, one night, the student union was showing 'The Doors' movie at the amphitheater, and we showed up late. The only available seats were right in front. We snuck down to the seats to watch the movie," Lauren says.

I chime in. "Lauren didn't know what was going on in the movie, so I began whispering the plot to her. Can you believe she's never seen that movie? Anyway, the guy behind us didn't appreciate all of the whispering and shushed us. Lauren turned around and told him to mind his own business and shut his piehole." I curl my fingers into air quotes. "He told her she was cute, and they ended up sharing popcorn and Twizzlers together." I make lovey-dovey eyes at Lauren and give her a big smile.

"So, you insult Will and end up with a boyfriend all in the same night?" Ethan asks. "That's hysterical!"

"I like a girl who isn't shy, and Lauren's one of the most outgoing people I know. She also pointed her little finger at me as she was yelling at me. It was adorable. Of course, I *was* on my third beer," Will laughs.

"HEY NOW!" Lauren cries and playfully pinches him on the arm.

We place our dinner order with the server, and I relax and sit back. The restaurant walls are covered with dark paneling and intimate pendant lighting hangs over each table. All of the servers wear starched, white button down shirts with ties and long black aprons. The wine collection is displayed behind the bar, and the bartender uses a rolling ladder to reach the bottles on the high shelves.

"Lauren, Kari mentioned you work for the city. What do you do?" Ethan asks and takes a sip of the 2007 Cakebread Merlot.

"I am the director for the Community Development Department which oversees neighborhoods, planning and development. Basically, permitting, working with builders, community planners, and projects. Quite a mouthful, huh?" Lauren says, grinning.

"So, if someone wants to build a playground at a park, or if there are disputes among neighborhoods, you are the lucky mediator," Ethan says.

Lauren is impressed. "Exactly. Except, when the mayor gets beat up by the public for something, so do we. It's a love/hate relationship. We all want a safe and healthy community. Folks have different ideas on how to achieve it."

"Portland was similar. It's hard to keep morale up when the mayor first takes office," Ethan says in agreement. "I volunteered on the task force on homelessness, and the city employees were so passionate. If you ever need help with anything, let me know."

"Wow, Ethan. Thank you so much! I'll keep it in mind," Lauren says and kicks my shin under the table. Double ouch. From the way she's smiling, I can tell she's already planning our wedding.

The server delivers the salads, and we turn our discussion to upcoming winter events. Ethan suggests we all attend the Beer & Barley Wine Festival together. He saw the ad for it in the weekly entertainment newspaper.

"I'm definitely in," Will says. "It's one of the better festivals, and free cab rides home for everyone who wants one. Lauren and I make pretzel necklaces, so we have something to munch on between beers."

Ethan laughs. "I love it! Let's plan on it for sure."

He and Will talk about their favorite beers, and the best local breweries in Anchorage and Portland. They seem to have much in common, and the conversation flows easily. See? That's a big difference between guys and girls. They just fall into a friendship so easily. Girls are busy checking out each other's outfits, et cetera. You know, making sure they're compatible in the caste system first. Sad, but true.

I catch Ethan's eye, and he smiles at me. He's having a good time, and he's also rubbing my leg with his hand under the table.

After the salad plates are cleared, Lauren and I excuse ourselves. Once inside the ladies room, Lauren can't contain her excitement.

"Ethan's fabulous! He's smart, considerate, and clearly likes you." She gives me a hug.

"I know, right? I can't believe my luck! And, we *just* met, and it's already wonderful," I smile and touch up my lipstick.

Inside, I am praying that he's The One, and he has no hidden dealbreakers. I mean, he doesn't seem like the pet ferret type, and I think he'll buy a house in Anchorage, not in the Valley forty miles away. I exhale deeply.

Lauren continues chattering on about Ethan. "He and Will get along, so that's a plus. He ordered an expensive wine and seems to know a lot about beer. *And*, he suggested we all go out again! He's planning for the future. Remember how you said he gave you a weird vibe? I think that's just his personality. He's a planner like you and me!"

"I'm going to take it slowly and enjoy it. If I analyze it too much, I'll screw everything up," I say, crossing my fingers not to jinx it.

Lauren looks at me. "There's nothing to jinx. He's The One!" I smile at her and pray she's right.

We walk back to the table. Ethan and Will are talking about the Seattle Seahawks season thus far and discussing the quarterback's statistics.

Our entrees arrive, and I'm excited for the lamb chops. I rarely order lamb, but I splurged since it seems like a special occasion. Ethan shares some of his porterhouse with me, and all of the entrees are cooked perfectly. Lauren and Will share a pasta entrée and declare it's the best dish ever. Wow. I'll have to share this foodie experience with Jack. He would love it here.

After dinner, we skip ordering dessert there at the restaurant, and go to Sugar, the dessert café. Lauren and Will fall in love with their cranberry spice crème brulee and red velvet cake. Ethan and I once again split their divine cheesecake and sip on espresso.

With promises to do this again, we say goodbye to Lauren and Will, and drive back to my apartment. Ethan asks if he can come up, and we relax on the sofa.

"Kari, you have delightful friends," Ethan says, while nibbling on my ear. I groan and rub his back and inhale his aftershave.

"Thanks, Ethan. They loved you," I say, kissing him fully on the mouth, forbidding any more small talk.

I take his hand and lead him into the bedroom, leaving his tie trailing on the floor behind us.

20

E than and I arrive to the cooking class a few minutes late due to another round in bed. We both like morning romps and dozing in between. It's becoming routine … lazy naked mornings, now for several weeks.

The other attendees wear red aprons, and they are paired up at cooking stations. After checking in with the chef instructor and putting on aprons, we take our place at the last cooking station, looking a little sheepish. I quickly fasten back my curly hair into a ponytail, and we wash our hands.

Our class is Mastering French Cuisine. Ethan surprised me with the class as a gift. We will make Boeuf Bourguignon, Sole Meuniere, and Cassoulet. Since class lasts all day, the chef will feed us lunch, classic roast chicken with potatoes and haricot vert.

Pilar, the chef, tells us about the origins of Boeuf Bourguignon, and we pull the ingredients off the rack near the refrigerator. We follow her instructions and begin to dry off the beef cubes with paper towels and then season them with salt and pepper.

"Do you love your surprise? All day in the kitchen making delicious food," Ethan says and watches me sear the beef. "I'm starving already. We should've grabbed breakfast on the way to class."

"And be even later? Did you see the way Pilar looked at us? We come traipsing in smelling like sex," I giggle and adjust the flame on the gas burner.

Pilar is walking around the cooking stations, assisting people and answering questions. She nods at me, as she walks by. I'm doing something right, I suppose.

After I take the seared beef out of the pot, Ethan dumps in the vegetables he chopped. We work well together, and I'm glowing. Not only from the sex, but I like feeling part of a couple.

Once all the ingredients are incorporated into the pot, Ethan places it in the oven, and we move onto the Sole Meuniere.

"I love cooking with my handsome boyfriend. How about I make a romantic dinner for you on Friday night?" I ask, while I wipe down our area before cleaning the fish.

"Umm … I can't on Friday. I have plans. How about on Sunday?" Ethan sounds vague, and I have this sudden sinking feeling in my stomach.

"What? Do you have plans with another girl?" I joke and dry my hands on a towel.

Ethan sighs and says quietly, "Kari, we haven't really talked about exclusivity."

I turn to look at him, my eyes widened by his statement. "Wait. Are you saying we're *not* exclusive? We've practically spent every night together these past two weeks." I'm devastated, and my stomach churns.

"Calm down. It's just, you know," Ethan says slowly and looks at his shoes.

"What? What do I know? You want to date other women while we continue to sleep together?" I hiss. When did he find time to date other women? Who else is he seeing? My mind is full of questions.

"Keep your voice down. I just moved to town, you know that. I want to meet and see other women," Ethan says and smiles awkwardly to the other attendees who are now eavesdropping.

Pilar drops off the sole to our station and moves on quickly. She's trying to recapture everyone's attention.

We are temporarily quiet while Pilar talks us through filleting the sole. I take the fish knife and follow her instructions, trying to squash the idea of cutting off Ethan's finger instead. Or some other body part.

After I'm done with the fish, Ethan dredges it in flour and spices and places it in the sizzling skillet.

"Can we talk about this later?" Ethan pleads. "Let's try to have a good time."

I pause for a moment. Part of me wants to kick him out of class so I can still enjoy the French Cuisine, and part of me wants to talk it out and see if we can salvage our relationship. Sure, I assumed we were exclusive, but I really don't think it's my fault.

Reminds me of a saying … Eighty percent of problems are from lack of communicating each other's expectations. I expected he will only sleep with me, not a myriad of women at the same time.

"Fine, let's stay," I give in. "But, we're talking about this at lunch when we have a moment to ourselves." I nod to the others, still obviously eavesdropping. Pilar has lost control of the class, and I feel guilty.

We taste the finished Sole Meuniere, and it's flaky, delicate and lemony. I relax a little bit and chat with the other attendees, ignoring Ethan. They are thankful our lover's spat is over too, if only delayed.

Pilar ushers the class into the dining room for lunch. One long table is beautifully set with white china, wine glasses and plum colored linen napkins. She and her cooking assistant serve the plated lunch, expertly prepared. It's fantastic, and we give them a round of applause at the end of lunch. Pilar also made crème brulee for dessert as an added bonus. I'm going to hit the gym hard after this fattening, but worthy day of feasting.

Since we were unable to talk during lunch, we suffer through the rest of the afternoon. I have several thoughts running through my head, and many involved punching him in the groin.

After class, Ethan drives me back to my apartment. We're quiet during the first few minutes of the car ride.

"Ethan, if you wanted to see other women, I think we should've talked about it first," I say and look out the car window.

"I know. I'm an ass for not saying anything. I assumed we would eventually talk about it, and I would tell you that I'm not the monogamous type," Ethan says, exhaling slowly.

Inside, I'm freaking out. "Okay, so you don't do exclusivity. Well, I *want* it. I feel like we have this amazing connection, and frankly, I'm not willing to share you. And I don't feel comfortable with you dating other women while seeing me."

Ethan pulls over to the side of the road. "Kari, please. I really like you! I just want to see other women, too. Won't you even consider another option?" He reaches over and strokes my hand.

"No, I'm sorry. I like you, but it's not going to work. Can you please take me home?" I sigh and pull my hand away. Tears begin to squirt out of my eyes. Ugh. I hate crying in front of people, especially guys.

How can this be? He seemed like the perfect guy, and he dropped this whole monogamy bombshell on me. When did he expect we would discuss it? When I saw him out with another girl at a restaurant or at Sugar? I knew it! This whole thing was too good to be true. I truly have the worst luck in dating.

Ethan pulls back onto the road. We don't talk until we reach my apartment.

"Kari, please. Let's work something out. I don't want to lose you," Ethan says to me as I quickly get out of the car.

"Goodbye, Ethan. Please don't ever contact me again." I walk up the steps to my apartment, unlock the door, and close it with a thud. And then the real sobbing begins. I crawl into bed and stay there until the next morning.

21

My Sunday is spent on the sofa covered with two afghans, watching cooking shows, sniffling, clutching a box of tissues, and feeling downright sorry for myself. I knew it was too perfect! Who jumps into a relationship that quickly, falls into lust, and everything turns out like a fairy tale? No one! Absolutely no one!

Maybe I was just waiting for something to go wrong. No! I will not blame myself. It's all Ethan's fault. He should have told me we weren't exclusive, and he wasn't the monogamous type. He totally misled me! Yep, it was downright fraud, deceit, something like that. I'm sure he could tell how I felt about him.

My phone jingles with a text from Jack.

Jack: Saw Deirdre at Red Shed Coffee. 200 points.
Me: Funny
Jack: You okay?
Me: Sure
Jack: No funny retorts? I really get 200 points??
Me: That's ridiculous. Of course not.

I don't tell Jack about Ethan because I don't want to talk about it yet. Or let him see me cry tomorrow at the office. My heart is broken, and I can't handle anyone judging me or feeling sorry for me. I know it's not my fault, but I want some space and alone time. Let me have the pity party now, so I can get it over with.

The only thing I dread more is my weekly Sunday phone call with Mama. She will know something's wrong with me right away. I've raved to her about Ethan, and she'll be disappointed it didn't work out.

All day, I wondered if Ethan would call me, but he didn't. I guess his mind is made up, and I'm not willing to compromise. *And*, he must think I'm not worth the effort. Tears well up in my eyes again when I think about that. How could I not be worth the effort? We were having a good time. What is wrong with me? Why do I continually get dumped?

At four o'clock on the dot, my cell phone rings, and I pick it up without looking at Caller ID.

"Hi Mama," I say.

"Kari, what's wrong? I can hear it in your voice," Mama says, sounding concerned.

I open my mouth, and the story tumbles out. Between hic-cupping from crying, I tell her about our disastrous cooking class, conversation, and how awful I feel now.

"Kari Ann Covington. I'm going to tell you something," she says sternly. "He's not worth your time, not one iota of it. And, you deserve a man who will treat you like a princess. Obviously, Ethan is not that man."

"But," I start to say, and Mama interrupts me.

"But, nothing. Don't give him a second thought. Move on to some wonderful man who loves you and only you. Do you hear me? Listen to your Mama," she says sharply. "I won't have you whimpering over some loser who wants to play the field."

She continues. "Now then. Tell me what's new at work and what you've been cooking lately. I need some inspiration since it's too darn easy to eat out now since it's just your father and me."

I smile weakly. "I love you, Mama. Thanks for everything."

"Honey, of course. I want the best for you," Mama says.

I tell her about the food we made at the cooking class and the recent baking from my new cookbook by Dorie Greenspan.

By the end of the conversation, I'm feeling better and more positive about my decision to end the relationship with Ethan. Mama promises to call me during the week to check on me, and I'm smiling as I hang up from the phone call.

My pity party is coming to an end, and I'm feeling strong and back to my optimistic self. Screw Ethan.

22

The following evening at the gym, I tell Lauren about Ethan and our break up. She's surprised by his non-monogamous declaration, and she's ready to pummel him. Or at least send Will to do it. I can tell she's worried about me, but I assure her I'm fine. Almost fine, really…

"I'm still heartbroken, but at least I found this out early in the relationship and not six months down the road," I say miserably and inspect my legs to see if they are more muscular or thinner. I avoid looking Lauren in the face, or I may start crying again.

"Yes, but he could've mentioned it while you were getting to know each other. And you spent tons of time together. When did he have time to date other girls?" Lauren asks and sits on her bench.

"I know, right? I have no clue. You know what upsets me most of all?"

"What?"

"Having sex with him. I know we moved fast to the bedroom, and it's totally out of character for me. You know me! I don't want to have a long list of men I've slept with. I don't do one night stands or have sex with just any guy," I cry, frustrated at my choice to sleep with him. Ergh. I think back to how I led him to my bedroom, and

129

I want to kick myself for it. Well, there's nothing I can do about it now except move forward. That's it … think positive.

"I know, I know. Don't forget, I was your college roommate. You hemmed and hawed, and only added one guy to your list during four years of college. Other girls were adding to their list daily," Lauren says matter-of-factly.

"Exactly!"

"What did Jack say when you told him? Is he ready to hunt Ethan down and whack him upside the head with a ski?" Lauren giggles as she mentally pictures it.

"I haven't told Jack yet. He didn't ask about Ethan during our morning coffee run, and I certainly didn't bring it up."

"Although, he did have an interesting tidbit of gossip. He ran into Deirdre on Saturday at Red Shed Coffee, so they sat down and talked for a few minutes. Turns out, one of her shy co-workers got up the nerve to ask her out, and they've gone out twice."

"Really? How sweet! I bet she doesn't abide by your silly rule of no fraternizing with co-workers!"

"Ha ha. Very funny," I say, with a tiny snort.

"Listen, tell Jack about Ethan before Thanksgiving. I don't want any awkwardness on Thursday when he asks why you didn't bring him to dinner, okay?" Lauren says firmly.

"Will do, I promise. I'm looking forward to Thanksgiving! Good food and good friends. Sounds like the perfect time," I say, thinking about sweet potato casserole. Mmm … so sweet it's like eating dessert first.

The instructor enters class, and we clam up and make a face at each other. Lauren bursts out laughing, and I join in. Sometimes, laugher really is the best medicine.

On Wednesday, Jack and I eat lunch at Miller's Deli. They have a pulled pork sandwich that Jack really likes, so we go there often.

We're quiet for a few minutes as we enjoy our lunch and watch snowflakes fall. A white Thanksgiving. I don't mind the snow since it sets the scene.

"Looking forward to a big meal tomorrow?" Jack asks. "What dishes are you cooking?"

I finish chewing the bite of my grilled vegetable panini. "I'm on sweet potatoes and dessert duty. Tonight, I'm baking off the pies."

"Awesome! Is Ethan coming with you?"

Just get it over with. Be quick, vague, and move on.

"Actually, I'm not seeing him anymore. It wasn't a good match," I say quickly and eat a potato chip, looking at the floor.

"What? You guys were hot and heavy. Why didn't it work out? Does he have a secret ferret?" Jack laughs.

"Ha ha. No ferret. Do you want to drive over together tomorrow?" I ask and change the subject.

"Kari! What's going on? Are you okay? You can't just tell me you broke up with Ethan and then change the subject!"

"Seriously, it's not a big deal. We weren't on the same wavelength. Enough said."

I wonder how much snow will accumulate as I think about the errands I have to do after work. Driving in fresh snow automatically doubles the time it takes to go anywhere. The grocery store will be packed. I should have gone last night or even last weekend for my pie ingredients.

"Okay, I know when to back off. If you want to talk about what happened, I'm here for you, okay?" Jack says sincerely and takes a long look at me.

"Thanks, Jack," I say, relieved he didn't ask more questions. Time to move on.

23

I spread the steaming mashed sweet potatoes in the oval casserole dish. The pecan and brown sugar topping goes on next, and I double the topping. It's the holidays. Calorie counting goes out the window.

The chocolate pecan pie, pumpkin pie and chocolate pots de crème are packed and ready for the trip to Lauren and Will's home. After I finish assembling the sweet potato casserole, I'll duck in the shower and head out. Jack said he'll meet me there with red and white wine and a case of Natural Light beer. Leave it to Jack to bring the perfect party beer.

From my overstuffed closet, I choose a cashmere black turtleneck and soft carmel trousers with a wide cuff. The new Naughty Monkey pumps I picked up yesterday from the mall, pair perfectly. I decide to leave my hair curly and hit auto start to warm up my car.

I drive over carefully since November brought us a record thirty-two inches of snow so far. Jack's silver Tacoma truck is parked in the driveway along with a couple of other cars.

"Happy Thanksgiving!" Lauren cries when she opens the door, and she takes a pie from my hand.

Will comes up behind her, squeezes my shoulder, and heads to my car to grab the rest of the food. What a keeper.

"Happy Thanksgiving to you, too! The house smells so yummy!" I exclaim and take off my scarf and snow boots.

Slipping the Naughty Monkey shoes on, I head to the kitchen to meet the other guests. The kitchen sideboard is heavily loaded with wine, Natural Light and gin martini ingredients.

"Kari, this is Abby Morrison. We work on the same floor, different departments," Lauren says as she places the pie on the counter.

"Very nice to meet you, Kari! Love the shoes," Abby admires with a smile.

See? Good shoes say a lot about a person. The shoe inspection reveals her black Jimmy Choo slingbacks. I'm *so* jealous.

"Thank you so much! It's lovely to meet you," I say.

I surreptitiously look her up and down. Abby has long red hair, a perfect, slightly turned-up nose, and is wearing a black halter dress with pearls. Think glamorous Julianne Moore on Oscars night. Slightly overdressed for Thanksgiving, but she pulls it off easily.

"And you remember Don and Lynn, Will's parents? They drove down from Fairbanks last night," Lauren says.

"Hi Kari! You look wonderful as always," Lynn hugs me. Don waves as he pops open a Natural Light.

"Nice to see you both! How was the drive down?" I ask, lifting off the lid from the sweet potato casserole.

"Snow-packed roads, except a little icy around Denali," Don says and comes over to hug me. They are such dear people. When we all graduated from Clemson, they took everyone out for dinner and toasted the event. My parents still exchange Christmas cards with them.

"Kari! Glad you made it okay," Jack says, entering into the kitchen, Natural Light in hand, of course.

"Jack, you look very handsome," I compliment. He's wearing a light blue dress shirt and khaki's with a shiny brown belt.

"Will, how much longer for the turkey? The sweet potato casserole needs to bake for thirty minutes," I say peering through the oven door and licking my lips.

"About fifteen more minutes and then it rests for twenty minutes before I start carving," Will places the desserts on the counter and double-checks the timer.

I adore Will. He has been a lifesaver when I needed dimmer switches installed in my apartment along with other home improvement tasks. Tonight, Will is wearing jeans and a navy sweater. His short, black hair curls around the neck of the sweater.

"Perfect," I say and place the chocolate pots de crème in the packed refrigerator.

"Let's go in the living room where it's more comfortable. Can I get anyone another drink?" Lauren ushers us out of the kitchen.

"I'll take a glass of Merlot," I say, noticing Jack and Abby sitting on the loveseat by the fire. I give Lauren a look, and we walk back into the kitchen. The others sit down and chat.

"Abby's drop dead gorgeous! Please tell me she has a boyfriend who is just out of town for the holiday," I murmur.

"Nope. Single and looking for the right guy like you. She and Jack make a cute couple. Very dashing!" Lauren says and hands me a glass of wine.

"Hey! You said the same thing about me and Jack!" I hiss, wondering if I'm jealous. Well, yeah, I am.

"I promise this isn't matchmaking. They're both single. Who knows? They might not even get along tonight," Lauren says matter-of-factly.

I hear Abby laughing as Jack tells her about growing up in Seward. "What do you care? You're the one who told me over and over that you and Jack are only friends. Are you jealous?"

"No! It's just that I ... I've never seen Jack with another girl, so I'm thrown off, I suppose," I stammer defensively.

We walk back in the living room and join the group. Jack and Abby are chatting away, and Will and his parents are lounging on the couch, enjoying the warm festive mood and delicious smells coming from the kitchen.

"There you two are! Want to catch the end of the football game on ESPN?" Don says and picks up the remote control.

"Sure, Dad. Let's see how the Cowboys are faring," Will says.

I'm perched on the edge of the leather armchair and lean in to catch snippets of Jack and Abby's conversation. The television is blaring, and I can't exactly go squeeze onto the loveseat with them. Abby tells Jack about growing up in Kansas, and Jack listens intently. Her luscious red hair could be showcased in a Clairol commercial.

I excuse myself and head toward the kitchen, beckoning Will to join me.

"Will, I think we should check on the turkey," I insist.

"Sure thing. Excuse me, everyone," Will says.

Will checks the internal temperature of the turkey and declares it's done. He sets it on the counter and covers it with foil and a dishtowel while I place the casserole in the oven.

Will opens a Natural Light. "Jack's a fun guy and knows the right beer to bring." He holds up his beer and clinks it against my wine glass.

"Lauren told me about Ethan. Sorry, Kari. I liked the guy. Should I beat him up for you?"

"Very funny, Will. You're sweet to offer, but I'm over it. Yes, Jack's great … the perfect person to bring to a party. He's good at talking with everyone and quite likable. Abby and him look pretty cozy over by the fire," I comment.

"You think? They're only talking."

Guys are so clueless. Seriously.

I see Jack look at Abby appreciatively and then wink at me. Maybe his jaded attitude has shifted. And, why does he always wink at me? I used to find it endearing, but now it just annoys me. Why am I suddenly grumpy?

Lauren joins us in the kitchen and carries the side dishes to the dining room. She putters around, keeping an eye on me. I'm swirling the Merlot in my glass, trying not to think about Jack and Abby. Will's parents offer to help, but I tell them to relax and we'll announce when dinner is ready.

Will carves the turkey and loads it onto a platter, while I stir the gravy. I steal a taste of the cranberry orange relish Abby brought. It's delicious. Hmph.

"Dinner's ready! Come and join us," Lauren calls out.

Time to eat and be thankful!

24

"I'm the municipal prosecutor for the city," Abby answers when Don asks what she does for a living.

"Nice! I bet that keeps you busy," Don says, clearly impressed. He passes his plate to Will for another helping of turkey.

"Yes, it does. I have no social life, and all of my girlfriends are lawyers, so they never have time to go out." Oh, pity party. OMG! Kari, change your attitude! This is a day for friends, family, good health, and more. If Mama were here, she'd knock me upside the head and tell me to smile.

"Everything is delicious!" I exclaim, changing the subject. I pour more Merlot into my glass and pass the bottle around the table.

"Yes, who made the cranberry sauce? It's wonderful," Jack says.

Abby raises her hand slightly. "Guilty. I know it's not the traditional kind, but I like to add ginger and zested orange. I don't really follow recipes. Just throw something together and go with it!"

Hey! There's nothing wrong with recipes, especially in baking!

"I better save room for dessert," Jack says as he pushes his plate back. He's so sweet since he knows I made all of them. What he doesn't know is that I also brought chocolate pots de crème for him. He's in for a nice surprise.

"So, Abby, what do you like to do for fun? You said you have no social life, but I'm sure that's an exaggeration," Jack insists. OMG! That's totally like a first date question.

"I do yoga three times a week, and I'm training for a marathon next April. Although, I hate running on the treadmill. I already can't wait for spring, so I can run outside," Abby says and runs a perfectly manicured hand through her red hair.

"I agree! The treadmill is a pain. I have a kick ass music mix that gets me through it. Where do you go for yoga?"

"At Lotus Studios. Are you willing to share your music mix?" Abby asks sweetly with a smile.

I feel like a third wheel on their first date. Seriously. Doesn't anyone else feel that way? I make a face at Lauren, and she tries not to laugh.

"Sure, give me your deets after dinner," Jack says, grinning.

"Lauren, your home looks lovely," Lynn says at the conversation break.

"Thanks, Lynn. I appreciate the kind compliment," Lauren says and lets out a relieved breath. She's passed the mother-in-law cleanliness test and begins to relax.

"And, the meal is delicious … just thankful we're here with you all."

"Thanks, Mom. We're so glad you and Dad could make it," Will says and pats Lauren's hand. Lauren smiles broadly and begins to pass around the food for third helpings.

The men are on dish duty, so the girls retire to the living room. Lauren and Lynn discuss some upcoming home improvements on Lauren and Will's home. They are selecting new tile in the guest bathroom and painting the guest room.

I smile at Abby. "How long have you lived in Anchorage, Abby?" I want to know more about this girl who held Jack's attention during dinner.

"Three years. How about you? Lauren mentioned you're from Charleston. Are you finding the winters difficult?" Abby asks and takes a sip of her hot tea.

"A little over a year. I love it here, and the winters don't bother me at all. Do you visit Kansas often?"

"Not as much as I would like. So, I have to ask. Is Jack seeing anyone right now? I know you work together. Is he a good guy?"

Oh no, she didn't just go there.

How do I respond to this without sounding jealous, or do I grit my teeth and play matchmaker?

"Nope, he's single. He's a fantastic guy. Loves food and cooking, hanging out with friends, sports, and skiing," I say, while my stomach churns.

"Hmm. Thanks. I'll keep that in mind. He's quite handsome and easy to talk to."

Duh. Why do you think I hang out with him all the time?

"Well, I'm sure he'll call me. I slipped him my business card," Abby says confidently. She finishes her hot tea and heads into the kitchen offering to help. Brown-noser.

I. Hate. Her.

"Dessert time!" Jack announces. "Kari! You made chocolate pots de crème! I can't believe it. Did the restaurant share their recipe?"

"No, I found this recipe in one of my cookbooks," I say and begin scooping ice cream onto dessert plates, while Will cuts the pies.

We gather around the dining room table, and Lauren takes orders while Will and I dish up dessert.

"Kari, it's fantastic! Better than The Snowy Owl for sure," Jack compliments me.

"Oh, have you been there? My friend, Bethany owns it. We can go sometime if you want," Abby says pointedly to Jack.

Bold girl. Guess she isn't going to wait for Jack to ask her out. I admire her confidence and want to kick her at the same time.

"Sure! Kari and I went there awhile back, and the food was wonderful. Your apple pie is really scrumptious too, Abby. Nice and tart," Jack says, flirting.

Hey! Dessert is *my thing*. I'm the baker!

And, that's how Thanksgiving ended. Jack and Abby flirting and Lauren and Will visiting with Will's parents. Me? Sad and missing Ethan and his warm touch.

I am *so* going to stab Lauren with my spoon for inviting Abby.

25

Trying to get in the work mode after a long holiday weekend is hard for me. I don't want to wait for the coffee run with Jack, so I stop at Starbucks and pick up a grande vanilla latte with an extra shot. It's too early, too cold, and I can't face Jack this morning without caffeine.

In my office, I change out of my snow boots to the Burberry brown flats, and I log in to email. There's an email from Lauren asking if I'm okay. She sent me three text messages yesterday asking the same thing.

So what if Jack and Abby hit it off? It's not like I had dibs on Jack. I just need to focus on me and finding The One. For once, it's all about me. Not anyone else.

Jack walks into my office at 8:30 a.m., empty coffee cup in hand and stops suddenly when he spots the Starbucks cup on my desk.

"Heeyyy. What's that all about?" He points to my cup and frowns.

"Sorry, Jack. I needed coffee ASAP this morning, so I stopped on my way in. How was the rest of your weekend?" I ask and take a long sip of coffee.

"It was okay. I whipped up a big pot of chili mac yesterday and watched football with my roommate. What about you?" He lounges in the chair in front of my desk, tapping his coffee cup with his thumb.

"Fine. Hung out and relaxed. Checked in with my sisters and parents. We talked about my trip home at Christmas. I also went shopping and picked up a fabulous pair of heels to wear once spring arrives."

"You and your shoes. You know that spring isn't until May, right? It lasts about three weeks. Anyway, I'll go grab crappy coffee from the kitchen here. Are we on for lunch today?" Jack yawns and stands up.

"Let me see how this morning goes, and I'll ping you later," I say. Why am I suddenly passive aggressive? He hasn't even mentioned *her*.

"Cool. Oh, by the way, I'm meeting Abby for drinks later this week. She's really fun. So glad you invited me to Lauren and Will's for Thanksgiving," Jack says with a big smile. "Have a good morning!"

I slowly inhale and exhale. Relax. It's not like they're getting married.

My office phone rings, and I pick it up. My baby sister, Kate, chirps,"KARI! I'm engaged!" And, this is before I even say hello.

Now, my day officially sucks.

The afternoon flies by as I catch up on emails, attend several meetings, and work on drawings. I skip having lunch with Jack and grab a sandwich from the cafe next door. Better to keep my head down and stay busy, so I don't think about Kate, Jack, and Abby.

I send an email to Lauren before my last meeting of the day.
To: lauren.blackwell@alaska.gov
From: kcovington@bbarchitects.com

No gym tonight. My apartment at 7. Bring ice cream and oreos.

Kari

⤳

After stopping by the store for groceries, I change into a pink fleece hoodie and running pants when I arrive home. Then I tie back my hair and don an apron. My ultimate comfort foods are homemade macaroni and cheese, fried shrimp and blueberry muffins. I know, weird combination, but I like each food for different reasons.

Lauren rings the doorbell, and she hands me a bag with oreo ice cream, black raspberry chip ice cream and a package of oreos.

"Hey Kari! If we eat all this, we have to hit the gym hard next week," Lauren says as she kicks off her snow boots and hangs her coat in the hall closet.

"I promise we will. Thanks for bringing the perfect dessert," I say, walking back into the kitchen and stashing the ice cream in the freezer. The macaroni and cheese is in the oven, muffins in a bread basket with a stick of butter next to them, and I'm dredging the shrimp in a peppery cornmeal mixture.

"It smells divine! Anything I can help you with?" Lauren asks, entering the kitchen, rubbing her hands to warm up.

"Nah, just help yourself to wine and pick out some tunes. I was listening to Eva Cassidy before you arrived, so maybe something a little more upbeat?" I ask. The shrimp sizzle in the pan, and I set the table.

Lauren stands in front of my iPod and browses my music. She chooses the latest album by The Black Keys.

"A little more upbeat. So, what's the news? We skip the gym and you cook a big dinner. I'm dying to know. Are we celebrating?" Lauren asks impatiently and munches on chips and guacamole that I put out on the coffee table. "Oh, has Ethan called you?"

"Nope. I don't expect him to. So, I'm not going to waste any more thoughts on him. He's not worth it."

"Wise decision. I won't bring him up anymore, and I hope a snow plow runs into his fancy Range Rover," Lauren snickers.

"Lauren!" I scold her. "Come sit down, and let's eat!" I say.

I pour myself another glass of Chardonnay, spoon the shrimp on a platter and bring all of the food to the table.

"Dish up. Oh and brace yourself," I say dramatically. "Here's the news. First, Jack has a date with Abby this week. And second, Kate is engaged," I say miserably. My shoulders wilt, and I load up my plate with double helpings of everything.

Come here, butter. *You* are my friend.

"Kate? Really? Didn't she just start her senior year at UNC?" Lauren asks and gently blows on the steaming macaroni and cheese.

"Yep. She apparently met the love of her life at a sorority mixer, and he's from Savannah. She's lost her mind. Aren't you going to say anything about Jack and Abby?"

"Kari, I actually already knew," Lauren winces. "Abby stopped by my office this morning and gushed about Jack. I wasn't sure how to tell you. I figured Jack would mention it during your morning coffee run. Sorry!"

My phone chirps with a text message. It's from Jack and a picture is attached.

Jack: Braised Korean spare ribs!

I read the message and decide not to respond right now. Lauren watches me put the phone on the counter behind me. I shouldn't pout. It's totally not my style.

"It's okay, Lauren. You know, it's Monday, right after a long holiday weekend. Two big things to deal with. But, you will be glad to know that I made a decision this afternoon," I pause and take a deep breath. "I signed up for Speed Dating next week."

"What? Are you serious? That's super! I heard it's a great way to meet lots of guys without going out on a zillion dates."

"Thanks! I'm not going to stress about Jack and Abby. I'm happy for Kate and will support her, even though she's young and crazy to get married so soon after meeting someone. But, she's my baby sister and I love her. Instead, I'm focusing on *me* and taking control of my destiny," I say, popping the last shrimp in my mouth and pushing back my plate.

"Kari, you are so wonderful! I know you'll find The One. I guess your Mom is off your back now with Kate's news," Lauren laughs.

"Yes, she's excited and probably already picked out her mother of the bride dress. Goodness gracious. Are you done with dinner? Let's eat dessert on the sofa and catch up on *Homeland*. Sound good?"

"Perfect. I'll do dishes while you scoop the ice cream."

We carry the dishes and leftovers into the kitchen and chat about Lauren's job. I'm so glad Lauren is my go-to-girl. She supports and encourages me in everything I do.

It is a relaxing evening ... just what I needed. Good food, best friend, and drama-filled TV. I head to bed and pull a book from the reading pile, feeling more hopeful than I have in several weeks.

26

And so the wedding emails and phone calls flood in from Kate, Mama, and Kimberly, almost immediately. It's busy at work, so I send email responses and return phone calls during my lunch break or in the evenings after the gym.

Friday morning, I walk down to Red Shed Coffee with Jack, and he's whistling *again*. I guess his date went well with Abby, but he hasn't mentioned it and probably won't even if prodded.

"Good morning!" Lisa sings out as we enter and hand her our coffee cups.

"Hey Lisa! How's it going?" I ask and hand her cash to pay for the drinks.

"Fantastic! I'm done with final exams, and I met a guy last night," Lisa beams. "My friend, Rebecca had a party to celebrate fall semester ending, and she introduced me to him."

"That's awesome! Cute? What does he do for a living?" I inquire, and Jack hovers near me to listen in.

"Jordan's a freelance photographer and absolutely adorable."

"Congrats! Keep us posted. We'll see you tomorrow," I say as she hands us our steaming lattes.

"Thanks! Have a fabulous day!" Lisa says, smiling from ear to ear.

Perfect. Everyone is paired up now. That's okay. I'm going to meet some amazing guys at Speed Dating tomorrow night.

We walk back to the office, shivering from the single digit temperatures. I adjust my hat to cover my ears and pick up the pace, trying not to jostle my coffee.

"So, Kari, I feel like we haven't talked or barely seen each other since Thanksgiving. Did you get my text with the picture of the spare ribs a couple of days ago?" Jack asks, sounding concerned and a little hurt.

"Sorry, Jack. I was in the middle of dinner with Lauren and forgot to respond back. I've been really busy. Big news though, my sister, Kate, is getting married. Oh, and I'm going to Speed Dating tomorrow night," I say quickly.

"Slow down there. Isn't your sister still in college?"

"Yep, she's twenty-one and declared she's head over heels in love," I say miserably, trying not to sound bitter.

Jack lets out a whistle. "That's pretty young. When's the wedding?"

"June 21, next year. Aren't you going to tease me about Speed Dating?" I turn to look at him.

"I think it's great! You aren't becoming jaded over the whole Ethan situation. He must've really screwed up, so his loss. Back to speed dating, my roommate went to it last spring, had fun, and met a few nice girls. You'll have a great time."

Wow. No teasing? Actually, I'm not surprised. Jack is one of the most supportive people I know.

"Thanks, Jack. I'll let you know how it goes," I smile and exhale deeply. "Anything new with you?"

Wonder if he'll take the bait and give me some dish about his date with Abby yesterday. I only know it was yesterday because I calendar stalked him. They went to The Snowy Owl at 6 p.m., and he picked her up at the office.

"No, same old, same old. Work, yoga, and skiing."

Dang it. He's a vault. I'll email Lauren when I get back to the office and see if she has any gossip from Abby.

27

I arrive ten minutes early to McKinley's Bar for the Speed Dating event. I'm nervous and flip open the vanity mirror in my car to apply a fresh coat of lipstick.

"Why didn't I drag one of my other single girlfriends with me?" I lament.

I shiver as I step out of the car and shuffle across the icy parking lot. Deciding on what to wear was hard because I didn't know how casual or dressy people would be. I finally give in and choose black pants and a floral silk blouse.

I walk into the lobby, and Claire, the speed dating coordinator, greets me. She's sitting at a table with nametags, pens, and a stack of scorecards.

"Hi and welcome! My name is Claire. May I ask your name, so I can check you in?" Claire asks with a friendly smile.

"Yes, I'm Kari Covington."

"So nice to meet you, Kari! Tonight will be great fun! Here's a nametag. Just write your first name and last initial on the top line. Then write your favorite movie on the second line. It's an icebreaker … something people can read off your nametag and chat about with you. Hold onto this scorecard and pen, and I'll go over it later. We'll start the event in a few minutes, so feel free to mingle."

"Thanks so much," I say, wondering which movie to list. I decide on *Officespace* and walk into the bar area. My scorecard has a number seven written in the top left-hand corner.

Several girls and guys are milling around, commenting on nametags, and laughing nervously. I order a glass of Chardonnay from the bartender and glance around the group. I see several guys talking with one girl, who has long, curly black hair and an infectious laugh. Her nametag says "Phoebe S. Pretty Woman." Other small clusters of people stand around high top bar tables. I walk up to a table, smile, and say hello to the two girls there.

"Have you been to speed dating before?" I ask, shyly.

"It's my second time, and it is *so much* fun," Maisy says as she twists her hair nervously around her finger. She is petite with chin length brown hair and a raspy voice. She's wearing a burgundy cashmere sweater, grey pencil skirt, and black dress boots.

"It's my first time here, and I see no cute guys," Heather remarks with a frown. She takes off her black jacket and reveals a deeply cut tight red shirt. Heather tucks her long, brown hair behind her ears and sighs as she glances around the room again.

Okay, I don't see any outstanding guys either, but I'm still excited to meet some new people. Besides, my type of guy usually has facial hair, recycles, and constantly has the just-rolled-out-of-bed look all the time, complete with rumpled clothes. Completely opposite of the preppy guys at Clemson and in Charleston, much to the embarassment of my parents.

Although, now that I think about it, most of the blind dates this summer were with preppy guys. Ethan was the most clean-cut guy I dated this year. See? I tried to break away from the granola guys, and it didn't prove successful.

I remind myself of the snap judgment rule since I'll meet many guys tonight, but only spend a short amount of time with them.

Claire walks into the bar and shakes a little bell. People quiet down and turn their attention to her.

"Welcome and thank you for attending tonight! Couple of instructions before we start: You each have a scorecard. Girls have a number on top of their scorecard, and this corresponds to the table you will sit at the entire evening. We have ten tables, and each table has a number on it. The girls will sit at their table and not rotate, the guys will rotate. Any questions, girls? Okay, find your table and settle in," Claire instructs.

The girls scatter and find their tables, tucking purses and coats on the back of their chair.

"Now, guys ... you also have a number on your scorecard, that's the table you will start at for the first round. Then, you'll continue moving up one table in numerical order each time the bell rings. So, if your number is five, you'll start at table five, then move to table six and so forth. Any questions?"

"Everyone take a moment to look at their scorecard. It has numbers one thru ten on it and then yes or no next to the numbers. Mark yes if you're interested in seeing the person again, mark no if you're not interested. A word to the wise ... if you're here because you think you're guaranteed to have a date for next Saturday, you're here for the wrong reason. Please be open-minded. Marking yes could mean that you both ski and would like to go skiing sometime. Marking yes could also mean you have several things in common, but the bell rang too soon for you to talk about them. Marking yes does not mean you are bound to go to dinner, a movie, and meet his parents in one evening. Everyone understand?"

We all nod in agreement. A few people laugh at her speech.

She continues. "There are only two rules: Don't ask anyone their last name and don't ask what company they work for. Use general terms when you talk about your occupations. You'll have seven minutes at each table, and then I'll ring the bell for you to move on. We'll take a fifteen minute break halfway through. Everyone ready?" Claire asks enthusiastically as she picks up the bell.

She rings the bell, and the guys locate their starting table. They have a scorecard, pen, and drink in hand, eager to meet ten dates in one evening.

28

I fold my scorecard, so I can mark it discreetly and look up as Phil, Guy #9 slips into the seat. He has short, curly hair and is wearing jeans and a striped green t-shirt.

"Hi, how are you doing? I'm really nervous. Have you been to this before?" He stammers on.

"No, this is my first time here. So, what do you like to do for fun?" I ask, taking the lead. He doesn't seem the type to take charge in the conversation.

"Umm. I like to read sci-fi novels, play video games, and collect vintage comic books. What about you?"

"I like camping, hiking, and cross-country skiing. I also like to cook and bake." Awkward pause, as we have absolutely nothing in common. Oh boy, what did I sign up for? Okay, switch gears and think of something to say.

"What type of work do you do?" I ask, hoping this will turn into a six and a half minute response.

"Help desk at a cable company. I work second shift. Thought I would check out speed dating since I don't have a chance to meet women much," he shrugs, looking down and picking at his fingernail.

"What's your favorite video game?" I surreptitiously glance at my watch to see how many minutes are left. Nothing against Phil, but I read fiction novels, detest video games, and only read the Sunday comics. Baby Blues and B.C. are my favorites, but I decide against mentioning this tidbit.

"Halo 3."

I listen as Phil talks about the merits of Halo 3 and the upcoming Halo: Reach launch right before Christmas. The bell rings, and we shake hands. Pulling out my scorecard, I mark no. Yes, it's a snap judgment, but I don't see a date with him in the future that doesn't include a Wii and a pizza. Nice enough guy, but nothing in common.

The first half of the event flies by as I mark my card with a variety of yes and no responses. At the break, I head to the bathroom with the other girls. Maisy and Heather are chatting in front of the mirror about Marshall, #4.

"He owns a house and drives a Subaru. Stable guy. I marked him yes for sure," Heather says, clearly impressed by what she learned about him in their seven minutes. She brushes her hair and then applies powder to her nose.

"I like him too ... he's easy to talk to. Plus, he's cute, and I adore goatees," Maisy swoons.

My ears perk up as I listen to their exchange. After the break, he'll sit at my table. I pick up another glass of Chardonnay from the bartender. The wine definitely relaxes me and eases my nervousness.

Claire rings the bell and directs the girls to take their seat once again.

"Let's get started. Are there any questions before we begin? Several of you asked about match notification. I'll tally everyone's cards and if both people mark yes, I will send an email to you tomorrow with each other's email and phone number. It's up to you from there," Claire smiles. She rings the bell to commence the round.

Marshall #4 sits down at my table with a beer in hand.

"Hi, I'm Marshall. How's your evening going? Are you meeting some good people?"

"Yes, it's actually really fun. So, what do you do for a living?" I ask, noting how relaxed he seems to be. No need to beat around the bush ... see what he does and then move on to hobbies.

"I'm an IT Consultant. What about you?" Marshall takes a sip of beer.

"An architect. I recently moved up from Charleston, South Carolina. Did you grow up here?"

"Nah, I grew up in Chicago and then lived in rural Alaska for seven years before moving here to Anchorage. Are you enjoying Alaska? I bet it's a big change from the South."

"I love it here. People are so friendly, and there's something to do every weekend."

"Very true. Although, we could use some more live music in this town. I just heard that Cake is playing in Talkeetna on New Year's Eve."

"I love Cake! I saw them in Charleston, and it was a great show. You know, you're causing quite a stir with the girls here tonight. They were chatting about you in the bathroom ... rumor has it you're a good conversationalist and cute!"

OMG! I can't believe I said that to him! I instantly blush. What was I thinking? I really need to filter my thoughts before letting them fly out of my mouth.

"Really? That's so funny. Honestly, I just try to be myself," Marshall smiles and looks a little embarrassed.

Phew. Honest response, no big head and no smart ass response.

Marshall and I cover a wide range of topics during our seven minutes. We both love the nachos at Tahoe South Cantina, watching documentaries, hiking, and have similar music tastes. I mark yes to Marshall when the bell rings.

It's really nice to chat with someone who has shared interests. He does seem like a really decent guy, so I wonder what flaws he might have. Dang it, Kari. Quit dissecting him. He may not even mark you yes!

At the end of the evening, I turn in the scorecard to Claire. Out of ten guys, I marked four as a yes, and I'm hoping for the best when it comes to the tallying.

I'm so glad I took the plunge and signed up to attend. Driving home, I smile to myself. I met some interesting guys and had an enjoyable evening. I can't wait for the email from Claire tomorrow.

29

Arriving to work early, I log into email immediately to see if there's one from Claire. Jack enters my office with coffee cup in hand.

"Coffee run? I'm dying to hear all about speed dating," Jack grins at me.

"Sure, let me just check email quickly," I scan through my inbox. No emails from Claire.

We walk down the block, and I decide to wait until we have coffee in hand before spilling the details.

"The usual coffees?" Lisa asks automatically with a warm smile.

"Yes, please. How is your morning going?" Jack asks her. We hand over our cups.

"Good, busy. How about you guys?"

"Not bad for a Monday."

"Can I please get a cheese bagel, too?" I ask.

Lisa hands the bagel to me, and Jack hands over his credit card to pay.

"How long are you going to make me wait?" Jack asks impatiently. "Anyone worth marking yes? Did seven minutes fly by or drag by?"

"I had no idea what to expect, but it was actually fun! A little nervous in the beginning, but everyone there was nervous. You know, it's funny, if I had lots in common with the guy, the time flew by. On the other hand, nothing in common with the guy, and the time dragged by." I open the bag and tear off a hunk of the warm bagel to snack on while we wait for our coffee. Jack shakes his head when I offer him part of the bagel.

"How many people did you mark yes? Do you think they marked yes too? What kind of people sign up for Speed Dating? I mean, it's not something everyone is comfortable doing. Did you know anyone there?"

Slow down, Jack!

"I have no idea if they marked me yes or no. I hope so … we had some things in common. I marked yes to four out of ten guys. Claire, the speed dating coordinator, said she would send us an email with any mutual matches. There was one particular guy named Marshall who I really enjoyed talking to. He was kind of like you, without the smart ass comments," I tease.

We pick up our coffees from Lisa, say goodbye, and walk back to work.

I check my email again. Nothing from Claire. Patience is a virtue. The 9 a.m. staff meeting is about to begin, so I grab my coffee, last bite of bagel and head to the conference room.

The morning flies by with a walk through at the museum with our team. Jack and I sneak out for a late lunch.

"So, do you have an email yet with your matches?" Jack asks. We are eating grilled polish dogs from our favorite vendor who sets up a cart year-round, even in the blowing snow. After waiting in line for our food, we hurry back to the atrium and sit at one of the empty tables.

"I got it just before we left. Three matches, and I am *totally* excited to see Marshall again. He seemed like a really solid guy. Bonus points. We both love *Seinfeld* and *The West Wing*," I say and spread mustard on the polish dog.

"Great, so you can watch reruns together! Seriously, Kari. I hope it works out. You deserve it. You're one of the coolest girls I know. You're fun, adventurous, and up for anything. One of those yes people who will hang out whenever and do whatever. I'm rooting for you."

"Jack, you are so sweet. Thank you!" Awkward pause. Well, that's a first. Usually, we chatter non-stop about anything and everything.

"What do you think I should do about the matches? Contact them or wait until they email me?" I ask, so the conversation moves forward.

"Take the bull by the horns and shoot them a friendly email. Give 'em a boost of confidence to ask you out," Jack says and finishes the last of his potato chips.

"Maybe. I've been direct before, and it hasn't always worked out. In high school, I was always the one calling boys. It drove Mama crazy."

"You're not sixteen anymore. Just do it," Jack says and splits the cookie he bought and hands me half.

We walk upstairs to the office after lunch. I open my email, and there's a message from Marshall.

From: marshall@birchconsulting.com
To: kcovington@bbarchitects.com
Subject: For the love of Tahoe South Cantina Nachos

Hi Kari,

Hope your day is going well. Are you up for some nachos after work tomorrow? I would love to chat with you again.
Looking forward to hearing from you,

Marshall

My stomach does a little flip. I hit Reply and think for a moment on a response. I don't want to seem too eager, but we really hit it off last night.

To: marshall@birchconsulting.com
From: kcovington@bbarchitects.com
Subject: I love nachos, no olives!

Hey Marshall,

So nice to hear from you! Sure, I can meet up tomorrow. Meet at the bar at 5?

Kari

From: marshall@birchconsulting.com
To: kcovington@bbarchitects.com
Subject: RE: I love nachos, olives on the side

Great! Sounds like a plan. See you then.

/MB

I wonder if the B stands for Birch and he's the owner of Birch Consulting. Thanks to Google, I do a quick search and bring up the home page for Birch Consulting.

Looks like he's the owner and they have an impressive list of clients as well as a list of non-profits they support with free technical assistance. Wow. A nice guy who owns a house, good conversationalist, and involved in the community? This will silence Mama for awhile when I relay this during our Sunday phone call.

I add the date to my Outlook calendar. When Jack stalks my calendar, he will certainly ask about it when he sees it.

I don't receive any other emails from speed dating guys that afternoon. I'm happy with the email from Marshall and assume the remaining guys will call or email later this week.

$$\sim\!\!\!\circlearrowleft$$

After work, I meet Lauren for step class at the gym. We stake out our places in the back row, and the chatting begins.

"So, how was speed dating? I tried calling you at work today, but you weren't at your desk," Lauren says as she watches the other girls set up step benches around us. She frowns as one girl sets up her bench too close to hers. Must be a newbie.

"Sorry, today was super busy, and I was in meetings most of the day. Speed dating was fun! I met some nice guys, and I'm meeting one of them for drinks tomorrow night! His name is Marshall, and I already Google stalked him. Definitely some potential there," I say, smiling.

"Does he have a driver's license and a car? Any crazy ex-girlfriends? Give me some dish. I live vicariously through you now that I'm an old married woman."

"Ha! And this is why you're my best friend. You're always looking out for me. He seems perfect. I know it's early to say that, but we both like *Seinfeld*. It's a sign!"

"You and your *Seinfeld*! And your signs … remember that guy who owned all the seasons of *Seinfeld*, but wouldn't show you the inside of his house? He spent all of his time at your apartment, and you never saw what his house looked like. I bet it was a mess. I think you said it was a sign when he mentioned *Seinfeld*, too. I'm just saying …" Lauren laughs.

"Yeah, Alan was a mistake. A two year mistake, actually. The cherry on top was when he dumped me before Valentine's Day, so he wouldn't have to buy me a gift. Loserville," I roll my eyes and think back to the money I wasted paying for most of our dates, too!

"Typical Kari dating fiasco."

"I know the right guy is out there for me, and I refuse to give up."

The instructor comes into class, and we finish our conversation before class begins. After the gym, I stop at the grocery store for ingredients to make spaghetti and meatballs for dinner. Super easy and goes well with a nice glass of red wine. Makes me stop and think about Ethan, but I quickly dismiss him from my thoughts.

After dinner, I open my closet and select a couple of outfit options for my date with Marshall. I'll come straight from work, so I don't want to look all wrinkled by the end of the day. Finally, I decide on a fitted, black sweater and grey wool pants. I'll wear a chunky, red necklace for some color and the Charles David black leather ankle boots. Then, I won't have to worry about snow boots.

I go to bed early to read, but it's hard to sleep. I'm so excited for my date. Hopefully the work day will fly by tomorrow.

30

"Do you remember the one where Jerry rents a car, and the car rental place runs out of cars? Classic," I laugh as Marshall and I talk about our favorite *Seinfeld* episodes.

We're sitting at the Tahoe South Cantina bar, drinking beer, and eating nachos with olives on the side (a compromise since he loves olives). I feel relaxed and comfortable chatting with Marshall. My nervousness disappears after the first few minutes, and he appears relaxed as well.

"Nice! Although my all-time favorite is the Soup Nazi. I love Elaine," Marshall says as he scoops up sour cream and refried beans onto a chip.

"She's so funny! So, tell me about your work. How did you get into IT?"

"I majored in Computer Science at Loyola and then moved to Bethel after college for an internship and stayed for seven years."

"Isn't Bethel in rural Alaska where they don't have running water?" I ask and shake my head slowly. I can't imagine not having running water and peeing into a bucket or using an outhouse during the winter.

"No, it's actually pretty developed for rural Alaska. Just a small town with lots of expensive Chinese food and pizza. There are a few little towns nearby without running water and kids drive snowmachines to school. It's a whole different world."

"Yes, I can't even imagine! I've never been on a snowmachine. We don't get much snow in Charleston, just occasional ice, so winter is all new to me, especially driving in it. Although, I have learned to do a courtesy wave to folks when I slide through intersections here on the ice," I laugh as I demonstrate my Princess/I'm sorry/ Please don't hit me wave.

"You mentioned learning to cross-country ski the other night at speed dating. Are you taking lessons through Parks and Recreation or the University?"

Impressive! He remembers our conversation and the fact that I'm learning to ski. Not only a good conversationalist, but a great listener, too. I feel like I won the lottery.

"Not really formal lessons. My friend, Lauren, and her husband are accomplished skiers, so they took me out several times last winter, and I bought some skis. It's been fun learning, and I'm a little less wary of big hills now."

"If you want to go skiing sometime, let me know. I'm always up for hitting the trails. There are trails downtown without hills and they're lit for night skiing."

"Cool, thanks. I might take you up on it."

We finish our nachos and order another round of beer. Marshall asks about my past dating history. I guess he feels comfortable enough with me to ask since it's kind of a sensitive subject and not something people generally talk about on the first date.

I consider mentioning the Ethan disaster, but decide to see what he shares. Too much information right away might scare Marshall off, and I'm really enjoying this date so far. I'll keep it light on details.

"My friend, Lauren, has set me up on four blind dates over the last couple of months. Honestly, none of them resulted in a second date. All the guys were nice and polite, but we didn't have an instant connection. Is that too much information?"

"Not at all. Sometimes you just have to hit it off with someone or be on the same wavelength. I will say … you are courageous to go on so many blind dates. I guess Lauren likes playing matchmaker?"

"She's relentless. She hands out my business card to random guys and she'll even ask our waiter if he's single. It's embarrassing sometimes, but I can't fault her. Lauren married her college sweetheart, and her goal is to match up every single person she meets. A big heart, but a little overboard sometimes."

"Lauren sounds like she's a good friend. In all fairness, you answered my question, so I'll tell you a little bit about me. I haven't dated anyone seriously in two years. I was dating this girl, and she suddenly said we had to get married or break up. That probably sounds dumb, but I wasn't ready to settle down. It was hard to bounce back from an ultimatum and the suddenness of everything. Speed dating was the opportunity for me to get back out there."

"How long did you date?" I ask, relieved that his history isn't checkered or filled with a crazy ex-girlfriend.

"We dated for eight months which is not very long at all. Met her when I was in Bethel. She was a nurse at the hospital. I really liked her, but we were still getting to know each other … we were in the honeymoon phase, and I was taking it slow. Funny thing is, she's still single. If she hadn't pushed me, we could've been married by now," he says, his shoulders sagging.

"Wow. I'm sorry, Marshall." I pat him on the arm.

"It's fine. I had a great time at speed dating, met you, and here we are! Eating nachos and chatting like old friends," Marshall perks up and grins at me.

Ouch. Did he just say old friends? Was that a slip of the tongue?

"Kari, do you want to have dinner and see a movie on Saturday?"

"Sure, that sounds wonderful." A second date! Lauren will be so proud.

"Awesome. I'll touch base with you later this week."

Marshall paid the check, and we walk out to our respective cars. He waits until I drive off before he leaves the parking lot. I try not to overanalyze the "old friends" comment as I drive home, but it left me wondering. Maybe he doesn't feel a connection? Why would he ask me out again? Seriously … I need a guidebook or road map to understand guys sometimes.

31

Lauren rings my doorbell as I'm taking the lasagna out of the oven. Will is out of town this week, so I invited her over for dinner. He's attending a conference in sunny, warm San Diego.

"Door's open!" I yell as I set the heavy pan down on the stovetop. I toss the garlic bread in the oven and close the oven door. It'll warm up while the lasagna rests for ten minutes.

"Smells heavenly. I'm starving!" Lauren says and hands me a hefty jug of Chianti. She takes off her coat and snow boots. "It's freezing out there. Thank goodness for your cozy fireplace."

"It helps. My heat is included in the rent, so I can keep it as warm as I want!"

"Dinner will be ready in a few minutes. Aren't you glad I dragged you to the gym tonight? We can eat big and drink big. The gym cancels out the extra calories," I giggle in a good mood.

Lauren sets the table, and I pour Chianti in juice glasses, like my favorite Italian restaurant, Scalini, serves it.

"What shall we toast to?" Lauren asks.

"To a second date with Marshall. Woo Hoo!" I cry. Our glasses clink, and then I carry over the lasagna, bread, and Caesar salad to the table.

"Give me all the details! How did it go?" Lauren asks and cuts the lasagna for us.

"Marshall's great. Conversation flows easily, and I'm totally comfortable with him. We're going to dinner and a movie on Saturday," I grin.

"Sounds like it went very well. What does he do for a living?"

"He's an IT consultant. Owns the business and also a member of Rotary, treasurer in fact! Very community-minded. I like that. He has two sisters, and he grew up in Chicago."

"Did you talk about past relationships?" Lauren asks.

"We did!" I admit, triumphantly. "Some girl broke his heart, so speed dating was his dip back into the dating pool. I like him already."

"I'm so happy for you! He sounds like a gem. Since he has sisters, I bet he knows how to treat a girl. I can't wait to meet him. How about I host a game night next weekend, and you can bring him?"

Her wheels are already churning and planning my engagement party down the road. Slow down, Lauren.

"Maybe ... let's see how the dinner and movie goes first. I'm happily optimistic about Marshall. Although, I haven't heard from the other speed dating matches. Oh well, I'm not too worried about it."

"What did you tell him about you?"

"You know ... the usual. I bake, cook, miss my family, but love it here. I told him about you setting me up all the time. He thought it was funny. I didn't talk too much, I hope ... kept it casual."

"Ha! It just shows that you're open-minded and willing to meet new people. By the way, how's Jack doing? Abby hasn't said a peep since their date after Thanksgiving. Are they hot and heavy yet?" Lauren asks and takes another slice of garlic bread.

"Jack is a vault. He rarely says anything about his personal life. I tried to talk to him about it, but no go," I shake my head. "He's been acting a little weird this week. He brought me a cookie and latte this afternoon, and he offered to pick up lunch for me yesterday since I was swamped at work."

"Yeah, but you're always eating together or going for cookie runs in the afternoons."

"I know, but he did it all without prompting or anything, and he sent me an email to check in and see how I was doing. He's always thoughtful and attentive, but it feels different this week. I wonder if there's some motive behind it," I say and carry our empty plates to the kitchen.

Lauren carries over the lasagna pan, salad bowl, and bread basket to the kitchen and then refills our juice glasses. "Maybe he's jealous of Marshall and your impending happiness."

"No, that's not it. Jack hasn't shown any interest in dating me. We've always just been friends, and suddenly I have this weird vibe from him. Maybe he thinks our friendship will change if Marshall and I become serious. His behavior didn't change like this when I was dating Ethan. Actually, I haven't even thought about what will happen to our friendship if either of us are involved with someone."

Okay, I admit I've had a few fantasies about dating Jack. They include cooking together, entertaining friends, and spending weekends together. And, I also dream about touching his amazing abs. Sigh.

"Ask him. Don't let anything interfere with your friendship. Be direct and find out, otherwise it'll make work life awkward …

suddenly your work husband will disappear! Maybe he'll open up and tell you about Abby. She's really nice, even though you don't want to believe it. She needs a guy who won't let her be a workaholic."

"I know she's nice. Plus, she has excellent taste in shoes." I carry out a lemon chiffon cake and place it on the table.

"I love that you look at everyone's shoes! Do you feel guilty having a separate closet for your shoes?" Lauren teases and licks her lips as I cut the cake.

"How do you have time to whip up cake *and* lasagna?"

"It's no big deal. This cake is one of those easy one bowl recipes. And to answer your question, I feel no guilt. Just sad that it's winter, and I can't show off my shoe wardrobe all the time." I serve Lauren a generous piece.

We carry our dessert and wine to the den and sit by the toasty fire. Lauren tells me about the latest mayor crisis and office gossip.

After Lauren leaves, I clean up the kitchen and tidy up the apartment. Then I lay on the sofa to relax and read a book before going to bed.

My cell phone rings, and caller ID displays Mama.

"Hi Mama!" I greet her.

"Kari, it's your Mama. What are you doing? Are you eating dinner? I never know what time it is in Alaska," she says, thoroughly confused.

"Mama, it's nine o'clock here. We're four hours earlier than you. Why are you up so late?"

"I'm working on the guest list. Lord knows, Kate doesn't know who all to include, so I told her I would take care of it."

"It's December. The wedding is not until June. Kate *just* got engaged. Why are you doing it now?" Seriously! I'm kind of thankful I'm not the one engaged since I see what Kate's going through … mostly because of Mama.

"Kari Ann Covington. I know what month it is. I have a million and a half things to do for this wedding. I'm calling to see if you're bringing a date."

"Seriously? Mama, I don't know. June is a long way off. Can I say yes and let you know?" I sigh, hoping this will not open a flood of questions.

"Are you dating someone now? Is that why you want me to mark you as a plus one? How did you meet him? Did Patrick ever call you?"

"I actually just started seeing someone. We met at speed dating. And no, Patrick didn't call. He's in the middle of a divorce, so I'm sure he has other things on his mind."

Please, no more questions. I can't handle it.

"I don't remember you saying anything about speed dating when we talked last Sunday. I've been so busy planning this wedding that I must've forgotten. What's speed dating? Is that some Alaska thing?"

"Basically, I met ten guys in one evening and talked with them for seven minutes each. It was fun."

"Sounds like some kind of orgy or weird Alaskan thing. Why on earth you moved there, I'll never know."

"Mama!" I cry. "It's not an orgy. They do it all over the United States. It's an efficient way of meeting people. And, I love it here. Although it's freezing cold right now, I still love it." I take a deep breath and slowly exhale. How many times do we have to talk about this?

"Fine, Kari. Listen, we need to talk about your trip here for Christmas. Kate is bringing Ashford, so he can meet the whole family. I want you on your best behavior."

Did she just say that? Huh … and you wonder why I moved so far away.

"Mama, I'm not six-years-old. I'm always on my best behavior. Does he really go by Ashford? Seems like such a formal name."

"I guess his family and friends call him Ash. Your Daddy and I are going to Savannah next weekend to meet his parents and talk about the wedding. What dates will you be here? I'm going to mark it on the calendar right now so I don't have to ask you a third time."

"It's okay. I'm coming December 20-28. Kimberly said she'll pick me up, so you don't have to worry about it. Don't stress over this wedding. It'll turn out perfect, and you have plenty of time to plan."

"Thanks! You know, Kate and I don't agree on the location, so it's a mess. She wants to get married on the beach, and I want them to have the wedding at Magnolia Plantation. They have such lovely grounds and a huge back lawn for the tent. What do you think?" Mama sighs.

Does she have everything planned already? Location, tent, guest list. I suspect the dinner menu is already written out along with Dad's toast to the happy couple. She is over the top. Seriously.

"Mama, I have to go. Lauren's calling me on the other line. Talk to you later." I lied. Straight out lied. There's no way I want thrown in the middle of Mama and Kate. They will have to duke it out on their own. Kate is very strong-willed, so I suspect she'll put up a fight and not give in to Mama and her ideas.

"Bye! Love you!" Mama sings out and hangs up.

Is there more wine?

32

It's just my luck I have to work late the rest of the week. Marshall wants to meet for Happy Hour on Thursday, but I have to decline since I'm on deadline at work. He has to cancel our dinner and movie date on Saturday because of a last minute job in Barrow, the coldest, furthest northern town in Alaska. Our stars are not aligned this week, and I'm disappointed.

I guess he could tell I was a little skeptical of the weekend work, but he assured me it was the best time to reconfigure a network during non-business hours. Makes sense, I suppose.

We chat about other random stuff, and he asks me to go skiing the following Wednesday. I agree, and he arranges to pick me up after work at my apartment.

"The best part of skiing and enduring the cold is a hot toddy after we finish, right?" I gasp, breathing hard.

I'm out of breath, as I reach the top of the small hill on the trail. Hmmm … I thought there were no hills on this trail.

Marshall and I are skiing on the downtown trails, and he's a really good skier. In fact, he gave me some helpful tips after I took a tumble for the third time. Yes, falling in front of him. Really graceful. However, he showed me an easy way to get up using my poles and pushing up from one knee, so it was worth it. I didn't look like my usual flailing sea otter with ski poles. Not a good visual picture, I assure you.

"Absolutely. There's a new tapas bar downtown. Do you want to check it out after we're done skiing?" Marshall asks. "Maybe it won't be too packed since it's only a Wednesday and not the weekend."

He stops at the bottom of the hill to take a picture of me cruising down the trail, somewhat gracefully. I asked him to snap a few pictures so I can send them to my family.

"Sure. I heard they have great food. Are we okay to go in our ski clothes?"

"Absolutely. It's winter, they won't care. I vote we ski back to the car and call it a day. This has really been fun, Kari. You're doing very well, and I hope you keep at it. There's some fun ski races in the spring."

"I don't know about doing any races, but it's great to be outside in the winter instead of lying on the sofa with chocolate chip cookies and TiVo."

I laugh and try to catch my breath. As I adjust my hat, I see my hair is frosted at the tips with icicles. I'm so glad I moved to Alaska. I'm so glad I moved to Alaska.

"Definitely. I've found the best way to survive nine months of winter is to keep busy and get outside every day, even if it's for only a few minutes. Keeps you sane!"

We ski back down the trail and take off our gear at his car. I'm looking forward to warming up. I brush the snow off my pants and rub lip balm on my dry lips. I'll never get over how dry it is in Alaska. I go through lotion, lip balm, and conditioner in huge quantities. Hoping my hat hair isn't too bad, I gently fluff up my hair and tuck it behind my ears, wishing I brought a headband or barrette.

Marshall loads our skis on the roof rack, and he starts up the car. No auto start. Boo. Not a dealbreaker, but almost everyone in Alaska has it.

"This was fun! Thanks for inviting me!" I say, rubbing my hands in front of the heater vent, praying the warm air will come quickly.

"Good times for sure. I'm ready for food and a glass of wine. So, how do you like Alaska now that it's your second winter? Do you think you'll stay here for the rest of your life?"

Wow. That's an interesting question. Does he want to stay in Alaska forever, I wonder.

"I really do like it, but I miss my family and friends in Charleston. Plus, I miss babysitting my nieces and watching them grow up. How old are your sisters?"

"My older sister is thirty-nine, and my younger sister is your age, thirty-two. Middle child all the way."

"Hey, me too! At least you didn't have hand me down clothes all your life."

"True, but my sisters definitely tortured me growing up," Marshall laughs and parallel parks along the downtown street.

We enter Sixth Street Tapas, and a hostess leads us to a table in the bar. She hands us menus, and I immediately see several items I want to try.

"What do you like best about living in Alaska?" I ask after we place our drink order.

"I love the people here. Everyone is friendly and outgoing. However, I do want to check out other areas in the Pacific Northwest. Some place a little more liberal."

"My friend lives in Bend, Oregon, and she loves it there. Not too many conservatives, I don't think."

"Right on. Do you want to choose items for the first round?"

"How about the salmon and sweet potato croquettes, the artichoke toasts, and the stuffed dates?" I say, licking my lips.

"Perfect," Marshall says and places the order with the server.

"Are you close with your family? Where do your sisters live?" I ask.

"We're super close. My older sister lives in Chicago near my parents, and my younger sister lives in Boston. Have you ever been to Chicago?"

"I visited a friend there one summer during college. Chicago has amazing architecture. I toured the Sears Tower and the John Hancock Center, plus a couple of Frank Lloyd Wright's homes. I had the most amazing steak in my life at Chicago Prime. Sorry, I really love food," I apologize, blushing.

"I kind of noticed … you seem to know all the places to eat in town and what to order there. I like that about you! I seem to go to the same places and order the same stuff."

"Thanks! It's nice to go out and try new things, especially food I wouldn't cook at home. I'm glad you suggested this place. It was on my list to try."

Hmm. He said he likes me. Well, kind of.

"Speaking of the same old places, since you're a big fan of Tahoe South Cantina and their nachos, what do you think about a standing dinner there on Sunday nights? It's a great way to start the week. We can invite friends or whatever, and it's something to look forward to."

"Love it! Do you have a lot of close friends here to invite?"

"A few, but most of my friends are married and have kids. What about you? Have you made a lot of friends up here?"

"A couple of close friends for sure. Lauren and Will are my best friends. Will is from Fairbanks and works for *The Alaska Courier*, and Lauren works for the City. They would definitely love the Sunday dinner idea. My other girlfriends, too!"

Come to think of it, I've left several messages for Deirdre, and she hasn't returned any of my calls. Perhaps dating the engineer co-worker is going really well.

The first round of tapas arrive, and we dive in. The dishes are excellent, and Marshall orders garlic shrimp, grilled chorizo, and crispy eggplant for the second round.

I'm having a lovely time, and I appreciate so many of Marshall's qualities. He is kind, considerate, and polite. The girls at speed dating definitely pegged him correctly. I wonder how many matches he had.

I bet he would have a grand time at my sister's wedding in June. Wait. Too soon. He hasn't made a move to kiss me, and this is only the second date. He does look like a good kisser though. Maybe tonight when he drops me off at home.

We end up having three rounds of tapas and talking about everything. We chat about work, college, past relationships, friends, and more. I'm feeling very relaxed from three glasses of wine and a little sore from skiing.

Marshall carries my skis up to my door, and leans in for a kiss ... on the cheek.

"Kari, thanks for a fun day! You're good people," Marshall says with a smile.

"Thanks for the skiing and dinner," I say, wondering what the heck is going on. Good people? What does that mean?

Marshall walks down the stairs and waves goodbye. I close my apartment door and immediately cry out, "ARGH!" Then, I dial Lauren's phone number for immediate analysis of the "good people" remark.

33

J ack and I walk quickly to Red Shed Coffee this morning since
it's snowing with a strong head wind. We stand in line, and Lisa
greets us with a big smile.

"Bit chilly out this morning, eh?" Lisa takes our coffee cups,
and I hand over my credit card.

"It's frigid! How are you and Jordan doing? Big plans for
Christmas?" I add in the tip and sign the receipt.

"We just celebrated our three week anniversary. He framed a
picture that he took of us when we went ice skating. And, we're
going to his parent's house for Christmas. They live in Homer,"
Lisa smiles. "I'm so excited to meet them."

"Great! Congrats on the anniversary," Jack says and high fives
her.

We sit down at a table for a few minutes and sip our coffee,
watching the snow plow go by. I take off my wool hat and unzip
my down coat.

"Jack, I want to ask your opinion, so be honest, no jokes," I
say seriously and sip on my vanilla latte.

"Sure. You sound so somber. Are you okay? Please tell me
you're not giving up on Alaska and moving back to Charleston,"
Jack pleads and points outside to the weather.

"No, not a chance. I love it even though it's cold and miserable right now. It's about Marshall. We've gone out twice now. We have fun, talk about everything, have stuff in common, and I like him. Last night at the end of our date, he kissed me on the cheek and told me I was good people. What does 'good people' mean? Lauren says it's the kiss of death, and he views me as a friend."

"Two dates, kiss on the cheek, and a compliment. Yep, you're in the friend zone. Are you okay with this?"

"Wait. Why does he keep asking me out if he's not interested in dating me?"

Guy behavior is so confusing. Seriously. I really need that guidebook and map now!

"Maybe he was trying to get to know you and then decide. I know that's not what you want to hear though. From what you've told me, he sounds like a solid guy. What will you do if he asks you out again?"

"I guess I'll accept. He *is* fun. Lauren thinks I should ditch him and not return his calls. I think that's rude, but I'm a little hurt. I like him, and he doesn't like me back. This really sucks. Seriously. First Ethan, now Marshall. Do I have the words 'please break my heart' written on my forehead?" I ask miserably.

I mean, he didn't have to go skiing with me. After our date at Tahoe South Cantina, if he wasn't into me, he could have left it at that. Why would he ask me out to dinner and a movie if he didn't like me? I hate to overanalyze, but his behavior doesn't make sense.

"Of course not, just a run of bad timing. I'm truly sorry, Kari," Jack says and pats me on the arm. I look into his brown eyes and swoon slightly. I can't help it. Jack is absolutely adorable.

"Let's walk back. I don't want to talk about it anymore. I appreciate your perspective," I say and stand up, tightening my pink scarf around my neck. Jack gives me a hug. I lean in closer to smell his aftershave.

We walk back to work with our backs facing the wind this time. I'm quiet and contemplative the rest of the day, and Jack stops by my office before heading home.

"Are you working late tonight?" Jack asks, zipping up his messenger bag and putting on a hat.

"Yes, I need to work on some designs for my latest project. It's the new administrative building at the University of Alaska."

"Nice! That's great. How about I run out and pick up some dinner for you?"

"Thanks, but I'll pass. I'm going to dig in for the evening. Have fun tonight at yoga with Abby!" I turn my attention to the computer monitor and hold back tears. I only know about Abby since I calendar stalked him and saw his yoga date for tonight.

Okay, I'm not completely torn up, but enough to have a small pity party. I feel like I've been out there meeting people, trying hard, and the one guy who I connect with doesn't like me back. A little disheartening.

Alaska is a tough place to live, and I'm so far away from my family. I want to meet a guy who makes me laugh and has shared interests.

I need a break: from Anchorage, from guys, from the cold weather, and from being alone. Christmas is two weeks away, and I leave on Friday. I can go home, drink sweet tea, play with my nieces, and recharge my batteries.

And no snow boots, wool hats, or gloves needed!

34

THE SOUTH

The place where … 1) Tea is sweet and accents are sweeter. 2) Summer starts in April. 3) Macaroni & Cheese is a vegetable. 4) Front porches are wide and words are long. 5) Pecan pie is a staple. 6) Y'all is the only proper noun. 7) Chicken is fried and biscuits come with gravy. 8) Everything is Darlin'. 9) Someone's heart is always being blessed.

"Aunt Kari! Aunt Kari!" My twin nieces, Anna and Ashley, shout as they scamper toward me at the airport. Their blonde hair is french braided and tied with a bright blue ribbon. They are wearing cute floral sundresses, not identical, thank goodness. My sister claims that dressing them the same will give them identity problems down the road. I think she read this in one of her many parenting books.

"Hi! Look how fast you're growing! Give me a big hug," I say and set down my Vera Bradley carry-on bag and purse. Bending down, I pick up both girls, and they each give me a wet kiss on the cheek.

"Kari! You look wonderful. Alaska suits you," Kimberly nods in approval. After I set the girls down, she gives me a hug and kiss on the cheek. Kimberly adjusts the sunglasses on top of her head, and her brown, curly hair springs up all around the frames. Kimberly is wearing white capri pants with a fitted, turquoise polo shirt and light brown espadrilles. Her brown messenger bag is filled with healthy snacks for the girls, her daytimer (to keep up with ballet lessons, soccer games, and Mark's schedule), and her iPhone.

"Thanks, Sweetie! Where's Mark?" I ask, looking around.

"Oh Lord, you know my husband, he's at the marina. Those Southern boys love their boats. The marina is having a Christmas decorating contest, so he has all these grand ideas for lighting up the boat."

"I can't wait to see him and everyone else. Let's go grab my suitcase. Girls, come this way!" I beckon them over with a wave.

"We're coming, Aunt Kari! Did you bring us a present?" They ask in unison.

"As a matter-of-fact, I did. I brought it all the way from Alaska. You're going to love it, but you have to wait until Christmas to open it." We take the escalator down to baggage claim. I brought them each an Alaska coloring book, homemade fudge (Kimberly will not approve!), a sled dog stuffed animal, and a t-shirt. Smoked salmon for Kimberly and Mark, too!

"Awww. Please, can we open it now?" Anna asks sweetly, batting her eyelashes at me.

She has the longest eyelashes. Why can't mine be that long?

"Nice try, Anna. You girls can wait. It's only a few days."

Anna and Ashley skip ahead to the baggage claim. My bag is already on the conveyor belt. I love flying into small airports!

I pick up my bag, and we walk out to Kimberly's Volvo wagon. The humidity hits my face as soon as the automatic door opens, and I breathe in deeply. I miss the South.

Kimberly buckles in the girls while I load my bags in the back of the car. I look around the airport parking lot and take a moment to appreciate the towering oaks with moss, the cars adorned with football emblems, and everyone dressed in capris or shorts.

On the way to our parent's home, Kimberly fills me in on the latest family gossip along with more wedding drama. I can't believe the wedding is six months away, and this many tears and tantrums have already happened.

"So, Mama tells Kate they won't pay for the wedding unless she gets married at Magnolia Plantation. Kate goes to Dad, and Mama throws a fit. I tell you, Kate should just elope over spring break," Kimberly insists.

"I still don't understand what the rush is and why they set a wedding date so soon. Why don't they enjoy their engagement for awhile? They practically just met," I say, admiring the green grass and blooming camellias in the neighborhood.

"You know Kate, impulsive and immediate gratification. I will say that Ash seems like an outstanding guy. He's gracious, and he gets along well with Dad. They've golfed together three times already."

"When is everyone coming over? Did Mama post a schedule? I know she likes bossing us all around."

"Whatever," Kimberly says and rolls her eyes. "Mama and her schedule. She drives me crazy with that thing, I swear!"

"Folks are coming over tonight, Christmas Eve, and Christmas Day. She scheduled shopping trips, meetings with caterers, and a wedding cake tasting in between everything else. You know what really bugs me? She didn't go all out like this for my wedding."

"She did. You've just blocked it from your memory. Don't you remember her telling the caterer off and saying she's eaten better food at Cracker Barrel? Goodness gracious, I almost died laughing." We giggle, thinking about Mama and how she doesn't hold back her thoughts on anything.

"That's right! I did forget. Mark was so over the whole wedding planning. He wanted to get married on the boat and sail off. Kate better practice saying no to Mama, or she'll end up with the wedding of Mama's dreams at Magnolia Plantation!" We laugh loudly and feel badly for our little sister.

Kimberly pulls up in front of the house. I love this house and have so many fond memories growing up here. It's on the historic register and within walking distance of downtown. My Dad has lovingly restored every part of it over the years.

The door flings open, and Mama runs out with Dad trailing behind her.

"Kari Ann! I'm so glad you're here! My, you look so pale. Don't they have sun in Alaska?" Mama says, frowning and pushes my curly hair out of my eyes, looking me up and down.

"Oh Vi, she looks fine. Give your ol' Dad a hug!" Dad says and opens his arms wide.

I grin and admire Dad's year-round tan. His snowy white hair is thinner on top, but he's still lean and in good shape. Spending most mornings on the golf course certainly helps, and he always carries his own golf clubs. No caddy or golf cart for him.

"I'm so glad to be here. You both look fantastic and so tan!" I hug and kiss them both on the cheek, admiring how little they've changed since I last saw them.

"I'll take your suitcase to your room," Dad says and heads out to the Volvo to gather my luggage. "Anna and Ashley, go on in, your Grammy baked you a special treat."

The twins can smell sugary homemade treats from a mile away. Kimberly monitors their sugar intake and is overly fanatical about it, according to Mama.

"Mama! If they eat cookies now, then they won't eat anything at dinner," Kimberly says with a huff and takes off after them into the house. She rolls her eyes at me as she calls to the girls to wait up.

35

Mama and I walk into the house, and I admire the Christmas decorations. Christmas is Mama's favorite holiday and with her masterful eye, she turns the house into a gorgeous warm and inviting Christmas postcard.

The banister is wrapped with garland, red berries and white lights all the way up to the third floor. An eight-foot tree is in the living room decorated with crystal ornaments and red accents. And, a small tabletop tree sits on the hallway table. This is just what I can see from the foyer.

"Now Kari, I made a schedule like usual, so everyone knows what's going on. You know that's the only way our family will function and show up at all the right times for everything. We have an appointment tomorrow morning at the seamstress for your bridesmaid gown," Mama says as we walk into the kitchen.

"What? I'm a bridesmaid? Kate hasn't asked me," I say and take a cookie off a tray sitting on the granite kitchen island.

"Of course, you and Kimberly are bridesmaids. Kate just hasn't had a minute to ask you. She had final exams last week," Mama says and pours me a glass of sweet tea and squeezes a lemon in it.

She smiles at the twins who are happily munching away on sugar cookies shaped like snowmen while Kimberly makes a face at me.

"Well, let's see what Kate says, okay?"

"Oh Kari, don't worry. Here's a copy of the schedule. I made a special note at the bottom of your copy."

"Patrick is coming to dinner tonight, so please be on your best behavior," I read aloud.

Kimberly snorts and raises up a magazine to hide her expression.

"Mama, what are you up to? I don't want to see him. It's been years since high school. Why on earth did you invite him?" I take a sip of sweet tea, the house wine of the South.

"Because he's available now and you used to date. What's the matter with that? He's excited to come over tonight. I was thinking you should leave your hair curly tonight."

"I know you like to straighten it sometimes, but it looks so much better curly. And don't wear one of your bright lipsticks. It's too much."

Mama is driving me crazy, and I've only been here for ten minutes. I see Dad slinking away to his office. Lucky guy.

"I'm going to go freshen up since I've been traveling all day," I say and pick up the glass of sweet tea to take on my escape upstairs.

"Okay, Kari. After you clean up, can you help me in the kitchen? Everyone's arriving tonight at five. We're going to watch the sunset and have cocktails before dinner is served," Mama says, checking the schedule posted on the refrigerator.

"Sure, Mama." I walk up to the second floor to my old room. I overhear Kimberly telling the girls they can't have any more cookies to eat. Whining soon follows, and they are shooed outside to play.

My room looks exactly like I left it when I went away to college. My white iron bed is adorned with a Laura Ashley pink and white flowered comforter, and pink paper lantern lights wrap around the headboard. Butterfly stickers decorate the corner of the room near the window, and my desk still has notebooks and a pencil sharpener sitting on it. The walls are painted light pink with a border around the white chair railing.

The only new addition is a five foot Christmas tree with blinking green lights next to the white armoire. I walk over to admire it, and I notice the ornaments. The theme is outdoors and Alaska. Leave it to Mama to make me feel comfortable. I especially like the ornament of the bear wearing red pajamas with the back flap undone.

I unzip the overstuffed suitcase and unpack my clothes and nine pairs of shoes. It was fun packing warm weather clothes and cute strappy sandals. Opening the closet door, I see Mama posted another schedule above the full-length mirror with the note about Patrick highlighted in bright orange. She really is relentless and obsessed about me getting married.

After showering and checking email on my laptop, I join Mama in the kitchen. Kimberly and the girls went to pick up Mark, so I'm on my own.

"What's for dinner, Mama? What can I help with?" I ask, peeking in the refrigerator and snagging a couple of pieces of cheese to eat.

"Lowcountry bouillabaisse, cheese grits, french bread, and a big green salad. I need your help with the appetizers. Homemade pimiento cheese with crackers, sausage balls, deviled eggs with pickled jalapenos, and warm turnip greens dip," Mama says with a flourish.

"Okay, which appetizers do you want me to make?" I ask, impressed as usual with Mama's menu planning. She taught me how to cook, so I love spending time in the kitchen with her. We spent a good portion of my childhood in the kitchen, so I know how she likes things done.

"The sausage balls and pimiento cheese, please. All the ingredients are in this fridge or the one out in the garage," Mama says as she places eggs in water to boil.

I pull her recipe binders down from the shelf above her desk in the corner of the kitchen and flip to her famous pimiento cheese recipe. She serves it cold, but I prefer to make a grilled cheese with it. Perfect comfort food.

"Your new granite countertops look magnificent," I say as I search the refrigerator shelves for ingredients to start measuring out for the recipes.

"Thanks, Kari. Your Dad put them in this fall for me. Much better looking than the old ones, don't you think?'

'Did you pick out a nice outfit for tonight to impress Patrick?" Mama says, setting the timer. "You're not wearing that, are you?"

I glance down at my outfit. Khaki capris, white dobby cotton short-sleeved shirt over a pink tanktop, and brown thong sandals. Perfectly acceptable.

"Mama! What's wrong with what I'm wearing? And for the last time, I have no interest in dating him and doing a long distance thing," I insist. I swear, she has selective listening. How many times do I have to tell her?

"Of course, you won't have a long distance relationship. You'll move back. Didn't you bring any cute dresses? We can squeeze in a shopping trip tomorrow and buy you some new clothes. Obviously, there aren't any decent stores in Anchorage."

"Enough about my clothes; I'm not going to change them. You seriously think I'll move back for Patrick? Mama. I *like* living in Alaska. I wish you'd accept that fact and move on. I'll be polite to Patrick tonight, but I really wish you hadn't invited him," I say firmly and look her in the eye.

As usual, she gives an exasperated sigh. I'm so glad I moved to Alaska. I'm so glad I moved to Alaska.

I pull out the measuring cups, knife, cutting board, and a big bowl from the white painted cabinet.

"Let's change the subject. Do I need to whip up a dessert, or do you have that covered?" I ask.

"I have banana pudding and deep dish pecan pie. Do you think we need something else? It's our family, Grandpa, Grandma, and Patrick. Oh, and Kate is bringing Ash. You'll love him. He's such a gentleman," Mama gushes. She cuts up collard greens and measures out mayonnaise.

"I'll make some lemon bars," I say, happy to contribute my baking skills to dinner tonight.

"They're your Dad's favorite dessert, so he'll appreciate it. How's work going? Have they seen your wonderful talent and given you a big raise?"

"Work is going really well. I love my job, co-workers, and the projects I'm working on. It's so different from here. We have to design buildings to withstand earthquakes since we have small ones all the time. Pretty crazy, huh?"

"I'm very proud of you, Kari. You are so talented and cre-ative. I know the right man will appreciate all you have to offer," Mama says. She comes over to hug me while I'm shredding cheese and gives me a peck on the cheek.

I wipe the red lipstick off my cheek with the back of my hand and smile at her. She's never been shy on praising us growing up and has always encouraged us in everything we do whether it's trying out for the school play or running for class president.

"What's new with you and Dad? Any other home projects?" I ask.

"Oh, you know. Lunch with my friends every week. I've also started volunteering at the Food Bank. They are such a big help to folks around here, so I go there every Thursday and sort food. Sometimes, your Dad joins me if it's raining too hard, and he can't play golf. I also want to remodel the master bathroom next spring. Take out the jetted tub and add some fancy tilework," Mama says and pours the turnip green mixture into a casserole dish to bake.

"Sounds great, Mama. I'm glad you're getting Dad to volunteer with you."

"I do have some good news for you, honey. You've been asking us to visit, and we want to come up for the Iditarod in March. How does that sound? Is it a good time to come see you? I would love to watch the mushers and see the dogs."

"That's fine with me, but it's going to be cold. Wouldn't you rather come in the summer when we have non-stop daylight, and it's a little warmer? In March, it's cold and dreary," I say.

I'm astonished they are committing to visit. I've begged them to visit for months now. They haven't come up since I moved there. In fact, none of my family has come up. But, I don't blame them too much. Two layovers and all day travel from here isn't very appealing.

"Your Dad wants to see the snow and igloos, so winter is the best time, right?" Mama asks and starts laughing.

I roll my eyes. Typical assumption we have igloos and even live in them, depending on who you ask.

"Mama! We don't have igloos. You know that," I shake my head. "People think that all the time. We have regular homes just like here. Not a lot of brick, but they're regular homes."

"You live in an igloo?" Dad says, walking into the kitchen and dipping a finger into the pimiento cheese. I swat at him, and he grins.

"Dad, we don't have igloos in Alaska. Mama just told me you're visiting next March. I'm so happy!" I give him a big hug and move the pimiento cheese away from him and his wandering fingers. "I can't wait to show you my apartment and all of Alaska. And, take you to one of my favorite restaurants for the best nachos. Oh, and there's a new dessert café in town with the most delicious cheesecake."

"Sounds great! You know I love desserts. We thought seeing snow and the dog race sounds like an adventure! And avoid the summer hordes of tourists," Dad says and walks over to see what Mama is cooking, so he can sample it.

"I'll check to see what day the race starts and what other activities are going on during that time *and* request time off work," I say, making a mental list of stuff to show them. I need my daytimer, but it's upstairs, and I'm in the middle of rolling out sausage balls with my hands.

"Last year, I watched the ceremonial race start with Lauren and Will. The mushers run along the downtown trails while everyone cheers them on. We brought camp chairs, hot chocolate, and gave out cookies to the mushers as they passed us. It was so much fun, and now you'll get to do it with us!"

Dad fills me in on his latest golf game scores as I finish the sausage balls. He tells me about how the country club fired three caddies last Saturday for theft.

His eyes light up as I start zesting lemons for the lemon bars, and he pats me on the shoulder. He brings out the plans for the master bathroom and asks me a couple of questions on the design.

I'm happy in the kitchen with my parents. I try not to think about dinner in a few hours with Patrick ringing our doorbell like he used to when we dated in high school. Oh well, I'll grin and bear it. Considering the awful blind dates and heartbreak over Ethan and Marshall, I'm toughening up and ready for anything.

36

"So, Kari, how long are you in town for?" Ash asks politely and passes me the bowl of cheese grits. Kate sits on the other side of him beaming and glowing. Her long blonde hair is held back with a slim, black headband, and she's wearing a cotton, black sundress with spaghetti straps and a pearl necklace. Our parents gave us matching pearl necklaces when we were teenagers, and we all still wear them.

Her engagement ring sparkles on her hand. It's a stunning, two carat, pear-shaped diamond on a white gold band.

Ash is nice just like everyone said. I talked with him in the kitchen while I was plating the appetizers for cocktail hour. He's majoring in Computer Science at UNC and lives off campus with three other students. He doesn't look like the typical Southern guy, blonde, good-looking, clean-shaven, fraternity tattoo, and six pack abs. Ash has thick, black hair, wide-set brown eyes, and a nose a little too big for his face. It gives him character, and I immediately like him.

"Until Saturday. I'll return to Anchorage for New Year's Eve," I say and pass the grits to Patrick, who is sitting next to me. Damn Mama and her trying to fix me up. I admit Patrick looks as handsome as ever, exactly like he did in high school, but I am *not* interested. Plus, he knocked back three gin and tonics during cocktail hour. Really? Slow down there, Patrick.

"Do you have big New Year's Eve plans? What do y'all do up there to celebrate in Alaska?" Patrick slurs a little bit.

"My friend, Jack, is having a fancy dress-up party with lots of food," I say, leaning away from Patrick. I remember he can get a little free-spirited with his hands when he's been drinking. This is the second time I've moved his hand off my knee under the table.

"Is this the Jack you always mention when we talk?" Mama asks. "Is he still single, too?" Ouch.

"Yes, that's him, and he's single. He's one of my best friends up there," I say. Someone please change the subject.

I ask Dad to pass the bouillabaisse and remove Patrick's hand from my knee again. He's going to get punched soon if he doesn't control himself.

"Kari, your Grandpa and I went on a cruise to Alaska back in 2005. It's the most beautiful place on earth. All those glaciers and wild animals," Grandma Covington says and reminisces a bit. "Herman, remember when we saw those whales bubble net feeding right next to the boat?"

"I surely remember, Gracie. I'm not senile yet," Grandpa Covington jokes.

"You're lucky to live there. Too damn far from here, but I expect you needed a change."

"Thanks for your support. I miss you all like crazy, but I like living there," I say.

My grandparents live ten minutes from my parents, and they've been present at every birthday, celebration, and Sunday dinner as long as I can remember. They are in relatively good health and take a walk every morning to the bakery for coffee and a pecan sweet roll.

"Ash, tell Kari about our plans after graduation," Kate says and rubs him affectionately on the arm.

"We're going to take a year off and travel around Europe before we settle down. Gives us a chance like you, to spread our wings and see some of the world," Ash says. "Kate really looks up to you, and it was all her idea. She has the trip already planned out."

Kate grins at me and leans over to kiss Ash on the cheek.

They really are cute together. At cocktail hour, they sat with Grandma and Grandpa Covington and chatted about how they met and the wedding plans. Luckily, Mama was fussing over dinner and didn't have an opportunity to knock heads with Kate over the wedding venue. Again.

"That's exciting," I exclaim. "Are you coming back to Charleston to live?" I sneak a look at Dad. He'll be heartbroken if his youngest daughter also lived far away.

"Possibly. We're thinking either here, Savannah or Atlanta," Kate says quickly and looks at Dad. "Not far, I promise. We want to live near our families. All of Ash's family lives in Savannah."

Dad exhales the breath he was holding. He and Mama look relieved and also surprised about their news to travel for a year. Guess Kate held out on telling them since she wasn't sure what their reaction would be.

"Mama, dinner is fantastic!" I say, since no one has commented on the big meal we made.

"Thanks, Kari. I appreciate all your help making it. Everyone, there's plenty of food, so don't be shy," Vivianne says and passes the salad to Mark.

"I always wanted to move to Colorado, but my ex-wife refused to leave Charleston," Patrick says slowly and drains his glass of white wine.

205

"Patrick, darling. I'm sorry to hear that, but now you have a fresh start! How about visiting Kari in Alaska? It's similar to Colorado," Mama suggests. I turn and give her the death stare.

"Mama! Alaska isn't like Colorado at all," I cry, mortified at her suggestion for Patrick to visit me.

"We're going there in March to watch the Iditarod. I guess Boyd will have to break down and buy me a fur coat to stay warm," Vivianne says and winks at Dad. The others laugh.

The twins are excused so they can go play in the bonus room. Mark goes with them and chases them up the back stairs. I can hear them all laughing.

"Kari, how about it? I come up next summer, and we can go camping. You can show me the *real* Alaska," Patrick says with a wicked little grin.

"Umm … sure, Patrick," I say and stand up to clear plates. Kate and Kimberly help me take the plates and food into the kitchen. Everyone else retires to the living room for an after-dinner drink.

"The look on your face was priceless when Patrick asked to visit you. Wish I had my camera," Kimberly laughs and begins to load the dishwasher.

"I can't believe Patrick showed up with a bottle of Tangueray as a hostess gift and then proceeded to drink from it," Kate laughs. "Poor guy though. His divorce is obviously hard on him."

"I don't care. I can't believe Mama invited him to visit me. Seriously," I say with a sigh and lean against the counter. Jet lag catches up with me, and I'm exhausted.

"Don't worry. You'll be dating someone next summer, so he can't visit," Kate says, with a smile.

She wraps up the leftover food and places it in the refrigerator. I sit on the stool and snack on the leftover pimiento cheese.

There's just enough for a grilled pimiento cheese sandwich for me tomorrow if Dad doesn't snag it before me.

I laugh. "I love the way you think and your constant optimism."

We wipe down the countertops, wash the remaining dishes, turn on the coffee, and gossip for a few minutes before joining the others in the living room. Kate tells me the latest wedding drama with Mama and rolls her eyes several times. Kimberly fills me in on the twins and their adventures at pre-school.

I sneak upstairs to my room for a few minutes to myself. I pick up my cell phone to text Jack, and there's a message from him with a picture of three pizzas.

Jack: Homemade pizza night at my house. Bon Appetit!

I hit reply and send him a text back.

Me: Yum-O! My mama invited my HS boyfriend to visit me next summer.
Jack: Seriously?
Me: Yep
Jack: Hang in there. Cook anything Southern tonight?
Me: Pimiento cheese dip and sausage balls
Jack: Delicious!
Me: For sure. Have fun!

I smile as I put the phone down on the bedside stand. He may receive a lot more texts from me before this night is over.

Mark and the twins are playing with Barbie dolls, and I peek in and snap some pictures with my camera. I miss them all so much! I tell them dessert will be served shortly and give each girl a big hug and kiss.

As I walk down the steps, I hear Patrick telling my family about his ex-wife cheating on him with her male co-worker, and he starts laughing loudly. My parents laugh awkwardly. I feel sorry for Patrick. It sounds like the divorce is taking a toll on him, and he's bitter.

"Everyone ready for dessert?" I ask and walk into the living room. I see my sisters sigh with relief, and they jump up to help me. Ash offers to help as well and heads into the kitchen with us.

"Poor guy. I feel for him," Ash says.

Kate reaches into the cupboard for coffee cups and plates. "I'm glad Mama invited him though. I hate to think of him alone during the holidays."

"I'll see if he wants to grab coffee sometime before I leave," I say thoughtfully. Maybe he needs someone to lean on.

"Maybe he'd like to play some golf while I'm here. What do you think, Kate?" Ash asks.

"That's so sweet! I love you, Ash. You're the most considerate guy ever," Kate says and kisses him.

Wow. They really do make a perfect match.

We gather up the banana pudding, deep dish pecan pie, lemon bars, and vanilla ice cream and set them on the sideboard in the living room. Kimberly sets out plates, and Kate takes orders while I dish up the desserts. My sisters and I make a good team.

Ash gives Patrick a cup of black coffee and chats with him about playing golf over the next few days. Mama looks at Ash appreciatively and nods her head in approval.

There is silence as we sample the desserts. We listen to the crickets and the occasional clip-clopping from the horse-drawn carriage rides passing our house.

"The lemon bars are delicious as always, Kari. Thanks for making my favorite dessert!" Dad says, munching on his third bar. "I've missed you and the lemon bars."

"I agree. Kate said you're a whiz in the kitchen. What's your favorite dish to make?" Ash asks.

"Thanks, Ash. I love making lasagna and some of the more Southern dishes like shrimp and grits and pulled pork. Keeps me from being too homesick. Growing up, I spent a lot of time in the kitchen with Mama since I wasn't into sports like Kate and Kimberly," I say, thinking about all the time I spent in the sunny kitchen surrounded by cookbooks and Mama singing along with the radio.

Both sisters were heavily involved in soccer, basketball, and lacrosse during school. Since I didn't have any interest or skill in sports, I kept busy cooking, reading, and spending time with friends. Dad carted my sisters all over town for their games, and he even coached soccer for several years. In fact, Kate received a scholarship for basketball to UNC.

"Vivianne, you make the best banana pudding this side of the Mississippi. Your pudding is part of the reason I married Kim for sure," Mark says with a laugh. "It surely is the best in town. I bet even Paula Deen would agree."

"Oh, Mark, you're just darling. My mama passed down the recipe many years ago, and it has a secret ingredient in it," Mama says. "Everyone, please help yourself to more dessert. I'll send the leftover pudding home with you, Mark."

My grandparents excuse themselves since it's getting late. Dad takes them back to their house since they no longer drive, and I start clearing the dessert dishes. Patrick comes into the kitchen with the plates and coffee cups.

"Kari, it was really nice seeing you. My deepest apologies for talking all night about my ex-wife," Patrick sighs. "I'm going through a difficult time."

I give him a little hug. "No worries at all. It's good seeing you. Maybe we can meet up for coffee before I leave."

"I'd love to, and I promise to be in a better mood and not mention my ex-wife. I want to hear more about Alaska and how you like it," Patrick says sincerely. "I'm around this week. Spending Christmas Eve and Christmas Day with my parents, so call me." He writes down his cell phone number on the pad next to the phone.

He thanks my parents for dinner, shakes hands with Ash and Mark, and waves goodbye to the rest of the family. Ash called him a cab earlier and promised to take him to his car tomorrow. Another act of kindness and consideration. Kate really chose a good guy.

Kimberly and Mark gather up the twins and say goodbye, and I promise to babysit this week while they finish Christmas shopping. It's been a long first day back in Charleston, and I go to bed as soon as the front door closes.

37

My week here will fly by quickly, thanks to Mama's busy schedule, including two trips to the seamstress for the bridesmaid gown. Kate apologizes for not asking me first, but she wanted to do it in person and not over email or the phone. Of course, I agree and give her a big hug. I bite my tongue and try not to lecture her on marrying so young. I relax and enjoy my time with her and the rest of the family.

The bridesmaid dress is a short strapless coral-colored dress. It will look glorious on all six bridesmaids, even on me, the only one who isn't a perfect size eight or less.

"I picked this color because it'll look nice on everyone when we get married on the *beach*," Kate says loudly as she looks at Mama. We're at the seamstress for a second fitting. Kate browses through the veils while I'm trying on the dress.

"Kate, I do not want you getting married on the beach. It's tacky. People will have to take off their shoes to walk in the sand. Is that what you want to see in your wedding album? Barefoot people?" Mama sighs and looks at wedding magazines while the seamstress pins the hem of my dress.

"Mama! It's up to Ash and me. The beach wedding is what we want. Not under a white tent at an old, boring plantation. Every other girl in high school gets married at Magnolia Plantation, and it's not our style," Kate says firmly, determined to hold her ground.

"You are *not* getting married on the beach. Your Dad and I are not going to pay for a wedding like that. Sand on everything, in the food, it could rain. Do you really want to me to list more reasons why it's a bad idea?"

"Are you threatening not to pay for the wedding? We'll gladly pay for the wedding we want. Or elope and not invite any of you," Kate starts to cry and turns her back on us. Uh-oh.

The seamstress stands up and discreetly leaves the room, while handing me a box of tissues on her way out. I walk over to Kate, pat her arm, and give her the tissues.

I whisper in her ear. "Don't do anything rash. I'm sure you and Mama can work this out. Please don't elope."

"I did not raise my daughter to sass me like this! We want everyone to be happy, but I feel a beach wedding is not the way to go. Surely, we can come up with a compromise," Mama says, determined not to give in completely.

"The beach is what we want. I see no compromise. I'm calling Ash," Kate walks out in a huff.

"Kari, what do you think? There are too many uncertain factors in getting married outside. She hasn't even thought it through," Mama says and looks at me. I vow to keep my mouth shut.

"Um, I don't know. Both options are nice," I say vaguely and look up at the ceiling tile, avoiding eye contact. Do not pick a side.

Kate strides back in the room, no tears in sight. "Mama, you and Dad are off the hook to pay. Ash said his parents will pay for whatever wedding we want."

"Wait, just a minute. We'll pay for the wedding, Kate. I just want you to think about everything that goes into an outdoor wedding. That's all. If you really don't want to get married at Magnolia

Plantation, fine. But, let's work together to make a beach wedding pleasurable for everyone," Mama insists and gives in.

"Really, Mama? Truly? Oh, thank you! I love you! I'm sure we'll have sunny weather. It'll be perfect!" Kate says and throws her arms around Mama in a grateful hug.

Mama sighs. I can see her brain working to make revised lists for the venue change and booking pedicures for everyone in the family. Sand, no shoes, praying for sunny weather.

"So, where are we going to next?" I ask, changing the subject. Small crisis solved with minimal tears. We've been Christmas shopping, visiting neighbors, and baking cookies. And, that's only this morning.

Mama pulls the schedule out of her purse. "Let's see. Next, we're dropping off cookies to the staff at the Food Bank and then a late lunch at the country club."

"Are you going to see Patrick this week? Poor man and his heart-breaking divorce. I think a trip to Alaska will cheer him up. He did seem rather pitiful at dinner the other night. The gin certainly didn't help."

Kate catches my eye and gives me a warning look. And now the spotlight is on me. Great.

"Mama, it's really nice that you invited him to visit me, but summer is a long way off. I *am* going to meet him for coffee tomorrow morning, but I have no interest in dating him," I say as gently as I can.

"Why not? He seems so lonely. I think he still has a crush on you," Mama insists. Kate covers her mouth and tries not to laugh.

"Look, I want to meet some guy in Alaska with a cabin, a goatee, and a snowmachine. Not another Southern boy who wants to live close to his parents and not leave Charleston. No offense,

Kate," I say. "Just lay off Patrick, okay? Please?" I look at her with pleading eyes.

"Fine. I just miss you so much and don't want to fly halfway across the world to visit you and future grandbabies every year," Mama says with a sniff. So dramatic! Grandbabies? She's planning a little too far ahead for my taste.

"Okay, moving on. What's next on our schedule?" I ask and change the subject. I quickly change clothes and hand the dress to the seamstress.

We head to the Food Bank next, and Mama introduces us to the staff there. The executive director tells us how much they appreciate Mama, and I see Mama beam with pride. They thank us for the basket of cookies, homemade jam, and fruit.

"Mama, I'm so proud of you. I can see how much they like you and value your time," Kate says as she drives us to the country club.

"Me too, Mama. You're amazing. Remember when we used to volunteer at the soup kitchen every Thanksgiving? It was fun, and I enjoyed it even though I probably complained about it," I laugh.

"Girls, I think it's important to volunteer, and I'm glad I've instilled it in you both. Folks need to learn to give back at an early age and keep doing it. That's why Dad and I made you volunteer at Thanksgiving. It was also a good bonding experience," Mama says.

We talk about memories of volunteering all through lunch, and I'm proud to be part of such a strong and committed family.

The next morning, I meet Patrick at Market Street Coffee. He's sitting at a small table by the window when I arrive.

"Hi Kari! What kind of coffee would you like?" Patrick asks as I sit down. He pulls out his wallet while I glance at the café's offerings, written on a colorful chalkboard above the counter.

"A Market Street Latte, please," I say.

While he orders the drinks at the counter, I look around the cozy café and see pictures of The Battery and Rainbow Row. The bakery case is filled with homemade teacakes, coconut cupcakes, and chocolate-filled croissants along with fresh squeezed carafes of juice. A large glass urn of sweet tea sits at the end of the counter.

Patrick comes over with the coffees, and I wrap my hands around the steaming warm mug. It's nice to enjoy coffee at the café and not in a travel mug while you work on schematics at your desk.

"Kari, first of all, I want to apologize for my behavior the other night. I was a little tipsy and not very good company. A bad first impression after all these years," Patrick says, apologetically and shakes his head.

"Not a big deal, Patrick. I'm glad you were able to join us," I say. "Have you kept in touch with many people from high school?" I hope changing the subject will help, and we can reminisce about high school.

"I see people here and there. Still hang out with Billy a couple of times a month. We're still tight. Kari, what's your favorite memory from high school?" Patrick asks and takes a sip of his Americano.

I think for a couple of moments. "Prom. Remember how we showed up two hours late? My parents were sitting in the hotel lobby watching everyone arrive in pretty dresses and tuxedos. We show up late and completely drenched from the rain outside. Mama threw a fit. It was fun and unexpected," I continue. "Neither of us really wanted to go and dance anyway. It was all about the after-prom party."

"That was hilarious! Your white dress was wilted, and we had to go take pictures with the photographer." Wait. He remembers my dress was white? Wow. Good memory.

"Yeah, I didn't really like high school that much. Maybe it would've helped if I played team sports or was more involved, but it seemed so clique-y. Everyone was driving BMWs, Miatas, and Mercedes to school. I had to catch rides with my older sister in her Volkswagon Rabbit," I laugh.

In fact, I really hated high school. If you didn't have all the right clothes and the right Liz Clairborne purses, you were an outcast. Our family is middle class, and with three kids, my parents didn't splurge on name brand clothing from The Limited and give us each a BMW to drive to school.

"That's right! The Rusted Rabbit. I remember that car."

"Kari, why did we end up breaking up? It was in the middle of our senior year, right?" Patrick asks, wrinkling his brow.

"*You* don't remember? You were the one who broke up with me!" I cry.

"Come on. Refresh me."

"Patrick, you broke my heart because I wouldn't have sex with you," I say, looking down at my latte.

It seemed like I was the last virgin in high school. Girls weren't exactly bragging about going all the way, but you knew who did. Patrick was pressuring me, and I wasn't ready. He had stuck a note in my locker and said we were going to go to his house (his parents were out of town) for a romantic evening. Uh-huh.

When he came to pick me up, I told him that I wasn't ready for sex, and I didn't want to go to his parents' house. And, I didn't want him to think I was leading him on. Despite my many protests, he probably thought I'd give in. He stormed off the porch, said we were done, and we didn't talk for three weeks. I cried for days, and Mama knew what happened even though I didn't tell her anything. She just hugged me, fed me homemade macaroni and cheese, and gave me space.

Patrick was my first serious boyfriend. He was on the high school football team, wrestling team, and had a dazzling smile. He was funny, charming, and I was truly smitten. We got along well, and I loved his parents.

"Kari, I'm sorry. I was dumb and stupid. Will you please forgive me?" Patrick pleads and looks ashamed at his behavior back in high school. "I think the world of you, and I'm sorry it ended with me as a jackass."

He truly looks sorry and a little embarrassed. "Of course. You were my boyfriend, my love of my life. I'm just sorry you never signed my yearbook," I laugh, lightening up the mood.

Patrick laughs, and he looks younger as he pushes his hair back from his forehead. We talk about my life in Alaska, his work as a mechanical engineer, and his parents.

When I stand up to leave, he gives me a hug and a sweet kiss on the cheek.

"Thanks for meeting me. Merry Christmas to you and your family!" Patrick says.

"Merry Christmas! Please tell your parents hello for me," I say and wave as I walk out into the sunshine and humidity.

I feel better now after my time with Patrick. He has friends and family here for him as he finalizes the divorce and moves forward with his life. I'm rooting for him to fall in love again.

38

Christmas Eve arrives before I know it. In the afternoon, I babysit my nieces while Kimberly and Mark do some last minute shopping.

"Aunt Kari, let's play Barbies. Here's Ken," Ashley says as she separates doll clothes into piles.

We're sitting on the floor in their playroom, which is decorated in pink and purple. Perfect girl colors. There are pastel colored bins and shelves along one wall to keep toys organized. Pink bean bag chairs sit in front of an entertainment center in the corner of the room. Two dormer windows facing south have white eyelet curtains.

"Sure. Why is Ken naked, and where are his clothes?" I ask, frowning at Ken's anatomically incorrect boy parts.

"Here they are, Aunt Kari," Anna says and brings over a plastic case from a bin. I open it to reveal Ken's wardrobe, two pink hairbrushes, matchbox cars, and three dice. Quite a random assortment.

I choose blue pants and a white shirt for Ken. Classic look for the young man. Anna and Ashley are busy choosing clothes for their Barbies, and my mind wanders for a minute to Jack and Abby.

I didn't ask Jack if he's still seeing Abby or if they're spending the holidays together. He probably wouldn't give me a straight answer anyway.

I *am* looking forward to his New Year's Eve party though. At the last minute, I asked Marshall if he wanted to go with me, and he gladly accepted.

"Okay, so Ken has a date with my Barbie and a date with Anna's Barbie the next night. Put Ken in the car and come pick me up at the dollhouse," Ashley instructs. She moves over to the dollhouse and places Barbie in her bedroom in front of the mirror and fiddles with Barbie's hair.

"You always get to go first," Anna whines and pouts.

"Girls, we'll take turns. Why am I Ken? Okay, let me jam Ken into his red Corvette, and I'll come pick you up," I say, wondering how they know about dates. Ugh … I feel old.

We play Barbies for an hour until I declare it's snack time. In the kitchen, I give them juice, crackers, and fruit that Kimberly left out for me. The girls tell me about their teacher, Miss Stephanie, at school. Sounds like recess is their favorite subject, although I know from Kimberly both girls excel in reading. They inherited that from me. Ha!

Kimberly and Mark arrive home while we're still sitting at the table chatting about their friends and who has the best pool in their backyard.

"Thanks for babysitting, Kari. We really appreciate it," Mark says and gives me a squeeze on the shoulder. "Kim's putting away the packages." He pours himself a glass of sweet tea, joins us at the table, kicks off his shoes, and rubs his aching feet.

"How was shopping? Did you get everything you needed?" I ask and snag an apple slice from the plate.

"I think so. Kimberly was super organized with a list. The stores were a madhouse as usual. People just starting their Christmas shopping, I suspect," Mark laughs.

"Glad I'm not the only one who does a list. I know she and Mama live by their lists. What time is dinner tonight?" I ask since I tossed Mama's schedules in the garbage on my first night here.

"Church is 5:30, then dinner after," Kimberly says, walking into the kitchen and giving the girls a kiss on the head. "Did you have fun with Aunt Kari this afternoon?"

"Yes, Mommy. We told Aunt Kari to move back. We promised to be good and let her babysit us anytime she wants to," Ashley says and gives me a big smile.

"Please, Aunt Kari. Move back here," Anna begs.

My heart breaks. I miss seeing their sweet faces. My eyes become misty, and I get up to refill my sweet tea.

"Girls, she likes Alaska. Besides, maybe we can go visit her next year. Doesn't that sound fun?" Kimberly says.

The girls cry yes in unison and start asking when, what to pack, and what animals they'll see. My apartment will be filled with many visitors next year.

"I would love for you all to visit. Sorry, Mark, we don't have a football or baseball team you can write about, but our hockey team is pretty decent," I say.

"No worries. I'm excited to do some fishing up there. I read about combat fishing for salmon on the Kenai River," Mark says.

"You bet. I have a couple of friends who will gladly take you fishing. Well, I better go home and get cleaned up for church. See y'all in awhile," I say and give everyone a hug and a kiss.

I drive Mama's Honda Accord home and make a stop at Southern Shooz for a quick look at their shoes. They also carry

Vera Bradley bags, so I pick up a travel cosmetic bag for Kate for her European adventures. I'm glad they're taking a year off to travel and have fun before settling down and letting married life consume them. Before they know it, life will consist of country club lunches, golfing, boating, and baby showers for all their friends.

I arrive home to a quiet house. Mama and Dad are on a walk downtown, and Kate's having coffee with her girlfriends. I take a long, hot shower and lay on the bed with the towel wrapped around my curly hair and read the novel I brought with me. I text Marshall to confirm we're on for New Year's Eve.

> **Me:** Merry almost Christmas! How are you?
> **Marshall:** Cold. Chicago feels colder than Alaska
> **Me:** Seriously? Wow. Are you having fun with your family?
> **Marshall:** Yes, what about you?
> **Me:** Yep, although I miss Alaska
> **Marshall:** Are we still on for NYE?
> **Me:** Can't wait. Good times for sure
> **Marshall:** Safe travels back on Saturday
> **Me:** You too

Even if Marshall isn't interested in me beyond friends, I know we'll have fun on New Year's Eve. He's the type of person you want to take to a party where you don't know anyone. I wonder if he will at least kiss me on the cheek at midnight.

That evening at church, our family takes up an entire pew. The kids put on a Christmas skit about gift giving and Christ. The handbell choir is my favorite.

I wear my new Dior patent leather peep toe shoes to church. No snowy weather here to impede wearing cute shoes.

At home, I help Mama with dinner preparation. Her tradition is a light meal on Christmas Eve since she cooks up an enormous meal on Christmas Day. The rest of the family is in the living room listening to the Josh Groban Christmas CD and talking about the church service. Grandpa and Grandma Covington are positively glowing, surrounded by all of the family.

I arrange deli meats and cheese on a tray, while she cuts up vegetables and fruit. Then I slice open rolls for sandwiches, and she warms up chicken tenders in the oven.

"Thanks for making the desserts earlier today, Kari! The chocolate shortbread and mini pumpkin whoopie pies look delicious," Mama says and unwraps the tray I placed them on.

"Sure, Mama. Anything to help out," I say. Tomorrow, I'm in charge of the cornbread dressing, sweet potato casserole, and dessert.

"How was coffee with Patrick?" Mama asks. She pours ranch dressing and barbeque sauce into small bowls.

"It was fine. He apologized for his drunken state the other night, and we talked about high school. He keeps in touch with several of our mutual friends. Much better than I do, even with Facebook and email."

"Good. I hope he makes it through the divorce okay. I saw his mama at the marina last month, and I know she's worried about him."

"He'll be fine. Okay, the deli tray is ready. Should we call everyone in?" I ask. We decided to serve dinner buffet style and sit in the living room near the Christmas tree and twinkling lights.

Mama calls out, "Everyone, dinner is served. Come on and make a plate."

After everyone fills up a plate and finds a cozy place to sit, we talk about plans for Christmas day.

223

"I'm driving back to Savannah tonight, so I can spend Christmas with my family. I'll miss your good cooking, Vivianne," Ash smiles and heads into the kitchen for second helpings.

"What time is the big meal tomorrow?" Kimberly asks. I know she and Mark plan to spend the morning with the girls.

"We'll do a late lunch at two o'clock, and then the usual sandwich spread for dinner," Mama says, as she crunches on cucumbers dipped in ranch dressing.

"Girls! We'll open gifts at home and have chocolate chip pancakes for breakfast. Then, you can choose one toy to bring over here to play with, okay?" Mark says.

"Okay, Daddy!" The girls say and sneak a shortbread into their pocket. I don't know how they managed to pick up a shortbread without Kimberly seeing.

"Anna and Ashley, after dinner, you can open one gift from us," Mama says.

"And one gift from us, too," says Grandma Covington.

I load up my plate with second helpings of chicken tenders and fruit. "Ash, we'll miss you tomorrow. Has Kate filled you in on the Covington Sandwich Spread ritual?"

"No, she hasn't. I was going to ask about it when Vivianne mentioned it," Ash says as he eats his third mini pumpkin whoopie pie. I love a man who eats dessert and isn't bashful about it.

I set down my fork. "Leftover turkey sandwiches are one of the highlights of our Christmas celebration. We put out a full spread just for them. Four types of mustard, leftover cranberry sauce, pesto mayonnaise, avocado, bacon, heirloom tomatoes, caramelized onions, olive tapenade, fresh vegetables, and more! It's a contest for making the best sandwich."

"Kari, you forgot the pimiento cheese, horseradish mayon-naise, and the roasted red peppers," adds Mark. "The horseradish mayonnaise seals the deal for me."

"Wow! Now, I'm really sorry to miss out. But, I'll look for-ward to it next year for sure," Ash says in amazement.

He puts his arm around Kate and smiles. I'm pretty sure they'll spend every Christmas with us, after hearing about the contest.

After the men clean up the kitchen, Mama selects two beauti-fully wrapped gifts from under the Christmas tree and gives them to Anna and Ashley. Mark grabs his camera, so he can capture the moment.

"Those gifts are from us," says Grandma Covington.

The girls rip open their gifts to reveal brand new pink pajamas, each a different style. One of them is a nightgown, and the other is a shirt and shorts.

"Thanks Grammy and Grampy Covington!" say the girls in unison. They both run over and give Grandpa and Grandma Covington a hug.

Dad selects two more gifts and gives them to the girls. They say thank you before even opening the gifts. Bless Kimberly and Mark for teaching them good manners.

The gifts from Mama and Dad are pink robes with warm fuzzy socks. Perfect! They will look so cute in their new outfits on Christmas morning as they open gifts.

After coffee and another pass at the dessert buffet, Ash stands up to leave. Kate gives him a kiss, and he promises to call her when he arrives to Savannah.

"Herman and Gracie, may I take you home tonight? It's my pleasure," Ash says. I think Mama almost swoons at his kind offer.

"Thank you, Ash," Grandpa Covington says and stands up. He then helps Grandma Covington out of her chair. Kate walks them out to the car after we all say goodbye.

"Ash is a winner. He's part of our family now," Mama says firmly, and I agree with her whole-heartedly. Kate has my full blessing.

39

I drop the suitcase inside my apartment door and kick off my red Dansko Mary Janes. Welcome back to Alaska.

Christmas Day was entertaining as usual. Grandma Covington made her annual fruitcake and rum balls. We played the Apples to Apples game, and Kate battled Dad for the win. We talked about wedding plans, and Mama showed enthusiasm about the beach location. She made new lists and started praying for good weather.

Of course, the best part of the day was the Covington sandwich spread, where everyone created the ultimate sandwich to win bragging rights. Grandpa Covington picked the winning sandwich, and Mark won the coveted prize for the third year in a row. I took a picture of his sandwich and texted it to Jack. He was impressed. Turkey, melted brie, avocado, horseradish mayonnaise, and tomato all toasted to perfection on a garlic butter, parmesan ciabatta roll.

I set down my Vera Bradley carry-on bag. It's heavy from cookie care packages (thanks, Mama), rum balls (thanks, Grandma), and the two Smitten Kitchen cookbooks from Kate. My favorite gift came from Kimberly and Mark. They gave me a copper pepper-mill with a crank handle. I can't wait to use it!

After I turn on my fireplace to take the chill out of the air and click up the heat, I unpack my suitcase, and carefully unroll the five

Penzey spices wrapped in tissue paper from Mama. She and I both love their spices, and she picked out several unique blends. My grandparents gave me a subscription to Southern Living magazine to remind me of my Southern roots.

Realizing I haven't talked or emailed with Lauren since Christmas, I dial her cell phone.

"Hey Lauren! How was your Christmas?" I ask.

"Kari! Happy New Year! Are you back in town?" Lauren says. I hear grocery store sounds in the background.

"I just got home. Long day of travel. Where are you?"

"I'm at the store, picking up stuff for stir fry tonight. Do you want to come over for dinner?" Lauren asks.

"Thanks, but I'll pass. I'm exhausted. Did you have a good Christmas?" I ask again since she didn't say anything about it. Yikes, I hope it went well.

"It was good, but freezing in Fairbanks at Will's parents' house. I'm so glad we flew up instead of driving all the way. On Christmas Day, the thermometer registered 30 below."

"OMG! That's really cold. I hope you didn't have to go out in that weather. We can talk more at the gym tomorrow night. Have a good dinner! Bye!"

"Bye and welcome home!"

Speaking of dinner, I wonder what's still edible in the refrigerator. Before I left town, I tried to eat most of the perishables and gave some leftover, homemade vegetable soup to Jack.

I rub my hands in front of the fireplace and do a few stretching exercises to ease my aching back from the plane ride. The last two days of the trip, I was antsy and ready to return. I missed Lauren, Jack, Marshall, and work!

Opening the refrigerator, I see parmesan cheese, so I cook fettuccine, plus sauté a few anchovies and minced garlic. I fill my new peppermill with peppercorns and top the pasta with pepper.

Sitting on the sofa in my warm pajamas and dinner in hand, I catch up on *Top Chef* and feel happy at home in Alaska.

～෨

The following evening, I meet Lauren at the gym. I hope to burn off some of the sugary desserts I ate in Charleston. It's so easy to snack on cookies when you're surrounded by them.

Lauren has our steps set up when I enter the exercise room. She's chatting with the other girls.

"Hi Kari! Welcome home!" Lauren gives me a big hug. "I missed you. Did you have fun with your family? How are your nieces?"

"I missed you, too! The trip was good, but I missed Anchorage, despite the negative temperatures here. My nieces are growing up so fast!" I say and sit on the edge of the bench to stretch.

"What did Will give you for Christmas?"

"Sparkly diamond earrings and auto start for my car. It'll be installed next week," Lauren says excitedly.

"What about you? Any favorite gifts? Did you eat your fill of Southern food?"

"Kimberly and Mark gave me a new copper peppermill. I love it! I definitely ate my share of Southern food, especially fast food which you can't get up here: Chick-fil-A, Krispy Kreme, and Cracker Barrel. I definitely gained weight last week."

"I miss Chick-fil-A. Maybe one will open up here eventually. At least we finally got a Macaroni Grill," Lauren laughs.

Anchorage is short on two crucial items. Good chain restaurants and clothing shops. We have fast food chains, but not many other nicer chain restaurants. Since I like to eat out, it was a real adjustment for me when I moved here. As far as shopping goes, Nordstrom is the most upscale store in town. Our two malls don't have the huge anchor department stores like typical malls.

Class begins, and we work out hard to combat the holiday weight gain. After class, we sit at the smoothie bar and chat about New Year's Eve plans.

Lauren takes a sip of her strawberry smoothie. "We're staying at the Anchorage Historic Hotel, and I made dinner reservations at Riversong Restaurant. It's supposedly the best place in town. Have you been there?"

"No, but it's been on my list to try for months. Definitely let me know how it is. Are you up for a little shopping tomorrow at lunch? I want to buy a new dress for New Year's Eve," I say.

"Sure. Are you looking forward to going with Marshall? Does he know Jack's party is dressy?"

"I told him about it. He seemed excited to dress up."

"Did Abby mention going to the party?" I ask, cringing at how beautiful she will look in comparison to me. Stop it, Kari! This is not a beauty pageant. Oh wait, isn't life always a beauty pageant or contest in some manner?

"She's in Kansas visiting her family, so I haven't talked to her." Lauren looks at me. "Are you okay? You've said all this time that you and Jack are only friends, but do you secretly have a crush on him?"

"Lauren!" I cry. "No, I'm just overly protective of him because I know how great of a guy he is, that's all. I'm not jealous or anything." Seriously. I mean it.

I've thought long and hard about Jack this past week. And, I realized that I really cherish his friendship. That's it. He can date whomever he wants.

"All right. Where do you want to shop tomorrow? The usual places?" Lauren asks and finishes her smoothie.

"Yes, let's start with Classic Consignment and Nordstrom. I already have cute patent leather peep toe shoes, so I won't need to look at the shoe department this time," I giggle. Lauren rolls her eyes at me.

"Maybe I need an obsession to throw my money at. You have shoes. What do I have?" Lauren says and grabs her gym bag.

I pick up my pink gym bag, and we stand up from the bar, saying goodbye to the gym staff. "Your money goes into your beautifully decorated home. I really need to hire you to do something with my living room. It's all beige and needs some color."

Lauren laughs, and we walk out of the gym to our cars, calling to each other to drive safely.

40

I walk into the office, drop off my purse and messenger bag, and walk directly to Jack's office. He's on the phone, so I fidget with my coffee mug while I stand there and wait.

"Okay, sounds good. I can't wait to see your dress," Jack says into the phone. "Have a good morning, and I'll call you this afternoon. Bye."

Hmmm. I bet he's talking to Abby. How sweet.

"Welcome home, Kari!" Jack says and comes over to hug me.

"Thanks, Jack! Did you have a good Christmas with your family?" I ask and shift restlessly. I need coffee *now*.

"It was awesome not travelling to Seward this year! Everyone came to my house for a change. Let's grab coffee," Jack says and grabs his down coat and coffee mug.

We walk out into the subzero temperatures. Thank goodness for no wind this morning.

"Any great gifts from the family?" I ask, shivering, despite ear warmers, leather gloves, and a wool hat. I'm so glad I moved to Alaska. I'm so glad I moved to Alaska. I chant silently and speed up my pace.

"My parents bought me a new Fry Daddy. It's twice as big as the one I had. Also got a vertical chicken roaster and a pizza stone, thus the picture I sent you of the pizzas. I opened that gift early, so we could make homemade pizzas with everyone," Jack says and speeds up to match my walking pace.

"Nice. What are you going to cook first in your Fry Daddy?"

"I broke it in last night with chicken wings and battered halibut for fish tacos. Unbelievable! I would have sent you a picture, but I was too busy eating!" Jack laughs. "Did you spend a lot of time with your nieces?"

"Yes, I played Barbies, read books with them, and had so much fun. I can't wait until they learn to write, so we can be pen pals."

After we pick up the drinks from Lisa, we sit down at the counter for a few minutes and sip on our drinks.

"So, who is coming to your New Year's Eve party?" I ask conversationally.

"Darren, some skiing pals, Sean and Victoria from work, Abby, you, Marshall, and some other random people ... a good mix. I'm making a bunch of appetizers for it, and you've got dessert covered, right?" Jack asks.

"Yep. I'm making a bourbon chocolate cake with malted buttercream frosting, cannoli, and mini red velvet cupcakes," I say and my mouth waters thinking about the cupcakes. Red velvet is my favorite cake, cupcake, whoopie pie, anything.

"Thanks, Kari! I'm sure everyone will love the desserts. I told everyone else to bring an appetizer or a bottle of champagne. I also bought a new festive tie to wear. Abby helped me pick it out before she left for Kansas."

"So, are you two hot and heavy?" I ask, hoping he'll share what's going on between them.

"We're dating, but that's all you're going to squeeze out of me," Jack says and stands up. Does he really think standing up to leave will magically change the subject?

"Fine, Jack. You make a cute couple," I say happily and mean it.

We walk back to work and sip on our coffee which is cooling off fast.

"Are you up for lunch today? Thought we could hit up Miller's Deli for a blue cheese steak sandwich," Jack says as he holds open the door for me to the atrium.

"Sorry, Jack. I have shopping plans with Lauren," I say and give him a sheepish grin.

"Jeez. Girls and shopping," Jack mutters on the way to his office.

Our first stop is Classic Consignment, and I hit the jackpot immediately. Lauren comes back to the dressing room with a vintage Valentino black lace dress with a wide dark red sash for me try on. It's a little snug, but with Spanx, it'll be perfect. And my signature pearls, of course.

"Do you think it's too dressy? It's not floor length, but the lace seems so formal," I say as I admire the delicate lace overlay.

"Kari, buy the dress. It's perfect for the party. Marshall will flip when he sees you in it. And, did you see the price tag?" Lauren says and comes over to take another peek. "$350! It's a steal at this price."

"Okay, okay. I'm buying it. I'll also wear it to Kate and Ash's rehearsal dinner next June, so it will do double duty. Did you see anything for you?" I ask as I change back into my work clothes.

"Not really. I have a red sheath dress that I'll probably wear," Lauren says and looks through the jewelry at the counter. "I'm trying to save money."

I pay for the dress. "Are you sure? We can go to Nordstrom and look at the sale rack. We have plenty of time left."

"No, it's fine. Let's go grab some lunch," Lauren says.

We catch up at lunch on work projects, New Year's resolutions, and family. Will's Mom still intimidates her. Lauren's hoping the New Year will bring her patience, calming qualities, and a "roll off your back" attitude when it comes to dealing with her.

41

I'm so glad I took New Year's Eve Day off from work since I have lots of baking to do. After breakfast, I change into jeans and a t-shirt. I tie my hair back in a ponytail, don an apron, and get busy.

The bourbon chocolate cake comes together nicely, and I whip up the buttercream until it's fluffy and light. After I frost the cooled sheet cake, I place it in the refrigerator to set the frosting. Before I leave for the party, I'll cut it into small snack-sized pieces.

Next up, the cannoli. For this dessert, I need to take my time and not rush, or it could be disastrous. But first, I need a little baking music. On my iPod, I choose Jared Woods' latest CD. He's a local musician and the nicest guy ever. After I make the cannoli shells and cool them, I dip the ends in melted bittersweet chocolate and chopped pistachios. Then, I fill the shells with the ricotta mixture, which is a painfully slow process, since I want them to look perfect.

I'll make the red velvet cupcakes later this afternoon after I take a nap. My phone jingles with a text and picture from Jack.

Jack: Halibut ceviche!
Me: Looks fab.
Jack: Tonight will be fun
Me: For sure

For sure? Did I suddenly turn into a Valley Girl? I think all the sugar has gone to my head. I lay on the sofa, covered with an afghan for a nap and have vivid dreams of the evening ahead.

As I bake and frost the cupcakes, I contemplate a hairstyle for tonight. The dress dictates an updo since it's so fancy. But, I want to look playful, flirty, and kissable. After trying a few different hairstyles, I decide to leave my hair curly and pin it up using glittery silver bobby pins. With Spanx on, the dress fits perfectly, and I'm pleased with the entire outfit.

Marshall rings my doorbell at ten, right on time. I open the door and he's smiling, holding a bouquet of pink roses.

"Kari! You look beautiful! These are for you," Marshall says and steps inside, shaking the snow off his jacket. It started snowing an hour ago, a light fluffy snow.

"Thanks, Marshall! The flowers are gorgeous," I say and walk into the kitchen to find a vase. How sweet of Marshall to bring me flowers!

Marshall is dressed in a black suit with a dark red paisley tie. He looks very handsome and boyish.

"You look great, too! Is that a new suit?" I ask and place the flowers on the sofa table.

Marshall unbuttons the jacket. "Brand new. Thought the occasion called for a splurge. I have a feeling this party will be better than driving up to Talkeetna to see Cake, especially since it's snowing out."

"I agree. I heard Cake loves playing in Alaska, so I'm sure we'll have other opportunities to see them."

"This is the one party with a fancy dress code that's worth it. He makes elaborate appetizers, and we drink bellinis and sidecars. I'm in charge of dessert," I say. The desserts are packaged and sitting on the kitchen counter.

"Make yourself comfortable. I'm almost ready," I say and head into the bathroom.

Marshall sits on the sofa by the fireplace. He flips through my *Bon Appetit* magazine and waits patiently.

"Ready! Thanks for waiting," I say, turning off the fireplace. We put on our coats and carry the desserts to his car. It takes two trips to haul them all out. Maybe I made too much cannoli. Wait, is there such a thing?

On the drive to Jack's house, Marshall asks about the guest list, and I describe the people I know who are coming.

When we arrive to Jack's house, there are cars parked in the driveway and along the curb. Looks like a decent turnout. We bring in the cupcakes and cake on the first trip.

"HAPPY NEW YEAR!" Jack cries as he opens the door. He's wearing a dark grey suit with a blue, striped tie. "Here let me take something for you." I give him the cake.

"Jack, this is Marshall. Marshall, this is Jack," I say, trying not to compare them side by side.

"Nice to meet you, Jack! Kari talks about you a lot," Marshall says and shakes Jack's available hand.

Marshall sets down the cupcake platter on the bench in the entryway. "Kari, I'll grab the rest of the desserts from the car. Stay here. I don't want you to ruin your party shoes."

"Are you sure? I can help you," I offer. Marshall shakes his head. He walks back out to the car. True. I skipped the clumsy snow boots and wore my black kate spades with three inch heels. Marshall pulled right up to the shoveled sidewalk, so I didn't have to wobble far.

Jack takes my coat and hangs it in the closet. "Polite guy. Seems solid."

I peek around the corner and see people lounging on the couch and standing around in the kitchen. Food is spread out on the dining room table. From here, I can see Jack's favorite blue cheese and walnut crackers, smoked salmon crepes, seared beef tenderloin with horseradish crema, risotto balls, fried ravioli with homemade marinara, and tempura asparagus. Looks like the Fry Daddy is broken in! There's an empty side table for desserts, and I bet the kitchen counter holds more savory goodies.

Marshall returns with the remaining desserts, and I hang up his coat. I unwrap the platters of cannoli and place them on each corner of the side table. The cake sits in the middle, and I arrange cupcakes on a tiered cake stand. Perfect.

Jack and Marshall are still standing in the entryway talking when I finish. I hear snippets of their conversation ... how poorly the Seahawks season was and the best ski trails in town. I'm glad they are getting along so well.

Abby walks over to them, and Jack introduces her to Marshall. She's wearing an emerald green taffeta dress with a short, flared skirt (aka the dress style Zooey Deschanel is known for) and Joan & David silver stilettos.

"Very nice to meet you, Marshall!" Abby says and places her arm around Jack's waist. "Please help yourself to food and make yourself at home."

"Abby, Happy New Year! You look lovely, as always," I say and smile as I join them. We take a peek at each other's shoes and start laughing.

"Kari, we must schedule some shoe shopping trips," Abby says. "Your dress is positively gorgeous."

I blush. "Thanks, Abby. A shoe shopping trip sounds great." I am sincere when I say that to her. She's genuinely sweet.

"Jack said you were bringing desserts and bragged about your baking skills. Let's go check them out, so you can tell me which to try first. Dessert is my guilty pleasure."

We walk over to the dessert table, and I say hi to a few people on the way. She's impressed by the cannoli and tries one immediately.

"This is so luscious! I love the pistachios. Are you willing to share the recipe?" Abby says, licking the ricotta filling off her fingers.

I laugh. "Absolutely. I'll email it to you."

I realize that I kind of abandoned Marshall, so I excuse myself and go look for him. He's talking to Darren and Chris about the upcoming football play-off games.

"Hey Kari!" Darren calls out. "Your guy here thinks the Bears will go all the way this time. What do you think?"

"Not a chance. I'm hoping the Falcons stomp them in the play-offs," I say. The guys chuckle. I see Jack join Abby at the dessert table, and she points to the cannoli. He picks one up from the plate and takes a bite.

Jack even decorated his house for the party with noisemakers, party hats, and I see a table in the corner with glasses, champagne, and Prosecco on ice.

"Kari, how about a drink? Sidecar or bellini?" Marshall asks. I see Darren and Chris have moved on to the dining room table, piling food on a plate.

I smile at Marshall. "A bellini, please. Thank you!"

While Marshall is in the kitchen, I introduce myself to some of the guests I don't know. We talk about the weather, resolutions, and their connection to Jack. Several folks are in his yoga class. I also see Sean and Victoria from work sitting on the couch, so I drift over to talk with them.

"Here you go, Kari," Marshall hands me a bellini with a pink umbrella in it. Festive. Jack went all out for the party, and I'm impressed.

"Thanks!"

"Marshall, this is Sean and Victoria. We all work together at B&B Architects," I say and smile. They are some of my favorite co-workers, and we occasionally go out for Happy Hour.

"Very nice to meet you both," Marshall says. "What do you do at B&B Architects?"

"I'm the Information Systems Manager. Basically, I keep their computers running, so they can keep chugging along, designing buildings, and such," Sean says with a laugh.

Marshall nods. "I know what you mean. I'm in IT myself. What about you, Victoria?"

"I'm an architect and mainly work on healthcare projects," Victoria says.

"Are you working with Anchorage Hospital System on their campus expansion?" Marshall asks.

Victoria is impressed. "Yes, it's my baby. It's been my life for the last 18 months."

"That's a massive project. They've tapped our company to set up the computer system in the cancer wing. Having a cancer treatment system up here will make a huge difference. People should be close to home and family during treatment and not down in Seattle," Marshall says earnestly.

"I agree with you!" Victoria nods her head and smiles at me.

They talk for a few more minutes about work, and then Marshall offers to get everyone a drink refill. Sean joins him in the kitchen.

"What a cutie! And so smart," Victoria gives me a nudge on the arm and a pointed look.

"I know, but we're just friends. Although, he better not leave me hanging at midnight! A kiss on the cheek at least," I joke. "Are you having a good time?"

"Absolutely. Jack always throws a fun party. I saved room for your desserts though. Have you had any food yet?" Victoria asks and places her empty plate on the end table.

"No, we'll grab a plate when Marshall returns," I say, my mouth watering.

"Definitely try the beef tenderloin and the fried asparagus. Both are fantastic!" Victoria gushes.

Marshall and Sean return with bellinis for everyone. We toast and clink glasses.

"Let's go check out the food," I say to Marshall. We excuse ourselves and walk over to the dining room table.

I pick up a plate and help myself to a little bit of everything except the mixed olives and the mini muffaletta sandwiches with olive tapenade. Marshall is careful not to take too much because he's saving room for a piece of cake and at least three cupcakes, according to him.

We snag two seats in the living room on the couch and set our plates down on the coffee table.

"The deep fried ravioli is tasty!" Marshall exclaims. "Actually, everything is really fantastic. You weren't kidding about Jack putting on a serious spread. Wow!"

I nod my head in agreement and eat a blue cheese and walnut cracker. "I don't want dessert, just more of these amazing little crackers."

We chat with the other folks sitting near us as we eat. Marshall gets up for a second helping of ravioli and brings back a couple of crackers for me.

After knocking back a third round of bellinis, we're feeling warm and super social. Marshall and I work the room and end up having quite a bit in common with several of the guests.

Before we know it, midnight is almost here. Jack and Abby are pouring Prosecco and champagne in glasses. Marshall and I help distribute the glasses to the guests. We watch his wall clock tick down the seconds, and then everyone is yelling "Happy New Year," hugging, and kissing.

Marshall clinks his glass against mine and gives me a hug. "Here's to the New Year! May it be a year full of fun, nachos, Sunday dinners, and good times with friends!" He kisses me lightly on the lips.

"Cheers, Marshall!" I say and clink his glass.

42

I wake up the next morning in my pink nightshirt with a pounding headache, and I check the clock on the nightstand. The sun is slowly rising above the mountains, and it's 10 a.m.

Ugh, it feels like I have fur growing in my mouth. I slowly get out of bed, throw on a robe and walk into the master bathroom. My curly hair is matted down and the bobby pins are nowhere to be found. I smooth it back into a ponytail and brush my teeth.

And, then I hear snoring. Wait ... what the what?

Now it comes back to me. Marshall and I took a cab back here, and he's sleeping on the sofa in a deep stupor, I bet. The worst part? Stopping at Taco Bell for tacos and then proceeding to eat right there in the cab.

No wonder my stomach is a little unhappy with me. It also explains the dried hot sauce on Marshall's cheek.

Marshall looks so funny! He's curled up on his side, halfway covered with my afghan, tie still on, and snoring like a semi-truck. I grab my iPhone and take a picture of him. He'll appreciate it later, once his hangover subsides.

I walk into the kitchen to make coffee and look for Ibuprofen. After drinking a big glass of water and taking two pills, I decide to whip up breakfast. Normally, I would go out for a greasy breakfast to cure my hangover if I was out too late with my girlfriends, but I decide to cook for us instead.

Speaking of girlfriends, I still haven't heard from Deirdre. I hope she doesn't turn into one of those girls who lands a man and then dumps her girlfriends. I make a mental note to call her again at work tomorrow.

Working quietly, I chop up mushrooms, ham, onion, and green pepper for omelettes. Next, I dice up potatoes to fry. Then, I slice up cinnamon chip bread for french toast. I hear a groan from the sofa as I'm cracking eggs into a bowl to dip the bread in.

"Oh, my head. Tell me … did we have fun last night? Did I make an ass out of myself in front of your friends and embarrass you?" Marshall mutters and slowly sits up.

I take him a glass of water and Ibuprofen. "We most certainly had fun, and no, you didn't embarrass me at all. In fact, you charmed everyone there with your amazing conversation skills. You have a little bit of Taco Bell sauce on your left cheek." I laugh.

"Thanks for the medicine and water! If I gain use of my legs in the next hour, I'll go wash my face."

"Well, I'm cooking us a big breakfast to combat the hangover. Are you ready for coffee? You take it black, right?" I ask and walk back into the kitchen with the empty glass.

Marshall groans again. "Yes, black coffee sounds great. Thanks, Kari. This is Southern hospitality at its finest."

I stir the vegetables in the pan, and then fill up a coffee cup for Marshall. He's rubbing his bleary eyes and stretching.

He takes the coffee and smiles. "Cute robe. You really like pink, huh?"

I laugh. My robe is pink and white polka-dotted along with my sleepshirt. "It's my favorite color. Go wash up, breakfast is almost ready. I'll fill you in on last night's adventures over breakfast." I flip the french toast in the pan and warm up syrup in the microwave.

Marshall makes his way to the guest bathroom, and I hear the sink water running.

After refilling our coffee cups, I set breakfast on the dining room table, and we serve ourselves generous portions.

"This looks delicious. Thanks for breakfast," Marshall says and takes a big bite of buttery french toast drenched in maple syrup.

I take a bite of the eggs. "So, do you remember *anything* from last night?"

"I remember counting down to midnight and eating an ungodly amount of fried ravioli," Marshall says slowly.

"That's a start. Midnight came and went and we were still partying. Some people left, but we stayed until the bitter end. Around 3 a.m., Jack got out Guitar Hero, and you challenged him to a play-off. It was hysterical!" I laugh and spear another piece of french toast onto my plate.

"What song did I rock out to? Please tell me I at least played well or chose a worthy song."

I put my fork down and stand up to imitate him. I do a little air guitar and start singing *Sunshine of Your Love* by Cream.

Marshall drops his head into his hands and cries out, "Oh. My. God."

I laugh and sit back down. "You actually did very well and won! Poor Jack couldn't believe it. Beat at his favorite video game in front of his friends. His song was *Seven Nation Army* by The White Stripes."

"Anything else happen?" Marshall asks and takes another helping of fried potatoes.

"Well, I begged the cab driver to stop at Taco Bell. Both of us ate a couple of tacos, which I regret," I say and rub my stomach.

"Phew. I guess it wasn't that bad of a night, then."

Marshall pushes back the plate and sips on his coffee. He's feeling better since the Ibuprofen has kicked in.

"One more thing, when we got home, you wanted to make a snowman with all the fresh snow, so we went outside and were kind of loud and obnoxious. The neighbors probably aren't too happy with us right now. I took a picture of you and the snowman," I say and show him the picture on my phone.

"Did you have a fun night despite all of this craziness?" Marshall asks with a smile.

I punch him in the shoulder. "You bet. The best New Year's Eve hands down."

We take our dishes into the kitchen and clean up. After pouring coffee in travel mugs, I take him to pick up his car at Jack's house. I promise to email him pictures from the night, and he gives me a big hug before getting into his car.

Once home, I sit on the sofa in front of the fireplace, downloading the pictures from the evening. There's a good picture of Jack, Abby, Marshall, and me gathered around the desserts. Jack has his arm around Abby and a red velvet cupcake in his hand. And, Jack took one of Marshall and me laughing. I love the candid, in-the-moment pictures.

The picture of Marshall with the snowman is funny. Marshall has a goofy smile on his face and his arm wrapped around the snowman, which is clad in my pink scarf, pink mittens, and a red velvet cupcake (icing licked off, courtesy of Marshall) as his nose.

I email the pictures to Jack and Marshall. It was an entertaining evening, and Marshall was the perfect date.

43

New year, new beginnings right? And definitely some new adventures for everyone.

Jack and I are eating lunch in my office. We braved the cold weather for a polish dog from the usual vendor. Poor guy, he was wearing Bunny Boots to keep warm while grilling hot dogs and sautéing onions for the long line of hungry people.

"Were you terribly hungover on New Year's Day?" I ask and dump the bag of chips onto my plate.

"Not too bad. I drank a lot of water before I passed out. Brought out the Fry Daddy and made chicken fried steak with eggs for breakfast," Jack says and spreads relish on his polish dog.

"Nice. I hope Marshall wasn't too obnoxious about his Guitar Hero win."

"He's a funny guy. Bad ass guitar player despite being three sheets to the wind. Did you know he licked the cream cheese frosting off a bunch of cupcakes and then set them back on the table?" Jack laughs.

"I'm so sorry about that!" I blush. Marshall will die of embarrassment when I tell him about the cupcakes.

"No worries at all. Glad you came to the party and had fun! After you and Marshall left, Abby and I bundled up and went for a long walk. It was so peaceful with all the fresh snow," Jack says and takes a sip of his Coke.

"She's pretty incredible. I really like her," I say.

"Me, too. So, any resolutions?" Jack says and changes the subject.

I finish the last bite of my polish dog. "Actually, I do have a few." I pull out my daytimer and flip to a dog-eared page.

"First, stay optimistic when it comes to men. Ethan didn't work out. Marshall didn't work out. That's life. Dating is a sorting process, and it's not easy. I refuse to become jaded. Second, start saving for a house. And third, volunteer. I used to volunteer all the time as a kid, and I haven't volunteered at all up here. I'm going to check out a couple of charities close to my heart," I read from the list.

"Wow. Those are some serious resolutions. I really like the volunteering one. Good for you!" Jack says and leans back in the chair.

"What about you?" I ask.

Jack clears his throat. "I generally don't make resolutions, but this year, I made an exception. I'm going back to school for my Ph.D in Planning, Design and Environment."

"Congratulations! That's wonderful! Can you do it locally? Are you quitting your job to focus on school?" My mind is flooded with questions. Jack has never mentioned school before, so this is a surprise.

"I'm taking classes on-line, and I fly to Seattle once a month to meet with my group. I start next week. Pretty exciting!" Jack smiles.

"You're brave to do this while working full-time," I praise him.

Jack looks sheepish. "Thanks, it's been on my mind to do, and I finally decided to take the plunge and do it. I may bug you for help."

"Anytime, Jack. I'll help you out with anything!"

Our conversation turns to spring trips. Most people in Alaska take a spring trip to ward off cabin fever and break up the long winter. Jack is headed to Hawaii for a week in March with his family. I booked a week back in Charleston, so I can attend my nieces' sixth birthday in February. Plus Mama and Dad's trip here in March for the Iditarod!

〜◯

After lunch, I call Deirdre at work since she hasn't returned any of my calls or emails.

"Deirdre Weston," she says, answering the phone.

"Dee! It's Kari. I haven't heard from you in forever!"

"Hey Kari. I know, I'm sorry. Life is crazy lately."

"Jack said he saw you at Red Shed Coffee. Are you dating one of your co-workers? Seriously?" I ask.

Deirdre sighs. "It's true. Laurence asked me out, and we've been spending a lot of time together. It took him a lot of courage to ask me out, but he did, and I'm in love."

"Love? Really? That's great! Did I meet him on the halibut fishing trip?" I ask, trying to remember names and faces.

"He was the one wearing the Cincinnati Reds ball cap. And, the only guy who didn't get seasick!" Deirdre laughs. "Laurence said he wanted to ask me out way back then, but was too shy. We spend every night together now, cook dinner, grocery shop, and do errands on the weekend."

"I remember him. I'm so happy for you!"

"Laurence wants us to go to Hawaii next month. He found round trip tickets on Alaska Air for $299 each," Deirdre says.

"Wonderful! If you want to go shopping before your trip, let me know!"

251

"Thanks! Do any shops around here sell bathing suits in the middle of winter?"

"I'm sure we can find one. If not, you can always order on-line," I say. I love ordering on-line. Packages are delivered right to my doorstep, and I can order in the comfort of my pajamas and home.

"Cool, well I need to run. Laurence and I are going out to lunch. I'll talk with you later!" Deirdre hangs up, not waiting for me to say goodbye.

Uh-oh. I have a feeling I won't hear from her very often. She seems pretty wrapped up with Laurence. But, it's okay. I'm glad she's happy and in love.

44

Over the next couple of weeks, Marshall and I hang out often. We meet for Happy Hour, eat nachos, go skiing again, and attend the Beer & Barley Wine Festival with Lauren and Will. Luckily, I do not run into Ethan there.

Jack is busy with school and Abby. We still go for coffee runs, but our lunch outings are infrequent now. He spends his lunch hour studying or having lunch with Abby.

Life is quite content except for my single status, but I'm staying true to my resolutions and remaining optimistic. I also ask Lauren for her real estate agent's phone number and begin saving money for a down payment.

As far as volunteering, I donate my time at the soup kitchen downtown. Every Saturday, I volunteer in the mornings and assist the staff in the kitchen, making soup and sandwiches for the noon meal. It's a perfect fit for me, and I enjoy the high-spirited and engaged staff.

On Sunday afternoon, my cell phone rings, and caller ID says Kimberly.

"Hi Kari! Is it snowy there?" Kimberly asks.

"Yes, but the sun makes it so pretty! What's new?" I ask, sitting back down at the kitchen table, where I was in the middle of paying bills on-line and balancing my checkbook.

"Not much, just wanted to check in with you and say hi. Have you talked to Kate or Mama lately?"

"No, is there more drama?' I wince.

"Kate doesn't want a sit down dinner at the reception. She wants appetizers and a full bar since most of her college friends are coming. Mama's having a fit. She's threatened to not pay for the wedding. Again."

"Are you sure we're all related? They are having so many disagreements. Kate's young and has tons of ideas. Mama needs to let up and relax, don't you think?"

"Absolutely. I'm ducking their calls, so I don't have to take sides. This is your heads up," Kimberly warns.

"Thanks, I appreciate it. Let's change the subject. What would the girls like for their birthday?"

Kimberly sighs. "They're growing so fast! Remember how they were into Barbies at Christmas? Now, they want to play dress up in my clothes and put on make-up! Five-years-old and make-up?"

"So, flavored lip gloss and feather boas?" I tease.

"Very funny. They're too young to wear make-up! That's my mantra when they ask. How about getting them some board games or soccer balls? Both girls start soccer in April."

"Sounds good. I'll choose some games. I don't want to try and pack soccer balls in my luggage when I come home for their party. Have you chosen a theme?" I ask, knowing she's probably had a theme picked out for weeks.

"Cinderella. I have plates, napkins, and everything with Cinderella on them. The girls helped choose the theme, and they both agreed. A miracle in itself. I'm making pink cupcakes, and Mama is making the other food. We're grilling out by the pool at the country club. Hope the weather cooperates," Kimberly says.

"It sounds great! I can't wait to see you all! Anything else happening?"

"Well, I do have one other thing to tell you. I'm pregnant!" Kimberly says enthusiastically.

"Congratulations! When are you due?"

"The fourth of July! Right in the middle of the hot summer."

"Yay! I'm thrilled for you all," I say, smiling and already mentally picking out cute onesies to send her.

"Thanks! I better run. Anna and Ashley are at swimming lessons with Mark, so I should start dinner. Love you!" Kimberly says.

"Bye, Kim!"

Wow. I bet Mama and Dad are over the moon happy. I'm sure I'll hear all about it at during my Sunday phone call with Mama. We'll have to keep it short and sweet, since I'm meeting Marshall for dinner at six.

❧

Sunday night dinner at Tahoe South Cantina is now a tradition for Marshall and me. Often, we invite friends to meet us, but tonight it's just us.

My phone jingles with a text.

Marshall: Rock star parking up front.

He has this incredible knack for good parking right by the door.

I'm already sitting in a booth when I read Marshall's text and laugh. I order an IPA beer for him when the server drops off my margarita and wave at him when he enters the restaurant door.

"Did you see my text? I hit that parking spot every time. Where did you park? It's packed tonight!" Marshall says as he looks around the restaurant.

"I parked over in the back forty, thanks for rubbing it in!"

"How are you doing?" I ask as I set aside the menu. Every time I come here, I look at it, but I don't know why … I usually rotate my order between a half order of nachos without olives, a potato burrito, or the portabella mushroom sandwich.

"Good. I worked a lot this weekend, but it was okay. Didn't you have a date last night?"

"I don't know if you call going to the indoor batting cage a date. But it was a disaster. I mentioned to Steve I like going there to hit softballs as a stress releaser, and he shows up at the batting cage with two gloves and a bag of baseballs slung over his shoulder."

Marshall laughs loudly. He sets the menu aside to give me his full attention.

"How did you meet Steve again?"

"Last week, Lauren and I met for drinks after work at Sushi Maki. He was in the bar with friends and came over to our table. He ordered a salmon roll and had us try it because he insisted it was the best in town. I kind of liked his boldness, so I said yes when he asked for my phone number."

"So, how was the date a disaster? He listened to what you said and was creative on where to take you. No boring dinner or drinks," Marshall says and nods thanks to the server for the IPA. He takes a grateful sip and turns his attention back to me.

"We went to the batting cage and hit some balls. No big deal, it was fun. Different because the batting cage is indoors, but still okay. Right next to the batting cage is a basketball court, and there was no one using it. He threw me a glove and insisted we throw the baseball back and forth. I suck at catching! It was humiliating and not fun at all. I was running after balls, and he didn't get the hint. He kept saying I needed to work on my catching," I mutter and roll my eyes.

The server comes by to take our order. Half order of nachos, no olives for me this time around. Chicken tacos for Marshall this week.

"I'm so glad we drove separately to the batting cage. I shook his hand, said I had fun, got in my car, and drove off."

"I'm sorry to laugh, but that's really funny. I guess your snap judgment was wrong on him too, just in reverse. You thought he was great, and he turned out a baseball bully. Anyway, how's work going? Are you still working on the museum project?"

"Yes, but it's wrapping up. We should finish by the end of the month. What about you? Any new lovely ladies in your life?"

"Well, now that you bring it up. I did score a girl's digits. I went to do a bank deposit, and the teller was very attractive."

"Wait ... aren't most of the tellers in their early twenties? Marshall! You're thirty-four! Seriously!" I say and take a sip of my margarita.

"She seemed very mature. Honestly, I don't know how old she is, but she was flirty, so I asked for her number, and she gave it to me. We're meeting for coffee on Wednesday morning."

"I bet she checked your account balance. Then, she'll go have a Brazilian wax before your date because she's hit the jackpot!" I tease, knowing Marshall is saving to retire at age fifty-five and has a generous jump on his nest egg.

The server stops by to check on another round of drinks and says our food should arrive shortly.

"Kari, we're just going for coffee, it's not a big deal. The acceptable age to date is half your age plus seven. Haven't you ever heard of that?" Marshall laughs.

"Very funny. Like you're really going to date someone seriously who is twenty-four? Come on. A twenty-four-year-old still has so much to experience in life."

"I'm only teasing you. It would be nice to find a girl closer to my own age, but you know what I'm looking for."

"Yes, I know," I groan. "You're waiting to lock eyes with a girl and see fireworks. Marshall, you know that's kind of unrealistic, right? I'm just saying ... sometimes people become more attractive to you once you get to know them. Fireworks aren't everything and you shouldn't dismiss girls so quickly. You're kind of making snap judgments like me. And you lecture me all the time about my bad habit."

"Good thing I have you to keep me in line," Marshall says and finishes off his beer.

We continue chatting over dinner and make plans to check out the Girdwood Winter Festival next weekend. Marshall promises to call me after the bank teller coffee date.

45

I kick off my new UGG Button Boots, drop my pink laptop bag on the couch, and join Lauren in the kitchen. We ordered pizza and are staying in tonight since Will's out of town, and the temperature is below zero.

"Kari, do you want white or red wine? I have a really nice Malbec," Lauren says and grabs a wine glass from the cabinet. "I'm sticking with Diet Coke tonight."

"The Malbec, please. How's work going? You mentioned a possible promotion, right?" I ask and lean against the counter.

"My boss put in her notice last week. She's moving to Seattle next month. I'm interested in her job, but I'm not wild about the long hours." Lauren hands me the wine glass, and we sit on the couch.

"You already work long hours. Both you and Will. Two of the hardest working people, I know. You should totally go for it."

"Yes, but I'm also working on a little side project that may take more of my time…" Lauren trails off.

"What side project?" I squint my eyes and turn my head towards her, giving her my full attention.

"Will and I are trying to have a baby!" Lauren cries out.

I scoot over and give her a big hug. "That's fantastic news! I'm so excited for you both. Wow!" First my sister, now Lauren.

"We just started, and I went off the pill last month. You're the first person I've told. You know we've been doing some renovations to our home. It's all in preparation for a baby! I even painted the baby's room already," Lauren says.

"I'm hoping for a girl, but I know Will really wants a boy."

"That's so exciting, Lauren!"

The doorbell rings, and she goes to greet the pizza delivery man. I grab plates and napkins in the kitchen, and we load up our plates and sit back down on the couch.

"Great idea to stay in. It's way too cold outside to venture out for food. Thanks for the pizza!" I take a bite of a breadstick.

"I want to ask for your help. I'm going to give on-line dating a chance. I've never tried it. Can you help me set up a profile?"

"Sure! I would love to help you! Brave move. What inspired you to give it a try?" Lauren asks as she takes a bite of pepperoni and mushroom pizza.

"Well, Jack has Abby. Deirdre has Laurence. Marshall has his harem of twenty-year-olds, and I need to keep trying. I refuse to give up."

"You are the *most* tenacious person I know. Way to go! Let's work on it after dinner."

"Thanks, I knew I could count on you."

We talk about baby names during dinner, and Lauren's face is animated and wistful as she thinks about the baby. After we clean up, I put my laptop on the kitchen table. Navigating to the AlaskaSingles website, I take a deep breath and click "Set Up Profile."

"What should I choose for a user name?" I ask Lauren, as she hands me another glass of wine. Confidence in a glass.

"A name that tells a little something about you. What about SouthernGal or SweetTeaLover or ClemsonRules?" Lauren giggles.

"Lauren! ClemsonRules? Seriously? I kind of like SouthernGal though." I type in SouthernGal and answer the questions. For music, I list Jack Johnson, Martin Sexton, Gwyneth & Monko, Mumford & Sons, The Quiet American, and Carrie Underwood. A random mix of artists. My friend back in Charleston supplies me with the latest CDs, plus sends me independent artists.

"Do you have a super cute picture to upload? What about the one from Thanksgiving or when we went snowshoeing?"

"The snowshoeing one might work. Or I have a picture from the summer when I went hiking. Then I'll look all outdoorsy and hard core," I giggle and upload the picture of me from the Turnagain Arm Trail. It's a good picture. I'm wearing shorts, a pink t-shirt, and my hair is curly and blowing in the wind.

"The final part is what you're looking for in a guy. Think about it before typing, Kari," Lauren lectures. She knows me well. I'll just type whatever enters my head and regret it later.

"Okay. Give me a minute," I say, closing my eyes and picturing my ideal mate. Aside from physical qualities, I think about combining Jack and Marshall's qualities. I know ... crazy and unrealistic.

Lauren grabs the plate of cranberry oatmeal cookies I brought and sets them in front of me. I chew on a cookie and type a few words, then quickly delete them.

"This is harder than I thought. I mean, when I think about my type of guy ... hippie, granola, listens to alternative music and thinks showers are optional. Is that really my type or just the guys I gravitate towards? Most of the guys I dated this year were not hippies, and none of them worked out," I say, frustrated.

"Don't focus on what they look like. Focus on the qualities of the guy. Like considerate, et cetera," Lauren says.

"Okay, I want a guy who is thoughtful, family-oriented, kind, supportive, smart, polite, and patient. Whew. That's quite a list. I think it will scare any potential guys."

"Nope, start typing it. Think of it like this ... it will weed out potential suitors."

I type the qualities I'm looking for in a guy. "Okay, done. My profile is uploaded, and my fingers are crossed."

"Yay! Keep me posted on the responses. I'm so excited for you!" Lauren gives me a hug.

"I'm more excited for you and Will. A little one with your good hair and his sense of adventure. It's late, so I better get going. I'll look at potential matches when I get home."

I put on my UGGs, pink wool beanie, pink mittens, scarf, and black wool coat. I'm so glad I moved to Alaska.

46

Marshall and I walk around the Girdwood Winter Festival, bundled up and sipping on hot toddies. Skiers and snowboarders enjoy the eight inches of fresh powder and wait patiently for their turn on the chairlift. In the parking lot, there are free sled dog rides for all ages. Festival attendees visit booths selling food, libations, and local crafts. The sky is bright blue, and we're enjoying the sunny, cold weather.

"This is one of my favorite festivals. I look forward to it each year even though it's freezing out!" Marshall says and moves a little closer to one of the outdoor heaters on the patio of the ski resort hotel.

"It's such a lovely day though. I'm so glad we're here. Hey, you never told me about your date with the bank teller," I giggle.

"It was fine, just coffee. She's young, nice, and forgot to mention her boyfriend when I asked her out in the first place," Marshall laughs.

"Sorry, Marshall, but it's kind of funny. How did she bring up the fact that she has a boyfriend?"

"We were talking, and then she just throws out, 'my boyfriend and I.' She could've declined when I asked her out, you know?"

Marshall sips on his drink and watches the skiers and snowboarders navigate the hill.

I take a deep breath and blurt out, "On to other news … I signed up for AlaskaSingles and created a rockin' profile. So far, 16 matches, and six of them emailed me already! Crazy! Have you ever tried on-line dating?"

"Yes, but the matches I get are foreign women looking for a green card who can't spell," Marshall laughs. "I even specify the women have to live in the same town, and for some reason my matches live in Slovenia."

"Marshall, that's crazy funny! Well, I'm hopeful one of the matches will work out. It's kind of fun emailing back and forth."

"Kari, promise me you'll be cautious. Go on group dates or meet in a very public place, okay?" Marshall looks me in the eye. "Seriously, it's not the same as Lauren matching you up with someone she knows."

"I promise. Don't worry. I'll meet them at the bookstore or a coffee shop. Let's go check out the ice sculpture competition."

We walk over to Girdwood Square where the blocks of ice are set up. Twelve competitors rev up their chainsaws, and we snag a seat on a bench near a heater. The timer rings, and they start carving.

"Is there a theme for the ice sculpture?" I ask while taking pictures. Difficult to do while wearing mittens, but I manage.

"Classic Alaska. Not sure what they'll end up looking like. A dogsled? Hopefully not an igloo or something corny."

We watch the competition and then walk around admiring their final sculptures. Marshall takes my picture next to the float plane. It is pretty amazing. I can't wait to send these pictures to my family.

I really love spending time with Marshall. I admire his kindness and sense of humor. Plus, he always says yes to activities. I can count on him to grab dinner at the last minute, do random errands together, watch the latest documentary on Netflix, or just drink coffee and people watch.

We stop for dinner at Tahoe South Cantina on the way home. I hear about his latest work project, and we make plans to attend a hockey game Saturday. The local team is on a winning streak, and we both like watching the fights between players.

In a way, I'm glad Marshall didn't like me back. Sure, it hurt for a bit, but I appreciate his friendship every day. It's funny how life works out.

47

Jack walks into my office and closes my door. He looks suspicious and happy. Hmmmm.

"Hey Jack. What's going on?" I ask and give my full attention to him.

"Kari, you're one of my best friends. I have news. I love Abby, and she loves me back," Jack announces and sits down.

"Well, that's fantastic! Congratulations! Seems a bit fast since you just met at Thanksgiving!" I say, a little taken aback by his declaration. My heart stops, and I'm pretty sure my mouth is still open in surprise.

"I know. We've spent a lot of time together since then. We have tons in common. She's an amazing woman. Hard worker, sweet, thoughtful, and gorgeous. The jaded Jack is gone, no more."

"Super! I'm glad you didn't let your jaded attitude get in the way of love. So, what's the next step for you two?" I pray he doesn't say the M word. If he does, I'm going to the store, buying oreo ice cream, and eating it in the car.

"Not sure yet. It's too early to propose, although I'm sure she'd say yes. I just wanted you to know about us. I'm incredibly grateful to Lauren for inviting her to Thanksgiving."

"Good, well I'm glad you shared this with me. Let's talk more later, okay?" I say, with a huge fake smile.

I want a moment to myself to let my heart recover, and I can sort out my feelings.

"Sure. Let's grab a cookie this afternoon," Jack says and walks out of the office with a big smile on his face.

Great. Everyone is in love. Well, not everyone. Marshall isn't. He's still searching for fireworks when he locks eyes with a girl. Okay, cheer up. You have lots of matches on AlaskaSingles, and you're happy, healthy, and have many friends. No time for a pity party!

I turn my attention back to the administrative building schematics and work on them the rest of the morning. I run out at lunch and pick up a sandwich from Miller's Deli.

When I return, there is an email from a new match, Spencer. He says he likes my profile and wonders if I have a cute Southern accent. Creative opening question.

I click on his profile, so I can learn more, but more importantly, see a picture of him.

The profile picture shows him on a mountain bike, wearing sunglasses and a bike helmet. He has a chiseled chin, and he's athletic. Not bad at all.

His interests are mountain biking, camping, fishing, spending time with family and friends, and training his Sheltie for agility competitions.

Hmmm. There's definitely some potential there. I really like his chiseled chin.

I heed Lauren's advice and think about a response before I start typing something off the cuff.

To: MountainBiker
From: SouthernGal

Hi Spencer,

Thanks for the email! Yes, I have a slight Southern accent.
I like your profile, and we have several things in common.
What is your dog's name?

Kari

I ask about his dog since I know a lot about him from his
profile. Out of the other guys I've been volleying emails with,
only a few stand out. Most seem to ask the same old questions
and none of them have asked to meet. I wonder if this is how
on-line dating is supposed to be. Are they are hiding behind their
profiles and emailing instead of meeting in person to have a real
conversation?

Lauren and I are meeting at the gym tonight, so I'll ask her
insight on the emailing versus meeting. After sending her a gym email
reminder with a celebrity quote from Lady Gaga, I return to work.

◦～◦

I set up two step benches in the back row and wait for Lauren to
arrive. I have so much to tell her, and with my luck, this'll be the
day she runs late.

It was an interesting afternoon at work. Spencer and I emailed
several times back and forth. He has a dry sense of humor, and

I find it quite entertaining. The best part is he asked to meet for coffee Saturday morning.

Lauren arrives in the middle of the first song, while we're stretching and warming up.

"Hi! Sorry, I'm late. My meeting ran over. Thanks for saving me a spot," Lauren whispers and sets her water bottle and towel down next to the wall.

"No worries," I say in between knee lifts. "I met a guy! We're meeting for coffee Saturday morning!"

Lauren cries, "Hooray!" The teacher gives us a warning look. "What's his name? Is he one of your on-line matches?"

"Yes, his name is Spencer. Cute, mountain biker, funny. We emailed each other all afternoon," I whisper excitedly.

"What does he do for a living?"

"Oh. I actually forgot to ask. We were talking about his dog, Cooper, and favorite hikes."

"Are you meeting in a public place? Will said for you to meet somewhere crowded, just in case he turns out to be a pervert or ax murderer," Lauren murmurs. She's breathing hard from knee repeaters.

I smile. "Will's so sweet! We're meeting at 10 a.m. at Barnes & Noble. I promise to leave ASAP if he's creepy."

The teacher calls out, "Girls, if you want to continue to have a full-blown chatfest, please do it outside!"

Ouch! This is our second warning this month for talking too much. Maybe we should attend class with a laid back, nice teacher.

Lauren rolls her eyes at me and motions to me that we'll finish our "chatfest" after class. I laugh and nod my head.

After class, we grab smoothies and walk to the toy store next door. I need to pick up Anna and Ashley's birthday gifts, plus we can avoid the teacher giving us the evil eye as she leaves the gym.

We're browsing in the game section, and I tell Lauren about Spencer.

"He likes camping, hiking, and his picture shows him on a mountain bike. He's wearing sunglasses and a helmet, so I can't see his eyes. But, he has this chiseled, strong chin," I gush and take a sip of my pineapple banana smoothie. "Just like Lance Armstrong."

"Sounds good so far. Did you ask him if he likes *Seinfeld*?" Lauren teases and picks up one of the games to look at.

"Lauren! I'm trying to be more open-minded these days. Not everyone has to like *Seinfeld*. See? Not a dealbreaker. He's training his dog for a show in San Diego next month."

"That's cool! Ask him what he does for work in your next email. What if he's unemployed or lives with his parents?"

I laugh. "Good point. I'll find out."

Looking at the games, I choose Sequence for Kids and Uno. Lauren wanders over to the children's books, so I join her with my goodies. She's paging through *The Velveteen Rabbit*.

"I am *so* buying this! Do you remember reading this when you were a kid? It's one of my favorite books," Lauren says, looking pensive. "I hope our child loves it as much as I do."

"Lauren, they will. No doubt about that!" I say and look at the books on the shelf.

Each birthday and Christmas, I buy the twins a book in addition to something fun. I grew up going to the library with Mama every Friday afternoon. As a result, I love reading every night, and I hope they will become lifetime book lovers, too.

After selecting two books from the early reader series, Lauren and I walk to the counter. She gives me an update on her latest project, the downtown city park. Our firm put together a bid for the project, but the city chose another firm. The project is moving along and will be completed by May, right in time for spring.

I promise to give her an update on Spencer, and we both head home for the evening.

48

I arrive early to Barnes & Noble, so I can spy on the café area and look for Spencer. I'm nervous, and I hope our in-person conversation flows as easily as our email conversations. Over the last couple of days, we exchanged several lengthy emails, and I like what he writes in the emails. He seems honest, funny, and perceptive, so my fingers are crossed.

Near the card rack, I have an unobstructed view of the café, and I see only one guy sitting alone at a table. Several other tables are occupied with couples or families. The lone guy is balding, tall, thin, and looking at a cooking magazine. Interesting.

It's hard to see his chin from here, and I wonder if this is him. Spencer's profile only had one picture, and I didn't consider asking him if he had a full head of hair or if he was bald under his bike helmet. Not that it really matters, I guess.

This guy is dressed nicely in pressed light blue pants and a white short-sleeve button down shirt. Really? All he needs is a pocket protector. Kari! Be nice … no snap judgments.

Hmmm. I'll wait a few more minutes over here and see if anyone else comes in.

While I'm waiting, I pick out birthday cards for my nieces and the latest issue of *Saveur* magazine. I decide to quit stalling and take another peek in the café. Blue pants guy is still sitting there, and he's looking around. Okay, should I just go over there and ask if he's Spencer?

Quit delaying it! Just do it.

I walk over to the table and smile.

"Hi, I'm Kari. Are you Spencer?" I ask nervously.

Blue pants guy jumps to his feet. "Yes, I'm Spencer. It's so nice to meet you in person, Kari! Can I get you a coffee or tea?"

"Sure. A mint tea, please," I say, sitting down and placing the magazine and cards in front of me. He was reading *Cooks Illustrated* magazine. Hmm ... does he like cooking? Another item we have in common perhaps?

What the what? He doesn't look anything like his picture. Sure, I couldn't really see anything from it, but this guy? He's not what I pictured. I envisioned Lance Armstrong in a yellow jersey waving to the crowd and calling my name, thanking me for supporting him.

Should I cut our coffee date short? Should I accuse him of false advertising? Should I sneak out while he's in line for our beverages? Ergh. I'm too polite to do any of those things.

"Here you go ... one mint tea. I wasn't sure if you wanted sugar or honey, so I brought some over just in case," Spencer says and sets the white mug in front of me. "That *Saveur* has some interesting articles in it this month."

My mouth drops open. Did he really say that? What's going on? Is he a secret chef? Own a food cart or something? Okay, don't flee yet. Relax, loosen the grasp on my purse ... breathe.

"Thanks! So, you like to cook?" I ask and remove the tea bag from my cup. Thinking back to our conversations, he didn't mention cooking. I, of course, told him about my love for baking and cooking, but he didn't say anything.

"I love it. I know you asked what I do for a living, and I told you I'm a furniture maker. The truth is…" He pauses. "The industry is pretty slow right now with the economy, so I'm working nights at Sixth Street Tapas as the sous chef."

Stop the presses. Are you kidding me?

"That's impressive. Where did you go to culinary school?" I ask in amazement.

"Johnson & Wales in Providence. I know you mentioned you liked cooking as well. Have you been to Sixth Street Tapas?" Spencer asks and takes a sip of his cappuccino.

"Yes, I went there a couple of months ago. It was fantastic! I especially liked the salmon and sweet potato croquettes. How many nights a week do you work there?"

"Three nights a week. Although, it doesn't feel like work, since I enjoy cooking. I'm glad you liked the croquettes. It's one of my favorite items on the menu, too."

We pause and take a sip of our drinks. Honestly, I'm blown away by Spencer. He's amazing, and I need to reconsider my first assessment of him. I wonder what he thinks about me. I dressed casually in jeans and a black funnel neck sweater. My curly hair is pulled back loosely in a barrette, and I'm wearing Franco Sarto black boots.

"How's business in the architecture world? Have you taken any hits from the economy?" Spencer asks.

"No, we're busy and have several projects in the queue. What kind of furniture do you make?" I ask.

"I mainly do functional pieces such as kitchen tables, armoires, and side tables. I'm working on a couple of small projects right now for some local clients. So, have you had success with on-line dating?"

"Not really. I signed up last week, and you're the first guy to ask me out. What about you?"

"It's been hit or miss. I think it's fine to email a couple of times, but then people should really meet in person. When I ask girls to meet, I never hear from them again. Do you think that's strange?"

"Kind of. Maybe they suddenly become shy or something. I also tried speed dating. Have you done that?" I ask and take a sip of my tea.

He shrugs. "I don't know about that … seems weird to have a bunch of dates all in one night. How did you like it?"

"It was good. You have seven minutes to talk to each person. But, sometimes you don't need that long to determine whether or not you want to mark them yes or no. In two minutes, you kind of know."

"Oh, so you're the type who makes snap judgments?" Spencer asks.

I turn my head to avoid his piercing gaze and think "OMG" to myself. Did he just say that to me? We barely know each other, and he insulted me. I can't believe it! What nerve!

Yes, I make snap judgments. I made a snap judgment the moment I saw his bald head and nerdy clothes. I knew from seeing Spencer in person, a second date is not a possibility. Everyone makes snap judgments!

Seriously! I can't believe he just called me out!

"Ummm … well, I have been known to do it on occasion," I stammer, looking at the floor.

"Interesting." Awkward pause.

The rest of the date, we talk about mountain biking, cooking, his dog, Cooper, and what it was like for me growing up in the

South. Inside, I'm fuming, and I can't wait to call Lauren as soon as the date is over.

"Kari, it was nice meeting you. May I call you later this week?" Spencer asks as we stand up to leave.

NO! No, you may not! Don't call me, you insulting Lance Armstrong wannabe!

"Sure," I say tentatively. "It was very nice to meet you, and thank you for the tea." We shake hands, and I walk to the counter to pay for the cards and magazine. Why did I say sure? What was I thinking?

Once I'm inside my car with the heat on full blast, I dial Lauren's cell phone.

"Hi Kari! Are you still on your date with Spencer? How's it going?" Lauren asks.

"Lauren! He totally insulted me! I can't believe it. Also, he doesn't look anything like Lance Armstrong! Not at all!" I begin to cry, tears squirting from my eyes, frustrated at the entire encounter.

"What happened? How did he insult you?" Lauren asks, thoroughly confused and sounding concerned.

"I was talking to him about speed dating, and I said that you talk to each person for seven minutes, but you really know in about two minutes. And, do you know what he said?" I continue on. "He said I'm the type who makes snap judgments!"

Lauren doesn't say anything for a few seconds. She bursts out laughing. "Kari, he totally called you out on it. That's hysterical!"

"Lauren! No, he insulted me by saying that. He doesn't know me! He's supposed to impress me, so I'll go out with him again. And, he says that right to my face! I can't believe it!"

"What did he look like? You said he didn't look like Lance Armstrong. Was he overweight? Bad teeth? Totally false advertising, huh?" Lauren starts laughing again.

"No! He had hairy arms and bad clothes. And, he's practically bald. Hair only on the sides of his head! He's thirty-five and balding!"

At this point, I start laughing. It's kind of funny. And, kind of typical for me. One dating fiasco after another.

"You know what? I'm going to see him again. That insult earned him a second date, despite my snap judgment the very moment I laid eyes on him. He was right on the money. Maybe that's what's been missing all this time. Someone who is honest and will not put up with my bullshit," I say thoughtfully. Maybe I can help him in the wardrobe department, too. He's probably used to either wearing Carhartts or a chef coat.

Spencer is the first guy to ever call me out, and I'm going to roll with the punches. He said he would call me later this week, so I'll wait for his call.

"Good for you, Kari. Sounds like you've met your match. I'll talk to you later. Do you mind if I tell Will about this? He'll get a kick out of it," Lauren laughs.

"Sure, go ahead. What a way to start off my Saturday morning! Bye!" I say.

That afternoon, I grocery shop for the week and think about the date with Spencer. The more I think about it, the more comical it seems, and I find myself looking forward to his call and seeing what else he says.

I'm tempted to call Marshall and see if he wants to eat dinner tonight at Sixth Street Tapas, so I can spy on Spencer, but I decide against it. I don't know what nights he works, and I wouldn't know what to say if I saw him.

Perhaps Spencer made that remark off the cuff, regrets it now, and won't call me. Or, maybe he didn't think I looked like my picture and won't call me. Who knows? He could've rejected me and was polite about calling me. Ugh. Why am I obsessing about this?

As far as appearance goes, it's not like I have anything against bald guys or even hairy guys. It's just that in my mind, I pictured Lance Armstrong, and it totally threw me for a loop when Spencer looked different.

All day Sunday, I try not to think about Spencer. I flinch every time the phone rings. During my Sunday call with Mama, she tells me about the latest wedding blow-up with Kate. She also informs me of the non-traditional ceremony Kate and Ash want. Something to do with blessing the rings and personal statements from Kate and Ash. To be honest, I tune Mama out and think about Spencer. What if he doesn't call me?

49

Monday came and went, and I'm starting to wonder if Spencer will call. Maybe he had to work late the last couple of nights at Sixth Street Tapas.

Jack and I are eating lunch at The Roadhouse on Tuesday. We decide to take a long lunch and catch up. He has been busy with school, and I listen to his concerns about the first group meeting in Seattle next weekend.

My cell phone rings right after we place our lunch order with the server. I glance at the number and don't recognize it.

"Are you going to answer that?" Jack asks, taking a sip of his Coke.

I frown. "I don't recognize the number, and I hate not knowing who it is."

"Just answer it. We don't have our food yet, so take the call."

I flip open the phone. "Hello?"

"Hi, Kari, it's Spencer. How are you doing?" He says.

I make a face at Jack and kick myself for not picking up the call right away. "Good, how are you?"

"Have I caught you at a bad time? I can call you back this afternoon," Spencer says. He can hear the restaurant sounds in the background.

"No, it's fine. I'm at lunch with my co-worker, but we just placed our order, so I can talk." I sound giddy. Slow down and relax.

"Where are you eating lunch?"

"The Roadhouse. I love their salads, especially their spinach salad with figs and warm bacon dressing," I say. Stop babbling. Seriously. Get ahold of yourself and let the guy talk.

"They put out some exceptional food there," Spencer says.

"Listen, I remember over email that you like to play Scrabble. Are you up for an evening of Scrabble tonight? I know it's last minute, but I just switched shifts at work, so I'm off tonight," Spencer says, sounding eager and nervous at the same time.

Adorable combination!

Jack's making faces at me, and I'm trying not to laugh.

"Sure, I can hang out tonight. Scrabble sounds fun!" I'm thrilled he called me for a second date! He had me sweating there for awhile.

"How about my place at seven? I'll whip up some food to go along with the game," he says.

He promises to email me directions to his house this afternoon, and I tell him I'm looking forward to it. We hang up, and I grin at Jack.

"Do you have a date? Give me the details. You haven't mentioned any new guys at all!" Jack says, clearly impressed.

"Spencer is one of my on-line matches. We met for coffee Saturday."

"And?? I guess you like him enough for a second date."

I giggle and blush. "Kind of. He sort of isn't my type. Jack, don't lecture me yet! He just looked a little different from his picture, which is totally my fault in a roundabout way. And, he called me out on making snap judgments. It was kind of an insult, actually."

Jack dissolves into laughter and looks at me incredulously. "Are you kidding me? He insults you on the first date? Why in the world are you going out with him again? Sounds like one bad date!"

"I know it sounds crazy! But, no one, except for you, has ever called me out on stuff. He's perceptive and smart. Honestly, I don't know. I'll see how it goes tonight."

Jack sits back in his seat and gazes happily at me. "He actually sounds really perfect for you."

"I know, right?"

"Hmm ... you can tell me all about it tomorrow morning at coffee," Jack says. "I look forward to it!"

After lunch, we drive back to the office, and I call Lauren at work to tell her about Spencer. I also tell her she's on her own at the gym, and she promises to still attend class. She reminds me to be on my best behavior. As if I need a reminder. Between her and Mama, I have plenty of parental role models telling me how to behave.

I leave work early, so I have ample time to shower and change clothes before heading over to Spencer's house. He emailed directions along with a cute, hand-drawn map. Turns out he lives fairly close to me, so it's a short drive. He also emailed me to see if I like mushrooms, olives (yuck), and calamari. I'm excited to try his cooking!

After showering and flat ironing my hair, I open the closet to choose an outfit. Something casual and comfortable. I choose jeans, white v-neck sweater and a cropped olive green jacket.

I offered to bring wine or dessert, but Spencer said he has it covered. What a nice change! One final glance in the mirror at my outfit and make-up, and I'm out the door right on time.

Spencer opens the door as I approach the front porch. "Hi Kari! Glad you found it okay."

I step inside. "Thanks, Spencer! Your map was really funny." He takes my wool coat and hangs it on a peg in the entryway.

Spencer's house is beautifully decorated in an Arts and Crafts style. The den furniture is a mixture of curly maple and ash. The long trestle dining room table is absolutely gorgeous, and I run my hand down it, relishing the smoothness. Large photographs adorn the walls, and I recognize Wonder Lake in Denali National Park as one of them.

Cooper greets me at the door, tail wagging hello. He is sweet and follows Spencer around as he shows me around. After he sniffs me sufficiently, he curls up on his dog bed by the stone fireplace.

"Your furniture is gorgeous. I love it. Did you make all the pieces?" I say and touch the side table next to the leather couch. I can't help it. The craftsmanship is superb.

Spencer blushes. "Yes, I made all the tables, but not the chairs. Too time consuming and a pain in the ass, actually."

"That's impressive," I say, astonished. "You're truly talented." I'm duly impressed, and I haven't even noticed the delicious aromas coming from the kitchen.

"Well, it's hard to make a living from crafting furniture, so I'm happy to fallback and rely on my cooking skills," he says.

"So, where did culinary school fit in? You're talented in furniture- making and cooking, what a combination."

"I went to culinary school right after high school and worked in New York City for ten years. Burned out from working eighty hours a week, so I moved back here to be close to family in Anchorage. I've always dabbled in woodworking ever since high school shop class," Spencer says. He walks into the kitchen to check on the food, and I follow him.

His kitchen is large, and he has generous counter space, which is tidy and clean. He flips over the salmon and sweet potato croquettes. They sizzle and pop in the hot pan.

"I hope you don't mind. I made the croquettes since you said you liked them," Spencer says. He lifts up a lid from a simmering pot of oil and throws in calamari dredged in garbanzo bean flour and spices.

I almost faint with happiness. He cooks. He made croquettes. He's family-oriented. He makes furniture. Pinch me, or don't wake me up from this dream.

"That's so sweet, thank you," I stammer. "Is there anything I can help you with?"

"Nope, just relax. What would you like to drink? I have wine, beer, juice, and water."

"A beer, please. At least let me set the table or something. I can't just stand here and watch you cook," I say.

Spencer hands me a Mirror Pond IPA and shakes his head. "When was the last time someone cooked for you, and you didn't have to do anything?"

I scratch my head and think. Hmmm. Christmas? Nope. Never?

"Yep, I thought so," Spencer remarks. Very perceptive.

I watch Spencer finish the appetizers and help him bring everything into the dining room. We sit down, and I take a moment to admire the delicious food, beautiful table, and Spencer's sweet face.

He begins to spoon food onto a plate for me, and I relax. I have a good feeling about Spencer. We lock eyes, and he smiles at me.

Everything about this feels right. I've found him, Mama. You can stop worrying about me, the remaining single daughter.

I'm very glad I moved to Alaska.

Epilogue

~

unday dinner at Tahoe South Cantina rolls around, and it's just Marshall and me. Lauren and Will cancelled at the last minute. Lauren isn't feeling well, and she's in her first trimester. I'm so thrilled for her and Will. They have names picked out already. Lindsay Ada for a girl and Joshua Henning for a boy.

"I don't know. I just imagined myself meeting a girl, falling in love, getting married, having kids, and living happily ever after. Here I am, hopelessly in love with a Jewish girl who has two children from a prior marriage, and I just met her!" Marshall exclaims and takes a sip of his IPA beer.

"Tell me again how you met Hannah. I'm fuzzy on the details," I say and settle in for the story.

Marshall clears his throat. "Our company is doing some work for the Anchorage Hospital System, and I was over there for a meeting on Friday. As I'm walking down the hallway, Hannah comes out of an office. She's drop-dead gorgeous with long brown hair, beautiful brown eyes, and a huge friendly smile. We lock eyes, she says hi, and I'm smitten right away. Fireworks explode. They really do. We start talking, and we instantly click. I don't know how to explain it. We had this amazing conversation, but she had to go to a meeting, so she gave me her business card."

"Wow. So, when did the two kids and religion come up?" I ask, amazed and a little embarrassed since I lectured him on multiple occasions about seeing "fireworks" with a girl.

"That's just it! At that same conversation, she told me she was Jewish and has two girls, ages five and eight. It didn't even faze me. I just wanted to keep talking with her," Marshall shakes his head in amazement.

The server comes by, and we order dinner. Potato burrito for me, and the carne asada burrito for Marshall.

"Did you call her yet?" I ask.

"I called her Friday afternoon when I returned to the office. We talked for an hour. Saturday, we went to lunch at The Roadhouse. Over lunch, we talked about anything and everything. It was totally comfortable, you know what I mean? She's easy to talk with and laughs at all my jokes."

"Super! What's the plan? When are you going out again?"

"I'm going over there tonight after dinner. Told her I would bring her dessert from Sugar," Marshall says and smiles, already thinking about Hannah.

"Is she pretty serious about religion? I think most Jewish people want to marry someone of the same faith," I say, trying not to sound like Debbie Downer, but I want him to proceed cautiously.

Marshall sighs. "We haven't talked about that yet, but I suspect yes. Maybe I'll convert. Who knows?"

"Marshall! You just met her! You're talking about converting? I've never seen you like this. I'm happy for you," I say, smiling.

"Thanks, Kari. I appreciate your support," Marshall says. "Enough about me. What's going on in your world?"

I clear my throat. "Spencer and I are really happy. Can you believe we've been dating for four months already? He met Mama and Dad in March, and they loved him. Next month, we have lots of hikes and camping trips planned all over Alaska. We're also planning to bike into Denali National Park on Labor Day weekend. I'm excited to do it. Biking is new to me, and he promises to help me train for it." I smile and think about him in his tight, black bike shorts, bike helmet, and chiseled chin.

"Kari, that's fantastic! Good for you! He's a good guy, and I wish he could've joined us tonight."

"I know, but since he's the Executive Chef now at Sixth Street Tapas, he has to work Sunday nights. It's okay though. I get to spend quality time with you!" I smile and think back to when I first met Marshall. Now, he's one of my best friends. He's embarking on an adventure that he didn't anticipate. Sometimes, those are the best ones.

"How's the wedding planning going for Jack?" Marshall asks.

"Abby has everything under control from what it sounds like. Small intimate wedding down in Seward at a lodge accessible by water taxi. Spencer and I will take a few extra days to explore the area after the wedding," I say.

The server delivers our food, and we dig in, plus order another round of drinks. Over dinner, we talk about work, fishing trips, and family.

Our Sunday night tradition continues, and I think it will grow over time as new friends come into lives. Life is funny that way sometimes ... all the ups and downs, but it's true friends who stand by and support you through love, life, and success.

The End.

Made in the USA
San Bernardino, CA
29 April 2014